Banished

Also by Betsy Schow

The Storymakers Series
Spelled
Wanted

Banished

BETSY SCHOW

Published by Sourcebooks Fire, an imprint of Sourcebooks, Inc.
P.O. Box 4410, Naperville, Illinois 60567-4410
(630) 961-3900
Fax: (630) 961-2168
sourcebooks.com

Library of Congress Cataloging-in-Publication Data

Names: Schow, Betsy, 1981- author.
Title: Banished / Betsy Schow.
Description: Naperville, IL : Sourcebooks Fire, [2018] | Series: Storymakers
    ; [3] | Summary: In a Kansas hospital, Princess Dorthea of Emerald
    struggles to regain her memory of what propelled her out of the land of
    Story, and how to get home, while Rexi, aided by Excalibur, continues to
    protect Story from the Wicked Witch.
Identifiers: LCCN 2017030948 | (13 : alk. paper)
Subjects: | CYAC: Fairy tales. | Princesses--Fiction. | Magic--Fiction. |
    Characters in literature--Fiction. | Storytelling--Fiction.
Classification: LCC PZ8.S3118 Ban 2018 | DDC [Fic]--dc23 LC record available at https://lccn.loc.gov/2017030948

Printed and bound in the United States of America.
VP 10 9 8 7 6 5 4 3 2 1

This book is for all of us who do battle with our shadows every day. Keep fighting. There is always light if you know where to look.

Off with Her Head

Rexi

Rain pounded against the shutters and ramparts, seeping between the crumbling stones of Camelot and dampening the cracks in the walls. More importantly, the downpour dampened the sounds of our footsteps down the hall. Honestly, we couldn't have asked for more perfect weather or better backdrop for our violent intentions.

The pretender had to go.

Don't judge me. A king has to make tough choices. Especially kings that were former palace kitchen girls who were forced to pretend they're a guy to sneak into the all-boys club, Camelot, and then accidently got crowned in the process so they have to keep pretending to be a boy or face the wrath of an angry mob and hang for treason. So yeah, as king of Camelot, a girl's gotta do what a girl's gotta do. At least that's what I told myself as I peered into the dark bedchamber, Excalibur in hand. I could barely make out a large shape in the bed, the blanket shifting ever so slightly, rising and falling with a slight nasal whistling of breath.

"So what's the—"

Mordred cut me off abruptly, one hand clamping across my mouth and the other bringing a finger to his lips in a shushing gesture. Then he tilted his head toward the door…waiting. The wheezing intake of breath continued uninterrupted.

I scowled and knocked his hand away, annoyed but silent.

Mordred was the military expert here, with more assassinations under his belt than I cared to think about. It didn't take a genius to know I was about to ask him what our plan was, so without speaking, he tried miming it out.

While I didn't know the proper hand signals among the knights, I prided myself on my charade skills, as there weren't a whole lot of entertainment options growing up in Sherwood Forest.

Mordred didn't share my talent.

He laid out a story with his hands, pointing, gesturing with dancing fingers. I tried to follow along, but the gestures were too fast and jumbled. At my vacant expression, he hit his palm against his forehead and started over, this time slower so I could follow along.

First, he pointed to himself. And then he pointed to the

left side of the bed. Next he pointed to me, and then made a two-fingered gesture like walking. Then he made the weird signals again, sort of like rock, scroll, scissors.

Bird? Horse? Sleeping princess? No, nuh-uh. I was not kissing anyone. But the last gesture was clear. *A slice across the neck.* Nodding, I gave Mordred the thumbs-up. I understood the beginning and the end.

Good enough for me.

He eased open the door, a hand on the hinges to muffle any squeaks. Once the opening was wide enough, we slipped inside. Since he was going to go left, I guessed I should go right. With my hand on the hilt of Excalibur, I made my way forward. Any direction of attack would work just as long as Gwenevere's head came off. That's the beauty of Hydra, a headhunter who had the magic to swap heads across bodies. Off with one head and on with the next. With each head Hydra wore, her personality changed. But while there were subtle changes in character, Hydra had always been Hydra. Different look, different speech, but always good-hearted and in control of her actions—until Gwen. Gwenevere lacked a heart, let alone goodness. Plus, her idea of being in control meant controlling everyone else, no matter what was best for Camelot. That's what made her dangerous.

If I used Excalibur to remove Gwenevere's head, the sword's holy magic would sever the connection to Hydra, and that vile, conniving Gwen would become nothing more than a decrepit skull. Of course, I had no idea what that would do to Hydra and if she would return to her old self with a new head on her shoulders. Before Hydra started using Gwenevere's head, Hydra had a few lucid moments a day, breaking through Gwen's tyrannical existence. Though it had been weeks since I'd seen a trace of Hydra's wobbly multicolored eyes shining through.

A hand grabbed my shoulder and jerked me, pulling me back to the here and now. Mordred gestured angrily. I did the same in return and mouthed, *You were supposed to go left, moron! You're in the way! Move!* I raised Excalibur to hurry him along.

He shook his head and pointed down the hall. A little cloud of glitter drifted across the floor. My gut frosted over. Gwenevere's guard beast was coming. If I listened carefully, I could hear the clip-clop of hooves.

Enchanted crystal cats decorated the room like a sparkly alarm system. They heard the clip-clop too and started sleepily meowing to alert their master.

"What is it, my little ones? Mummy's right here." Gwen yawned and stretched her arms.

"Hide!" Mordred whispered.

I turned to jump in the closet, but Mordred grabbed me by the collar of my tunic and yanked me to the ground. With a swift twist, he rolled us under the bed. The space was cramped, my back resting on Mordred's chest. I couldn't breathe. The feeling of claustrophobia was overwhelming. This was made worse by Gwenevere's large girth. Her weight taxed the bed's crossbeams, bowing them toward the floor.

The kitties yowled louder. "Yes, yes, I'm up." One massive cankle thudded to the floor. Then the other.

I half expected to hear, *Fee Fi Fo Fum.*

Mordred grabbed my hip and pulled me back, drawing me nearer to the center of the bed. Nearer to him.

Then in the distance, I saw it. More glitter. The painted glossy hooves that belonged to the pink, poofy, two-foot-tall terror, Mr. Fluffypants, the last remaining teacup unicorn–nightmare hybrid. Two weeks ago I made the mistake of mocking him. I still had the second-degree burns on my thigh to remind me of my error. From now on, even if a creature looks like a hot-pink pony, I'll remember that it can still change into a flaming, carnivorous, glitter demon in a snap.

Mordred tugged on my hip again, though not to bring me closer. His fingers deftly unlaced the pouch at my side. I smacked his hand, but he persisted. He was not to be deterred from the holy grail, which was disguised as an inkwell. I still didn't quite understand all the powers it had. But Mordred did. And he was obsessed with it. Obsessed with somehow using it to go back in time to beat Arthur and see his family. I'd thought he'd given that up in my service.

Guess I was wrong.

The hand wrestling came to a draw, or rather we both lost because the grail fell out of the pouch and skittered away from us.

"What is this?" Gwen reached down and picked up the glowing glass. "I wonder what else is down there." Her musing filled me with dread as she tossed a treat under the bed, which rolled right next to my leg. "Mr. Fluffypants, fetch!" Fluffy snorted and dived, his breath scalding. He licked up the treat up and bit down on my pants, dragging me out. Mordred let go quickly. He may have even given me a push.

It didn't save him.

Fluffy's braided mane turned to flame as he dived back under the bed and hauled out the dark knight, leaving scorch marks on Mordred's breaches.

"I see we have two rats," Gwen said, twirling the grail in her hand. "Really, I have to say I'm shocked."

"And here I thought my disgust was obvious." I scowled. "You think I haven't noticed that the only refugees you want to let in are all male and all cute. Day by day, you've been usurping the power of the throne and turning Camelot into your own personal fortress of fanboys. You don't care at all about stopping Blanc and Morte. So we came to stop you." Or at least I thought it was *we*. Now I wasn't so sure. Mordred stayed silent, his eyes still on the grail.

"I knew you didn't share my views of the future." She ran the back of her hand down my cheek. "I'm just surprised it took you so long to do something about it. And so poorly too. I thought I had taught you better. That really is a disappointment. However, it reaffirms my actions." She clapped, and her personal guard arrived. "Bring it."

"What are you up to?" I asked Gwen.

"I supported your claim to the throne. It was the easiest

way to retain my place in Camelot. But then I learned you had fooled me. You were not Rex, the once and future king, but a scullery maid in disguise. Now that the knights of the triangular table have returned, if they found out, they would form a coup and kick us both out. So I suppressed that witch Hydra so she couldn't spill my plans to get rid of you."

I snorted. "So you think that if I'm gone, they'll follow you?"

"No, I tried that when Arthur died." She traced the line of her neck. "It didn't end well. The people here are rooted in their myths and bound to the old ways. Therefore, I still need a king to my queen." There was a knock at the door. And then someone who looked exactly like me entered. But since I was standing right here, it had to be Mic, the Mimicman.

"That's pretty smart. Use his abilities to impersonate me, and he'll stay by your side and act like a good puppet because he's a coward." That barb was aimed at Mic. He didn't dispute it since it was the truth.

Gwen's smile twisted, making her look even uglier than normal. "And Mordred will not move against me as long as I hold the grail."

Mordred closed his eyes and sighed. "Aye. 'Tis true."

Every curse I knew streamed out of my mouth plus a few new ones I came up with on the spot. I continued spewing insults even after the guards snapped an iron mask on my face. I enjoyed seeing Mordred flinch as I unleashed them all.

"This way no one will see you for who you are, and I can still keep you nearby to use as a bargaining chip with Blanc."

Gwen clapped her hands. "I hope you are taking notes. That is how you actualize a plan. Visualize and follow through. Class is dismissed."

She waved me away, and the guards carted me off.

"Oh, I nearly forgot," she called and strode after me. "I'll be taking this." She pulled Excalibur from its sheath at my side. It glowed and glimmered. "I've always wanted this."

The sword vibrated, humming. Within moments it screeched and burst into dust.

I laughed. "Guess it didn't feel the same way about you."

"Take her to the tower!" Gwen yelled. "It won't be soon enough before I forget you're there."

"Being entirely honest with oneself is a very, very bad idea."

—Sigmund Fraud

We're All Mad Here
Dorthea

And what happens next, Ms. Gayle?" The man placed my tome gently on the table as if it would break. Or infect him.

I flopped back against the beige leather couch in his office and put my arm over my face. "I don't know. That's all I can remember from the vision."

"It's a dream journal."

Turning my head, I glared at my new nemesis—someone this world referred to as a head shrinker. The aging Dr. Baum fidgeted at his gray mustache with the small comb he kept in the brown, tweed jacket he wore every day. He peered at me from behind round bifocals, examining me like I was a bumpkin bug. Either that or he enjoyed taking apart my mind like a puzzle. I hated that. But even worse was when he told me what he thought I needed to do.

Well, what I *needed to do* was get home. The details of Libraria and my life there as the princess of Emerald were getting fuzzier by the day. My memories of enchantalors were being replaced with this world's elevators. Thoughts of magic mirrors now transformed into TVs that were powered by a lightning called electricity. This world shunned magic for something called science, and sorceresses were replaced by doctors. My mind quickly returned to Verte, the loyal Emerald witch—my teacher and friend—and the last time I'd seen her green warty face.

Maybe there are certain details I am better off forgetting.

"Whatever," I said and stared up at the tiled ceiling.

The doctor sighed heavily. "Why do you insist on lying on that couch?"

"Isn't that what people do in *therapy?*" Another new term I'd picked up in my time here.

"I wouldn't know. *Is* this therapy? I merely invited you to join me for my afternoon tea so we could talk about what's on your mind."

The sounds of clanking china were followed by the aroma of jasmine tea wafting my way. I still remembered enough of my royal manners to be horrified at the thought of letting a good cup of tea go cold.

With effort, I hoisted myself off the couch and ambled

over to the table, tightening the drawstring of my hospital scrubs so they didn't fall down around my ankles. I was going to have ask for a smaller size. I was literally wasting away in this world. This Kansas.

"There." I pasted a smile on my face, plopped myself into a chair, and grabbed my teacup. "Lovely weather we're having." I pointedly looked out his window at the mini monsoon. If I ever escaped, I might need a getaway boat.

Dr. Baum picked up my notebook and flipped through it again.

"So in your dreams—"

"Visions," I corrected.

His smile dipped a bit, and he took a deep breath. "These *lucid images*…"

I nodded, indicating I'd let that one pass.

He sighed, probably grateful for that small victory since we'd been having this same argument for a month. "I've noticed that these lucid images can be very violent."

I sipped my hot tea. I knew a trap when I heard one.

"Now you know that whatever you tell me here is confidential. But if I were to have reason to believe that you might be a danger to yourself or others…" He tapped the notebook and let his words—his threat—hang in the air.

I rolled my eyes. "Please. I'm not a threat to anyone. You've taken my shoelaces and given me only plastic silverware. My legs haven't seen a blade in so long I think I'm turning into a chimera."

I regretted the word as soon as I said it. *Kato...*

"But you must admit there is an underlying theme of death and violence in your more recent entries." The doctor watched the teacup like I might shatter it and take him hostage at any moment.

I set it down to ease some of the tension. "Look, there was this curse that made me 'evil queen' level psycho, but the grail cured me. Not to mention there's a war going on. So of course there's gonna be violence, though it's not like I personally want that." He passed the notebook back, open to the page of the attempted beheading. I sighed. "Oh, that. In my defense, Hydra is a head-swapping witch. So taking her head wouldn't actually kill her. Probably. And her current incarnation, Gwenevere, is a power hungry lunatic who totally deserves what's coming to her."

His raised eyebrows indicated that I wasn't exactly helping my case.

"Let's move on for a minute, Ms. Gayle. I've noticed that in these stories you are always this same girl, this Rexi. So do you find yourself interchangeable with her? Is she a part of you?"

"No," I corrected for the umpteenth time. "I'm not her. I just see things through her eyes. And as I've told you before, I can only do that because I used the Emerald curse to tie our souls together after she died. Blah, blah, blah."

He nodded slowly. "I see."

No, he didn't. "Look, I'm not a nutter. I know who I am,

and if I were Rexi, I'd be in the world of Fairy Tales and Myths with control of what was happening there, and I would do things very differently and better than she is. She's been king of Camelot for, like, a blip of a few weeks. She has no idea how to rule. I, on the other hand, have been royal my whole life. I was born to command armies." I crossed my arms, satisfied I'd made my point.

"You said something very interesting that I want to get back to. About control." Dr. Baum tilted his glasses down and jotted something in the folder he kept on me.

"Yeah," I said and repositioned myself in my seat, bracing for his examination. "So what?"

He stood up, taking his preaching stance. "If I may."

"Can I stop you?"

"Not really, no."

I spread my hand wide. "Then by all means."

He tapped his pen on his salt-and-pepper mustache and began to pace. "Have you ever wondered why you only started to experience this other world while you were in the coma after your excision surgery?"

I fingered the scar on my sternum where, as the doctor said, I'd had a bone tumor removed. It was the same place where Excalibur had pierced me.

Dr. Baum's pacing sped up. "And why is it that the only time you reconnect with this other world is in sleep or after a chemotherapy treatment? Perhaps these visions are your unconscious mind's way of expressing how frustrated you are at not having control of your own life. Perhaps the Emerald curse that eats away at you in these stories is simply a metaphor for the cancer inside you that grows without your control. Perhaps your connection to this Rexi is a desire to be someone else."

"Pfft. If that were true, I would invent someone with better fashion sense who didn't try to steal my prince," I snarked, refusing to let his doubts seep in.

Usually, he backed off, but not today. "Then why do your experiences mirror each other? Don't you find it odd that you would both love the same boy? Have you considered that this Rexi is the representation of the person that you really are? That after years of being the perfect child who fulfills your parents' expectations, you are finally letting lose and rebelling? An unconscious manifestation of multiple personalities is very common in a situation such as yours."

"A, Rexi and I are nothing alike. That girl has no sense of style. Or manners. Or tact. She's got all the grace of a hippo trying to do ballet. And…ugh." I got up out of the chair. "I'm done. I want to go back to my room."

He thought for a moment. "If you promise me that you'll stay safe and think about what I said, I'll call the orderly and let you go early today."

Stay safe. What was that supposed to mean? *Rexi* was the one in trouble, not me. Or maybe he meant *I* was in danger… from myself. My mind spun.

"Sure," I muttered, anxious to get out of this room, which

had suddenly become so stuffy that it was difficult to breathe. My guard showed up promptly and led me out.

"Oh, Dorothy," the doctor called as I reached the hall. "You only shared point A. What's point B?"

I didn't look back. "You don't have to believe me, but I'm not crazy."

He came up beside me, leaning down and speaking so quietly that only I could hear. "I meant no offense. All the best people have bit of madness. It's a sign of brilliance. You just need to learn how to take control of it."

His words looped in my mind as I was walked back to my cell. But I stopped short when I got to my room.

My mother was standing on my bed, pulling taped drawings off the wall.

"Why are you doing that?" I snapped. The walls of my hospital room were a nauseating shade of yellow, and I'd tried to cover them with my illustrations. My attempts to remember the world I needed to get back to. My friends.

My mother didn't reply. She merely continued to pull the remaining papers off the wall.

As she stood on tiptoes to reach the last and highest drawing taped to the ceiling—the one of a boy with tousled amber hair and an ice-blue gaze—anger swelled within me. "Touch that, and I will *never* forgive you." My voice held enough chill to give a snowman the shivers.

With a sigh, my mother's hand dropped, and she turned to me. Her face was as severe as the bun that kept her long, graying hair restrained. And though she lacked the gowns a royal would normally wear, she was not an ounce less regal in her simple cotton dress. Queen Em had been trapped here long enough to forget who she really was, *but some things will never change.*

"You need to stop this, Dorothy."

Like her need to tell me what to do.

"Stop what, Mother?" I asked innocently and with a smile.

"You know exactly what I mean, young lady." She swiped at the pile of sketches she'd collected, scattering them across the room. "Your father begs me to be patient with you, says that you'll come around in time. But I have tolerated this nonsense long enough. It is time to put away these childish fantasies and face reality. Focus on what really matters."

My fake smile faded into a hard line on my face. "That," I said, pointing to the drawing of Kato that still remained on the wall, "is the *only* thing that matters."

My mother's jaw set, her head shaking slightly.

I crossed my arms. "Well, you never understood me in Emerald. I don't know why I thought this world would be any pixing different," I muttered. Ignoring her, I bent down and started collecting my artwork.

Until I heard a sniffle.

Surely, I'd misheard. I looked up at my mother. At her unsteady lips. At the tears in her eyes that were on the brink of spilling over.

I froze. Astonished. In all my life, I had never seen the queen of Emerald cry. Not once. I honestly didn't think she could. A tear trickled down her face as she sat on my bed. Then a second. Then a dam seemed to break as she wept openly.

"Hey, hey," I soothed, dropping drawings and rushing to kneel in front of her.

Her shoulders shook, and her hands trembled as she held my face. The ache in my chest threatened to break me in two. The guilt over all the pain I'd caused. That I kept causing.

It was *my* selfishness that made the wish on the cursed star. *I* was the one who broke the magic of Fairy Tale and sent my parents to this mirror world called Kansas. *I* was the one who made my mother cry.

I laid my head in her lap and pressed my face into the folds of her dress like I used to as a little girl. "I'm sorry. I'm so sorry. I'll fix it."

"Oh, my baby." She ran her hands through my hair, her sobs growing quieter with each stroke. "All I want is for you to get better so you can come home with me."

Ever since I made that stupid wish—to be free of the rules of magic and story, free of my destiny, free of my parents—I'd wanted the same thing as my mother. I wanted to go home.

My father cleared his throat from the doorway. "I'm sorry to interrupt my girls, but if I stall this doctor any longer, I think he's going to strap us into wheelchairs and drag us out." He came over and took my hand, pulling me up into a hug. "My Punkin. Be whatever you have to. Just come back to us."

I hugged him back fiercely. *Now that I'd found my parents, I wouldn't let them go again.*

"Rule #91: Once the villain is vanquished, they are gone and never coming back to get you. So stop looking over your shoulder and think happy thoughts!"

—Definitive Fairy-Tale Survival Guide, Volume 1

Girl in the Iron Mask
Rexi

The walls of my cell were bare, unless you counted the slime. Not exactly quarters fit for a king. While I was used to forest accommodations after living in Sherwood with Robin Hood and the Merry Men, castle living had made me soft. Or being linked to the pampered Dorthea had infected me. Regardless, by the third night of my imprisonment, I would have traded everything I'd ever filched for a hexed stack of straw. No Rumpelstiltskin or spinning wheel required, just something to make the granite floor bearable.

I wouldn't mind a book either.

"Spells bells, now I know I've lost it. I'm actually asking to read." Anything would be better than trying to amuse myself by drawing pictures in the slime—for the thousandth time. I also longed for someone to talk to. I kept hoping a mouse might pop by to keep me company. But the worst part was the torture device that devil woman had locked onto my face, the metal mask.

My nose had been itching for days.

Light filtered into the tower cell. It only did that once a day when the second sun was at its peak. Nearly lunchtime. I turned to the small, barred square they called a window and let the sun shine on my face. After breathing it in for a minute, I opened my eyes. A furry blur streaked by. For a moment my chest froze, hoping it was Kato and Dot here to rescue me. But I knew that was impossible. Solitary confinement must have rotted my brain. I'd seen Morte take over Kato's body, turning him into a shadow host. And I'd shot Dot myself with Excalibur in pen form, filled with the holy grail ink to cure her homicidal pyromania madness. In the end, the reasoning didn't matter. She was still gone. Kato and Dorthea were both gone. And it was time I admitted they were never coming back.

Besides, the chimera that flew by the tower had a graying mane. And the only old-timer I'd seen like that was Bob.

Bob!

I clutched the iron bars and pulled my face forward, the metal mask clanking against them.

"Bob! Bob! In the tower," I yelled. "It's Rexi. Help me!"

I called and called. And while I heard his wings flapping, he didn't pass by the window again.

The hope that had sprung from my chest deflated, leaving me more depressed than before. No one actually cared that I was locked away. I spent the first day expecting Mordred, but he never came. Which made sense. I didn't have Excalibur or the grail anymore, and those were the only reasons he'd hung around. Now there was nothing special about me. I couldn't blame him for looking out for himself.

Verte, the real Hydra, Dot, even Oz, all of my friends… Gone. I may as well have been gone too since I was stuck up in this tower. A forgotten nobody. Though looking on the bright side, my imprisonment wouldn't last forever. Because any day I expected the evil Lady of the Lake, Blanc, to finish building her shadow army and kill us all.

I sighed. "That's me, Rexi, the king of silver linings."

Footsteps sounded outside the thick wood and iron door. Someone was climbing the steps to bring me the glop they called food.

"I'm sorry, I have strict instructions from the queen. No one passes through this door but me," the guard said in his gravelly voice.

It was the second voice that perked my attention. Because the voice sounded exactly like mine. "Surely, Gwenevere could not have meant me. After all, does not a king outrank a queen?"

The guard stumbled over his words, carefully trying to

avoid cause to be hung for treason. "Yes, sir. I mean, Your Highness. I mean, let me unlock the prisoner's cell for you."

"Please do," the voice that was mine but not mine said.

The door opened slowly, its weight making the old hinges groan in complaint. My double walked in, turned, and dismissed the guard. "Leave us."

"Yes, sir. Your Highness, um…yeah." The guard's boots clomped down the stairs, growing softer with each thud.

I relaxed against the wall, trying to appear far more at home than I was. "What brings you here? Oh, wait. I know. You need help. You can copy my face, but people are starting to notice that the real Rex doesn't walk around all stiff like a king with a sword stuck up his—"

"As of five minutes ago, the situation may have changed. So I suggest you hold that impertinent tongue of yours, or I will leave you to decay in peace," he said, starting to back out of my cell.

He was the first person to talk to me in days. I tried not to beg. I failed. "Wait, wait! Don't leave me alone." I launched myself toward him.

"That's better," he said, stepping back inside and shutting the door behind him.

"You said something changed," I said. "What? Why are you here?"

"You had a visitor."

Bob.

Mic tossed a small package at my feet. "He brought this for you."

I popped an eyebrow. "And you are playing courier out of the goodness of your heart?"

"No," Mic grumbled. "That chimera recognized immediately who I really was by my smell. But he didn't call me out. He made me swear to give this to you."

"Really? And why didn't you just keep it for yourself?"

Mic picked at his fingernails and mumbled out the side of his mouth. "It's enchanted so that only you can read it."

Ah, that made far more sense.

I bent down and retrieved the book, dusting off the cover. I'd seen it once before. In the Chimera Mountain. *Blanc Pages.* It was one of the few surviving e-books—enchanted books—that showed events that have happened. And sometimes events as they are happening.

After opening the book, I skipped the sections I'd already read, the parts where Blanc was the Lady of the Lake and lost Sir Lancelot to a nasty curse laid by Gwenevere. In revenge, Blanc declared war on the Storymakers, who were trying to rewrite her story—never mind erasing everyone else's in doing so. She was stopped and imprisoned for a long time— that is, until Dorthea and I let her out again.

I skimmed that whole part. I didn't need to be reminded of my stint working for team evil to save my own hide. Needless to say, when Blanc escaped, she took up her mission anew. And now she had Morte, the Grimm Reaper of the underworld, at her side.

I found the page I was looking for. The one just before the

empty pages. This page grew in color, the story unfolding right in front of us.

A black chimera stood in the background, looking completely at home among a field of glowing embers. The ground held few traces of the village it used to be. Sooty slaves dug deep into the earth, making a pit while flames licked the wooded sign that read *Nottingham's Museum of Magical History—Academy of Villains.*

Blanc, the woman in white, stood out like a diamond in a pile of coal.

"Are you pleased, My Empress?" the chimera that stole Kato's form asked. Morte looked like a breathing shadow, a beast all black from wings to horns except for his glowing eyes and a silver snake that acted as a second tail.

"Pleased?" she sneered. "Why ever would I be pleased with this disgusting, dirty display?" She raised her hands to the skies. The heavens opened to greet her, pouring her element, water, all around her. The liquid snuffed out the remaining sparks of the fire, the air growing hazy with smoke and steam. She breathed out deeply. "That's better. Now you best explain why you robbed me of my army of villains. Not that they were a very capable army, but I gained strength from taking their life sources with my powers. Now I have no minions and nothing to snack on."

Morte's gaze flared, a spark through the smoke. "There will be time for that. For now, we must eliminate the only power that can stop us."

Blanc waved a hand dismissively. "It was already taken care of."

"It is that attitude that has kept you from grasping what is yours. Ours," Morte corrected.

"And how will your ashes solve anything?"

"Behold."

He raised his wings to the sky, mimicking Blanc's gesture. But instead of water pouring from the sky, the ground shifted. The ashes on the ground coalesced and liquefied into ink. Then like reverse rain, the ink rose into the sky.

Morte grinned, exposing some teeth. "With the last relics of magic kept here, I finally have enough power from the dark grail to send a few spies to the other world."

"Are you saying that your mindless spies will have more success than I had in besting that child princess?"

"No, I have gained other powers too. And my spies won't be going alone." Morte pulled back his muzzle, showing full fang in a menacing smile. With a whip of his claw, he cut the silver serpent tail from his body. It writhed on the ground, gasping for air. Growing, changing until the snake molted. It shed its old body like a skin, leaving a naked woman behind.

Blanc slowly crouched down, extending her hand toward the woman. "Is it truly?"

"Shh, ssssister," the snake-turned-woman hissed. "We are not alone."

Morte shifted his gaze away from his work, his eyes going

dark, staring straight out of the pages. Staring straight at me. "Ahh. Little hero. Is that mask meant to make you fiercer? Or simply to hide your fear? I suppose I shall see you in person and rip it from your face soon enough. Then I can find out for myself." He nodded to Blanc, who wrung her hands in a complicated pattern. Water started flowing out of the pages of the book, blurring the picture like a watercolor that had soaked for too long.

"Don't let her in. Shut it now!" Mic cried, hands shaking as he reached out.

Yeah, he didn't need to tell me that. I'd slammed the book closed before he could finish his sentence.

Hurriedly, he took the book from me, whispering some words like a prayer before sitting on the book. "The grains of sand are just running out. Continue with your original plan. Remove Gwenevere from power and return Hydra. Hydra will help you go and get *her*."

He reached up, and with the touch of his bare hands, my mask fell off. He covered his own face with it, taking my place.

I should have run out of the cell without argument, but I had to ask. "Wait. Get who? Are you seriously that big of a coward that you're willing to swap me places and stay here in prison just so you don't have to face that snake, Griz?"

"No," he said, his voice muffled from the mask. "No, Griz is not the one you need to get. Don't you see? That portal goes somewhere. And Morte sent those abominations through it because she still lives. My Princess Dorthea is alive. And because of Excalibur and the grail, you are the only hope of bringing her back."

"Sometimes an ink blot is just an ink blot."

—*Rorschach Remedies and Snake Oils*

Down the Rabbit Hole
Dorthea

The clock ticked on, the hour coming to a close while Dr. Baum continued to read my journal in silence.

I looked back and forth between the clock and the man. "You do realize you haven't moved that cup from your lips for, like, fifteen minutes. Are you having a stroke?" I finally asked, standing. "I'll go get someone."

He sputtered and set down his tea. "No, no. I'm quite all right. Just enthralled by the details of your transmogrifijiggering. You are a gifted storyteller."

"It's not a story."

"Of course it is."

I rolled my eyes. "Why do I even bother talking if you don't actually listen to what I'm saying?"

"Because you want to get home and you need my help. So kindly hear me out for a moment." Dr. Baum gestured me back to my seat. "What I meant is that all of life is a story. And we are its authors. In your story, you control the narrative of what happens to you, of what is real and what is not. It matters not what anyone else believes, just what is firmly planted in your heart and mind. Your perception is your reality." He laid the book in front of me gently. "This. This is reality. At least to you." After turning his back on me, he went to his desk and pushed the button on the intercom. "Ms. Gayle is finished with her tea."

He said nothing else before I was led back to my room. Just let his words marinate in the murky soup of my thoughts. I didn't understand where he was going with this "Perception is reality" business. Did that mean he wanted me to believe in this reality and forget it all…like my mother begged me to do? Or did he want me to hang on to the reality in Libraria and keep writing about what happened to Rexi? He seemed to act like they could both be true. Which seemed impossible.

For the second time in a week, I returned to find a visitor in my hospital room. But not my parents. Rather it was a boy in hospital scrubs like mine. He stood at the window, with his back to me, looking outside. I couldn't tell the color of his hair since the only remnants of it was the light fuzz of regrowth along his scalp.

"They all talk about you, you know," he said, seemingly sensing that he was no longer alone.

"I'm sorry, but have we met?"

"Nope," he said blithely and turned. "But I know you, Your Majesty."

The hairs on my arms went up. My heart warred with itself, trying to determine if he was enemy or friend.

He kept his gaze down and put a hand to his chest. "I'm unsure of protocol when meeting a princess. Perhaps you were expecting me to bow." Head lowered, he swept his hands in an exaggerated greeting.

The whole "friend" thing wasn't looking good.

"What do you want?" I asked, staying on the balls of my feet in case I needed to bolt.

"I came here because I heard about your drawings and wanted to see for myself." He raised his head and pointed to the one high on the ceiling above my bed. "That one in particular."

Seeing his face for the first time, I gasped. While the features weren't an exact match, the eyes were his. I couldn't forget that ice-blue stare no matter how many lives I lived.

"Kato," I cried, rushing forward.

Before I could embrace him, he threw his hands up to catch my shoulders, keeping me at a distance. "Whoa there. I knew you were crazy, but no one told me you were a stalker too."

Seeing my face fall, he sighed and rubbed a hand over his scalp. "Look, I seem to remind you of somebody you know.

Sorry, but you have to admit it's creepy to find a portrait of yourself in some airhead's hospital room. So I'm just gonna take that drawing, and we can forget this whole stalking thing." He moved to climb on my bed.

His arrogance broke my silence. "Airhead? You don't even know me!"

"You're so special that you argued yourself into a private room in an overcrowded hospital. You think you're a princess from a far-off land. You're too high and mighty to take meals with the rest of us commoners, and half of these drawings are of shoes." He pointed around the room and then settled his gaze back on me. "Am I missing anything?"

"When you put it like that, I sound bad." I pointed at the ruby-heeled Hans Christian Louboutin. "But these shoes aren't only fabulously high fashion. They're magic too. And I need them to take me back to the land of Fairy Tale."

The boy nodded slowly, sidestepping past me with an eye on the door. "Okay…you have issues. And well, it's been unique."

I smacked my face with both hands. Moron. I hadn't meant to blabber about magic. I forgot I was talking to someone from this world because of the resemblance to Kato.

"Hey," he said, pausing at the door. "I don't get your whole deal, but for the sake of everyone around you, get over yourself. You will be better off if you let go of your fantasies and accept what's in front of you. Trust me, there's no magic that can save you when death comes." Then he left.

I scurried to the door to catch him, but he was gone. I looked up and down the hallway, but he'd disappeared. Who did I see? My parents. Headed back toward the doctor's suite.

Of course, I followed them.

Peeking around a corner, I saw Dr. Baum usher Mom and Dad into his office. His eyes narrowed in my direction, but that was probably my imagination. After he shut the door, I was worried I wouldn't be able to hear their conversation, but I nonchalantly stood outside his office like I was his next appointment. Luckily, the door didn't catch when he'd closed it, so I could listen through the crack.

"Mr. and Mrs. Gayle, I will get straight to the point. As you know, what your daughter and I talk about here is completely confidential. Some of it is philosophy, some theory, and of course, we have great tea…"

"The point, Doctor," my mother interjected. "You said you had one."

"Ah, yes." Dr. Baum coughed. "In recent days I've become more convinced that this isn't the right place for her. So if you wouldn't mind gathering up her things, I can start making transfer arrangements."

"You're trying to get rid of us?" my dad asked.

"Not at all. I'm simply trying to get her out of this hospital."

"What's wrong with this hospital, and why now?" my mother asked, her voice lowering.

There was a long pause before Dr. Baum said, "Dorothy's writings are becoming increasingly more paranoid and dark.

And to be perfectly honest, I'm afraid I can't keep her safe here anymore."

The sound of furniture scraping across the floor was followed by my mother's voice, which grew louder and closer. "Then I agree. She shouldn't stay here. I knew allowing her to find her way through this fantasy was a bad idea, and now you think she is in danger of self-harm."

"It is not self-harm that worries me. Rest assured, Mrs. Gayle, until the transfer is complete, I've arranged a strict security detail. We will have no mishaps after her radiation treatment."

Someone touched my shoulder, and I stifled a scream. It was a nurse.

"I've been looking for you everywhere, dearie," she said.

"I was just…" I found myself at a loss for an excuse.

"Eavesdropping and making yourself late for a very important date." She tapped her watch. "Come along now." She all but shoved me in a wheelchair and pushed me to the oncology section of the hospital. The chemo room.

"Don't worry about a thing. This treatment won't hurt at all, Dorothy dear."

Lies, I thought as the nurse readied the IV. Everyone lies to me. My parents. Dr. Baum. For once I wanted someone to tell me the truth.

This is going to hurt. A lot. The cure sucks and may kill you faster than the cancer. But hey, if you survive, bald is in fashion, and think of all the money you'll save on hair products.

Yeah, not a chance. The room was decorated with glitter stars and colorful little bunnies like a unicorn had thrown up rainbows and woodland creatures *everywhere*. But there was nothing that could brighten my mood. I saw the decorations for the lies they were. The cheer was all a screen. A desperate plea for patients to stay positive. Gotta keep your spirits up! Gotta look on the bright side! Too bad the dark side will stab you in the back, whether you hear it coming or not.

Outside, the weather affirmed my opinion. The emergency warning alert had sounded a half an hour before my therapy tea, the siren cutting into the kids' cartoons they insisted on playing during chemo. Tornado watch.

A flash of light flared into the room through the window. *One-one thousand. Two-one thousand. Three-one thousand. Four-one thousand. Five—*

Boom.

The nurse left, and my hand tingled and burned—a sure sign that the IV had started pumping. The green liquid was like fire seeping through my veins. Which meant the visions weren't far behind. My body felt light, and my mind drifted, calling me to my memories and a land that should have been full of Happily Ever Afters but was wallowed in war. And all because of me. I swear I could hear the screams from people fleeing the battlefield. Fleeing me.

If Dr. Baum was right, I was in charge of my story. And I was tired. Tired of everyone thinking I was crazy. Tired of making my parents sad. Tired of dreaming about the destruction of a world I couldn't get back to protect. "It's not real…"

In my mind, the wails grew louder. It's like I was back in the moments when the curse engulfed me, just before I was banished to Kansas. I could smell the people of Camelot burning in my Emerald flames.

That boy said I had issues. No pixing joke.

So I focused on changing my mental picture, rewriting the story. A beach. Maybe the stench was a bonfire. Despite my efforts to picture s'mores, the image of the charred bodies only got more vivid. I shook my head. "No, it's not real. I am in control."

"You wish," a voice cackled, high-pitched and off-key. "Or maybe not, since that's what got you into this mess."

I jerked my head around, searching the room. The monitors beeped quicker, making music out of my racing pulse. When I saw a face, I opened my mouth to scream. Then I realized it was me. A reflection on the glass cabinet door. Except for a second, the reflection didn't look like me.

Nonsense. The room was empty. I was alone. The only sound was the storm outside, wind howling and whipping the rain against the window.

Another flare of light.

One-one thousand. Two-one thousand. Three-one thousand. Four—

Crack.

The storm is getting closer. And then as if on cue, the lights went out, plunging my room in darkness. Within a second, the generator spells kicked in, bringing devices back to life and lighting the emergency hallway glow crystals. My room remained dark except for a small trickle of light from the hall.

"Hello?" I steadied myself on the edge of the reclining chair, leaning out as far as the IV tether would let me. I expected nurses and doctors scrambling in the hallway, but even grave-yards had more life than this hospital at the moment.

Where had everyone gone?

Underneath the irregular, percussive beep of my pulse monitor, there was another sound in the room. *Drip. Drip.*

It must have been raining hard enough outside that the roof was leaking.

Drip. Drip.

I focused in on the sound. The splash pitching deeper. I tracked the sound to the corner of the room and watched as the puddle grew.

The storm flashed again, lighting up the room. This time I didn't count. All of my focus was drawn to the puddle before me. It was black as ink. In a heartbeat, the room was plunged back into darkness.

No. It's not real. Not real...

I grabbed the glowing monitor and turned the screen toward the drip. The black puddle had spread, moving toward the wall. And up it. As if a figure was leaning against it. I closed my eyes, telling myself it was just a shadow cast off the IV pole.

"You're being stupid. Shadows can't get you," I told myself. I breathed deep and opened my eyes again.

The shadow had moved. It oozed and grew taller, separating from the wall to walk toward me.

"Found you." The shadow gurgled. "Run."

I didn't need to be told twice. Ignoring the pain, I ripped the IV from my hand and sprinted out of the room, taking the door away from the oozing, dark shadow.

"Nurse! Nurse!" I yelled.

Emergency lights on the ceiling swirled, and the spinning had a dizzying strobe effect. I staggered down the hall toward the illuminated exit sign. I pushed through the door and burst onto the landing. Then I looked over the railing. The stairwell leading down made my stomach lurch with vertigo, and I held my breath. A faint click sounded as the emergency lights started shutting off, floor by floor. The first floor went dark. Then the second. Then the third. I was on the fifth floor. Fleeing the darkness, I headed up to the roof, taking the stairs two at a time. I hit the exit door with a thud. It wouldn't budge.

I looked over my shoulder. The lights continued to snap off. Turning back to the exit, I could see a cyclone whipping through the city and toward the hospital through the small square window in the door. A streak of lightning shot down from the funnel.

Banished

The lightning was silver. And shaped like a woman.

"I told you I'd be back."

The last light in the stairwell went out, enfolding me in the darkness.

"Tip #1: If all your friends jump off a bridge, it might be prudent to look back and see what is chasing them."

—The Coward's Guide to Seeming Heroic

I'll Follow You into the Dark

The moans were deafening, a discordant symphony on an endless repeat, emanating from the Darkness. The enemies' battle cry, designed to pierce more than eardrums, pierced souls. These cries shattered people, broke their will, crushed their hope. And this is how the enemy won their battles before firing a single blast of magic.

While there were no words to their song, the sentiment was clear. Pain. Hurt. And blame.

Why didn't you save me?

Where were you?

You have forgotten us.

Only one person could be seen in the Darkness—Kato, his

hands outstretched. Fire crackled through his body, his skin flaking away to embers.

"I'm waiting for you," he called, his ice-blue eyes flashing. "Come to me, my love. Follow me home, and we can be together. Just walk through the darkness into the light."

The mournful song fell into decrescendo from its fever pitch.

Kato reached out again with a smile, no longer on fire. Whole again. "See? There is peace here. All you have to do is take one more step…"

Falling for You
Dorthea

D o. Not. Move."
  A voice rang out, clear and demanding in the dark. "I know I said you have issues, but this is not the answer."

The voice. The guy from my hospital room. The one with the eyes like *him*.

All at once, my vision snapped back into focus. I was looking down. And down. Down at the cars zooming along, splashing through the puddles in the street. At the people, the size of bugs, scurrying around below us. Some of them dropped their umbrellas, pointing up.

At me.

Only then did it hit me that I was standing on the other

side of the railing that separated the graveled roof from the concrete edge. My balance may have been steady before, but as soon as I realized my situation, my legs turned boneless.

"No," he called as I pitched forward.

I expected him to sprout wings. To transform to reach me in time.

He didn't.

Twisting my body at the last second, I grasped the railing. But the rain made it slick. Too slick to hold.

As my grip slipped, his hand shot down—his nails biting into my wrist, his other hand grabbing hold of my wet, tangled hair. With a heave, he fell backward, using gravity to haul me up. We tumbled over the rail and across the gravely rooftop.

He grunted underneath me. "Ugh. You're heavy."

"Yeah, I've heard that before," I said. My heartbeat quickened as the fog of my memory lifted. "Where is she?" I hopped up and searched the skies frantically for the storm witch.

"So you lack sanity *and* gratitude," the boy grumbled, standing up and picking the gravel out of his elbow. "It's not like I saved your life or anything."

I stopped for a moment. "Not the smoothest of rescues," I said. I rubbed my head where I was sure I'd find a missing chunk of hair. "But thank you anyway. Now I'll return the favor. We need to run."

I grabbed his hand and dragged him across the roof and

toward the stairwell door. Before we could get there, my mother and father threw open the door and crushed me in their embrace.

"We couldn't find you. And then the roof alarm went off, and nurses were rushing up here for a jumper. I thought I'd lost you again. I can't. I just can't," my mother said, sobbing. Then she held me out and scolded me. "What could have possibly been going through your head? Why would you run away like that? Why would you come up here?"

I tried to herd all of them back to the stairs. "I will explain when we are safe inside behind locked doors."

"No, you will explain now," my dad, never the stern one, commanded with a voice like steel.

I took a deep breath and said, "A shadowy ink creature crawled out of the ceiling in my treatment room, and he chased me to the roof, where the storm witch appeared out of the cyclone like lightning. She was alone, without her flying puppies…that breathe fire…"

The more I said, the more my parents eyes clouded with worry. Not about being fearful of Griz, but about me. I knew because I had been there, and what I was describing sounded fairy flipping crazy to me.

I searched their faces for understanding. There was none. "Please don't look at me like that." I pointed at my rescuer. "Ask him."

"Me?" he squeaked. "Nuh-uh. Leave me out of it."

"You should have thought of that before you saved me." I

grabbed him and pulled him in front of my parents. "This guy was here. He'll tell you."

"What does she mean you saved her? Is that true, young man?" my mother questioned.

He looked around for escape. But once my mother had you in her claws, you were stuck. "She went to the ledge and climbed over the railing like she was sleepwalking. I pulled her back."

I smacked his shoulder. "Not that part. The earlier stuff."

He looked at me with a blank, trapped expression.

"You had to have seen it. The tornado? If not Griz, then the darkness. The emergency lights going out in the stairway. Anything," I implored.

"I'm sorry. I really am. When the power went out, I saw you bolt, so I followed you. But nothing was chasing you, and there was no one else around. Just you." He backed away. "I think it's better if I leave you to your family." He opened the door and disappeared before I could ask why he had followed me. Before I could even find out his name. Before I could figure out why his eyes were so blue and made my pulse race.

My wonderings were interrupted by a flurry of white coats who flooded out to drag me back inside.

I looked at the chart my parents handed me. My chart.

Level-3 chemically induced hallucination triggered by a mal-function in chemotherapy dosing equipment from the power outage.

I put down the folder. "Really? These visions are common enough there are levels for it?"

My dad nodded enthusiastically. "Yes, apparently it's very well documented."

Mother took the folder and gave me another stack of paper-work. "Indeed, I've been researching. What you are going through is actually surprisingly prevalent."

"There's a list of people who've seen flying demon puppies and witches in cyclones?" Somehow I seriously doubted it, but if there was, I really wanted to see it.

Dad shot me a look. The stern one he rarely gave me. *Give us a break. Knock off the crap, kiddo, and be thankful you aren't in a straitjacket.*

I shrugged. "I guess I can see that. The whole shadow crea-ture is all really hazy like a dream." Both my parents let out the breath I didn't realize they had been holding. Relief. That maybe I wasn't broken beyond saving.

I wish I felt that way.

I thought I knew what I saw, but my grumpy rescuer hadn't seen anything. My gut said he was lying or blind, but the hospital administrators reviewed security footage of the stair-well and the roof in case we sued for negligence. While the video was glitchy from the power outage, the rooftop was empty. No witch. No cyclone. Just rain and me walking to the edge in a daze.

It was all there in my file, the one that got thicker by the day.

My mind played tricks on me, arguing devil's advocate.

If you were really from another world, how come you know so much about this one? How do you know about lawsuits…and cars…and reality TV?

I didn't have an answer. At first when I woke up in the hospital, I marveled at everything in strange world of Kansas, relying on magic to explain my surroundings. But my brain filled in the holes with knowledge of this world and the things in it. There were even pictures of me as a child. In Kansas. Evidence that I lived here was piling up and hard to explain away. Maybe everyone else was right, and I was wrong. Maybe I was the one who was delusional.

I stood up and reached for my drawings on my wall. "Maybe it's time to take these down and focus on getting better."

My parents stared at each other, clasping hands, sharing a look so hopeful and personal that I was at once embarrassed to witness it and happy that I finally brought them some happiness.

Dad squeezed my shoulder. "Imagination is a good thing. You have a gift for story, and that's nothing to be ashamed of."

"That's right. As long as you remember that it's just that—a story," my mother finished. She focused in on the last picture on the ceiling. My drawing of Kato.

I put my hand on hers. Her smile dimmed. "I'll do it," I insisted.

She nodded solemnly and backed away.

Banished

With a deep breath, I stepped on top of the bed and gave a small tug. The picture came off without resistance. I was disappointed. I don't know what I expected. Some magic proof I was making a mistake? For Kato's picture to be as stubborn as I remembered—no, imagined—he was in person?

I put his picture with the others and let Mother put all of them in the folder along with my notebook.

"Are you going to give those to Dr. Baum?" I looked at the clock. It was past the time when I normally saw him.

Dad crossed his arms. "Punkin, you won't be seeing Dr. Baum anymore."

"Why?"

Dad looked at Mom and then his feet. "You want to explain this one?"

She sighed and put a hand on my shoulder. "I won't lie to you. It seems Mr. Baum wasn't who we thought he was. He wasn't a specialist or even a doctor at all."

"What?" I shook my head, trying to make sense of what she was saying. What about all the things I'd shared with him? His advice? The tea?

"I had some suspicions after our conversation, and I asked the administrators to look into it. He faked his credentials. He has no history. It's like he doesn't exist." She clenched her fist, her hand shaking. "It's no wonder you weren't getting better. If I ever find that man, I'll…"

Dad put a calming hand on her arm. "You'll report him to the proper authorities."

The look on her face made me think we'd all better pray she never saw him again.

I was torn. If what Mom was saying was true, Dr. Baum—or whoever he was—had lied to me. I'd started to trust him.

Maybe because he always seemed so familiar—the way he spoke in riddles, the untidy brown jacket he wore, and his endless fiddling with his mustache—I started to believe he might be right. That I could control the story. But if he wasn't a shrink, if he'd set out to deceive me the whole time, what did he want from me?

"Rule #29: When deposing an evil queen, beware of dogs. As well as dragons, gargoyles, and flying monkeys. Wicked royalty is well known for idiotic yet deadly pets."

—*Definitive Fairy-Tale Survival Guide, Volume 2: Villains*

Off with Her Head...Again
Rexi

Mic and I had switched places yesterday, and so far no one had carted me off, so I assumed my secret was safe. I'd mostly kept to myself and tried to keep Gwen as drunk as possible. Which was easier than it sounded because she was a notorious lush. We were sitting in the dining hall, and she was already eight glasses in. I needed to make a move soon because according to Mic, Dorthea was still alive. But maybe not for long.

It sounded pretty far-fetched. I mean, I skewered her with Excalibur for hex's sake. I'd seen her disintegrate into green embers and float away. Then again, Oz had hinted in his obtuse way that she wasn't totally gone. He'd simply said, "She's exactly where she needs to be."

Well, if she was alive somewhere, I was going to bring her back to Story, to us. Not because I sent her away in the first place but because there was absolutely zero chance I could beat Blanc and Morte alone. So far I'd been on the defensive. I wasn't stupid. Water immunity or not, taking on that enchantress was suicidal. They couldn't reach us here in Camelot…yet.

Morte, the Grimm Reaper, was not stupid. I'd had a dream last night. One where all I could see was Kato in the darkness. He begged me to come to him, to step outside Camelot's protection spells. But I knew better, and Morte had used a dream of Kato to draw me out because he knows I won't kill him while he occupies Kato's body. It should have been me who had died, my body playing host to that demon. Except Kato sacrificed himself and took my place. Yet another impossible debt to repay added to the one I owed Dorthea. Hard to pay back the dead, though now maybe she wasn't.

"But really, what is it with those two and self-sacrifice?" I muttered, thinking of Kato and Dorthea. "Pffft. What good is true love if you don't stick around to enjoy it?" I had been in love with Kato very briefly, but it was really only an echo of Dorthea's affection for him through our bond. The experience was gutting. And if that was just an echo, I couldn't imagine what full strength of her emotion for him would feel like. "Grimm, preserve me from true love."

"Here, here," Gwen said, holding up her glass. "Play with them, twist their strings and make them dance, but never let them close to your heart. It will be the death of you." She took a swig of her mead and motioned for another. This time the serving wench who brought it was not a wench at all, but Mordred. She continued, "Who needs love when you have loyalty?"

Mordred said nothing as he refilled her glass.

"Isn't that right?" Gwen said a little louder, curling her fingers in his hair, pulling him closer.

Mordred bowed out of her grasp. "Of course. I am true to the rightful queen."

Loyalty. Ha! That little toad sold me out the first chance he got. No, I'd been a toad very briefly, and that creature was too noble for the likes of him. A slug perhaps. I should douse him and his grail with salt.

I stared at the salt shaker on the table and fantasized about beating him with it.

In my brief absence, Mordred and Gwen had stopped accepting storybook refugees—the survivors of Blanc and Morte's reign of terror—into Camelot. Gwenevere had used the grail she'd taken from me to keep the borders closed, and she seemed content to live it up with cake and mead and her loyal boy toys while the world outside succumbed to its fate. Now I was a fan of self-preservation, but I'd seen the hate that Blanc carried for Gwen. And there was no story or alternate world where the self-proclaimed queen of Camelot would be safe. It was only a matter of time before Blanc found her. And deep down, Gwen had to know it. Every once in a while, you could catch the fear as her eyes darted around at the smallest sound.

Gwen gestured sloppily across the table at me. "Drink! Do you think you're too good to drink with me?"

"Quite the opposite, my fair lady. This ale is for thine royal tongue alone and is far too special of vintage for one so low as he," Mordred said, sealing the braggart.

"Someone's gotten awfully full of himself," I grumbled.

"Boys, boys," Gwen said, swaying in her chair. "You can fight over me all you want, but…" She paused for a moment, trying to catch her thoughts. "No, that's it. I do so love it when men duel for my favors." With a hiccup, she broke into a giggle fit. Then she face-planted on the table.

Mordred let out the breath he was holding. "Stars and suns, that woman can hold her drink. Even with the sleeping draught I added, she still managed three quarts."

"*You drugged her?*"

"Someone had to, as thou were taking far too long to do it. By the steel of Excalibur, you've had an entire day." Mordred made a face and then started sifting through Gwen's pockets.

My jaw dropped. "Wait a minute. You knew it was me? When? How?"

Mordred looked up but still kept searching. "The moment you spoke. A rose by any other name would still have the same thorns."

For once, I thought his botched cliché was intentional.

"Though I realize," he grunted while he hefted Gwen to

rummage the other side of her, "'twas I who told you a ruler cannot afford to trust anyone…there are times when t'would be much more convenient if thou would trust me. I *did* say I was loyal to the rightful queen."

"How was I supposed to know that was a secret message? I'm the king, not the queen. Or at least I was when I had Excalibur."

"Hog sloth. The sword lives. 'Tis merely hiding again, waiting to be claimed. Forget not that I was around when the rule of kings was made, that only a man might have the strength to wield Excalibur, but even I think that 'tis archaic. Ye may have to pretend to be a man, Rex the King, to get the rest of the kingdom to follow thee, but ye never pretend for me. I saw. The sword chose thee. And I see ye as ye are. 'Tis enough for me." He stood up and huffed. "Now kindly assist me in searching the sensitive areas as thou art a woman and that is more proper."

Now it was my turn to pull a face. I looked at Gwen's cleavage threatening to break free of the far too small dress. "Boundaries, man. I don't think that's proper for anyone."

"Weren't we trying to behead her the other day?"

"Keep your hands to yourself and don't go changing the subject. I'm assuming you're looking for the grail," I said.

Mordred wrinkled his nose. "I've already searched her rooms. What else could I possibly want from the beast?"

"Hey, I don't judge," I said, putting my hands up. "Much."

Looking back down at Gwenevere, I saw a glint. The

sparkle of silver. A chain looped around her neck that disappeared within the plunge of her neckline.

"Aw, man. Do you think?" I asked, pointing out the chain.

Mordred tapped his finger to the rough stubble of his chin. "T'would be the safest place. Where no man would dare tread." He smiled and clapped me on the shoulder. "I leave this quest to you, brave knight. Good luck."

"Thanks," I grumbled. "Guess there are limits to what you'll do for the grail."

I slowly inched my hand forward. Looting a passed-out body seemed wrong, but she'd stolen my grail in the first place. Steeling myself for what was next, I gulped and moved the last bit toward the chain at her neck. A hand clasped mine before I touched her. "Ahh!" I screamed, and my eyes flew open. Gwen screamed back at me.

I smacked her hand. "Let go. Let go."

"What in newt were you doing? Trying to take my virtue, you scoundrel? I always knew you were a no-good, rotten, thieving—"

"Hydra?" I blinked and checked her eyes. They were rolling around a bit, but that could have been from the drink.

"'Course. That Gwennie is a lightweight 'ompared to me. Hic." She tried to stand, but she fell against Mordred. "Well, hello, hot stuff. Wanna take a ride on my broom?"

Mordred tilted his head to peek around her and glare at me. "Are you sure it's not her? 'Tis still as handsy as a sea star."

I sighed. It was *handsy as an octopus*. But close enough. "Yup, that's Hydra."

"I was swigging mead way before I shrunk my first head." She beat her chest proudly.

"Good for you." I thumped her back. "But we're kinda in a hurry. We can fill you in on the particulars after we swap heads. First, the grail please." I held out my hand and waited while she pulled and prodded. Fished and finagled. And finally produced the inkwell from her bodice and gave it to me.

Mordred's face paled, and he blinked repeatedly. "I fear I will never be able to unsee such horror."

"Bah, be thankful I didn't charge ya for the pleasure. Thought you said we was in a hurry. Move it already."

Between Mordred and me, we managed to help—or rather drag—Hydra back to her newly renovated model castle. She waved off the curious stares of those we passed. "Don't you gots something better to be doing?"

Luckily, the squires were used to Gwen's tirades and scurried off before she got really nasty.

When we reached her room, we plopped her on the bed.

"Okay, where can we find a new head?" I asked, getting straight to business.

"How would I know?" she said and yawned. "Ima just gonna rest my eyes for a second."

"Very helpful. Thanks," I said. "I'll take the closet. Mordred, you take the chest, but I think it's locked." Without a word, he sheered off the lock with his ax. "Show-off," I said in response to his triumphant smirk.

I wasn't careful. I just started chucking stuff out of her closet. Gwen was a slob. She had everything from takeout containers to potion bottles to old sports equipment heaped on the floor. The crystal cats scattered around the room started mewling, quiet at first and then louder.

"S'okay, little ones. Mummy's right here," Hydra said and then resumed snoring. Wait, little ones? Not Hydra. Gwen.

"We have to hurry," I said to Mordred.

"I had not noticed," he answered in a gravelly tone.

"Well, you don't have to growl at me," I complained.

"I didn't."

We both turned to the door and said in unison, "Mr. Fluffypants."

The pint-size glitter factory of terror, Gwen's guard-nightmare, stamped its hooves from the doorway. Smoke drifted out of its nostrils.

"Thaz right," Gwen said. "My fluffles is here. He'll save me. Won't you, sweetgums?"

Fluffypants whinnied in response.

"Aw, hex. We're rotted." For all his pink sparkle, I'd seen him devour a man who'd had the gall to wake the queen before noon.

I reached into the closet and grabbed the first object my hand touched. A croquet mallet. Okay, I could make that work. "Hey, Fluffy," I called, lining up my shot. "Go fetch!"

With a mighty swing, I took aim at Gwen's head, sending it sailing over the nightmare's head and rolling down the hall. Fluffypants couldn't resist his basic nature and tore off after the modified ball.

Mordred gawked.

"What? Plans are overrated. Now bolt the door. It'll be back," I instructed and returned to my own search.

With renewed frenzy, I yanked stuff from the never-ending closet. A beating started on the door. That was fast. Fluffy was back. And he'd brought his guard friends and Gwen's screeching head.

"Break it down! Blow it up if you have to. Just get in there!"

I guess getting beheaded sobers you up real fast.

Mordred leaned against the door, his ax at the ready in case they broke through. I hefted a bowling bag, hoping to use it as a weapon. It grunted. Fumbling with the zipper, I yanked it open. There was no ball but a mass of red hair. I had no idea which head this was, but it had to be better than the one screeching outside.

After pulling it out, I stuck it onto the prone body with a slurp. The walls of the model castle shook and shimmied, shrinking in.

"What in graces?" Mordred said, eyes wide. He looked out the window as if he was calculating the distance to the ground if he bailed out.

"Stand there and hang on," I reassured him. "Just wait for it."

The windows shattered as the room folded in on itself. And with a pop, we were gone.

The End of the World (No, I'm Not Fine)

Rexi

Fluffy white wisps drifted along the floor under the stacks of clutter and junk in the storage warehouse. A patch of white floor broke apart near Mordred's feet, giving him a view of the ground miles below. "By all that's unholy, what manner of sorcery be this?" Mordred wore a horrified look on his face when he realized he was standing on a cloud. Then the fierce dark knight shrieked like a nursery school kid as he scrambled on top of the nearest solid surface he could find.

I sighed. I could watch that all day. "If only I had a spell-phone to record you now," I told him.

"I'm sure I've got one here somewhere." Hydra fiddled with

her head, screwing it on properly with a squishy pop. "Ah, that's better. Now we're back in business." She picked up a marble from the ground and chucked it at a wall. It ricocheted around the pile of junk until it hit a piece of sheet metal. The metal flipped over, revealing the front of a sign: SPARE PARTS WAREHOUSE. "It's good to be back in control. And to show my appreciation, I'll give you the family price. Pay an extra ten percent above whatever the tag says."

"That doesn't sound like a good deal at all," I said.

She shrugged. "I never really liked my family. But I'm stuck with 'em anyhow, and now I consider you one of them."

"Um...thanks, I guess?"

With a grumbly noise in her throat, she spit into her hand and then smoothed out the white streak in her orange hair. "Don't mention it."

"How can thou be so calm about this?" Mordred balanced precariously on top of a three-legged chair. "We hath died, and this is heaven." He looked around at the expansive piles of junk. "Or hell."

"Oh, grow a pair. Or buy some. I have extras," Hydra said, shooting another marble right at one of the legs of Mordred's perch. It cracked off, sending him sprawling onto the fluffy white floor. When he didn't fall through, he stopped hyperventilating.

I helped him stand. "Things have changed since your time, old man. Welcome to cloud storage. Home to all manner of extra crap, giants, and basically anything else that doesn't really belong. Like us."

"But how did we come to be here? We were just in Camelot. Then a wink later, we were not."

Blink, but he was closer than usual.

Still, this was the first time he'd witnessed Hydra's head swap. I gave him a quick tutorial on the process. Hydra was a headhunter. Each head had its own personality and house that popped up when in place. And since we were in Gwen's house during the swap...

"We ended up here," I summed up.

Hydra tsked her tongue. "I knew I shoulda destroyed that Gwennie head ages ago. Barking mad and rotten when I found it, and age ain't mellowed the power-hungry cuckoo out of her." Bending over, Hydra stuck her head through the clouds, leaving her butt in the air. "Mrph morph morphing murr murr."

"Yeah, I didn't catch that," I said.

She popped back up, grabbed Mordred and me by the ears, and yanked us through with her. We could see the world below like an upside-down periscope.

I wished I couldn't.

Once upon a time, the view would have been spectacular. Now it was just scary as hex. Large swaths of land that should have been green with tiny dots of buildings and people milling around had been reduced to barren, blackened, scorched earth. Sherwood Forest was twisted and overgrown, more marshland than forest. I looked toward where the Emerald palace should have been. There was nothing. Not even sparkling ruins. Just white space.

"That spot there." Mordred pointed out at the blank space. "How did our enemies manage that?"

"They didn't," Hydra said matter-of-factly.

"It's because there's nothing left," I guessed. "The House of Emerald has been wiped out. Verte, Dorthea, King Henry, Queen Em…all dead."

"Close." Hydra disappeared, and I felt a hand grasp my collar and yank me back up. "Verte is the only one who is truly dead. The rest are in the world of the Storymakers. Our resident Storymaker, Dot, has lost her way, and this world is withering, vanishing as a result."

"You seem to be a great sorceress. Can you not do something?" Mordred asked.

Hydra shook her head sadly. "Even with my inventory, I don't have a Storymaker's heart."

A fire bubbled inside me. "Oh, spell no. I did not die a magillion times to spend my last life hanging around waiting to vanish, drown, or burn."

Mordred stood tall and straightened his tunic, all traces of uneasiness gone. His ember-sparked eyes stared into mine. "Normally, I would say 'tis not my fight. I only wish to change mine own past. Yet I cannot do so with my present and future falling apart. So I will be yours—ally, that is." Then he added as an afterthought, "And in return, you will owe me a favor of my choosing."

I sighed. "Of course I will."

Hydra clapped. "Oh, good. So an impossible quest it is.

Been forever since I took on one of those. Best stock up on supplies then." She plucked a knapsack from the heap and gestured to her vast hoarding piles, which seemed bigger than last time I looked. "I'll even give you a bulk price. Twelve percent over sticker."

"Rotted mercenaries the pair of you," I grumbled and started sifting through materials to find anything useful. "I'm the one who's supposed to be the thief."

Hydra's knapsack was similar to Dorthea's princess purses. There was a portal inside that led to a mini storage chest, so it held far more than the outside suggested.

Hydra packed a separate traveling salesman suitcase. She wouldn't let us see the contents. She said it was backup. Mordred picked through the stuff and also found useful things for our journey, including skeleton keys with the bones still attached. As for me, I need one thing…

"It's here, isn't it?" I could sense it. "Excalibur."

"Of course it is. It goes where it's needed to the master of its choosing. And it knows you're going on a suicide quest, so it probably wants to say good-bye," Hydra said with a shrug.

"Any chance you've seen a sword sticking out of a big chunk of granite?"

"Nope." She pointed to the locked glass case. "If I did, I would have marked it up since it would be a guaranteed sale."

"The sword is yours to command. Simply call it to you," Mordred instructed.

"Here sword, sword, sword. Come out, come out, wherever you are."

Mordred groaned. "Excalibur is not a hog. Ye must do it like this." He strode over and stepped behind me, taking my hand in his. "Put thine palm facing out. Good," he murmured, the stubble of his cheek brushing my ear. "Now close thine eyes. See it in thy mind like an extension of thyself. Order that it return to its master."

I did as he asked, which was not easy with an audience. His nearness was...uncomfortable. Blocking that out, I imagined I felt the hilt of Excalibur against my palm, and I called the sword home to me. I heard a clang as items shifted, and then I felt a rush of wind and something smack against my hand.

It was not a sword. Swords are not squishy. I was afraid to open my eyes, but I did anyway.

"Eww." One of Hydra's spare parts rested in my hand. A spinal column with some bits still attached.

I dropped it and wiped my hand on Mordred's sleeve. "Yeah, nice try. Thanks anyway."

Mordred tried to nudge the spine with his shoe, but it inched away. "I think it worked just fine."

"No way. You're kidding me. That can't be Excalibur." I gagged a bit, staring at it.

Hydra cackled, shutting her case. "Excalibur will manifest according to its master needs. And apparently, you seem to need more backbone."

Mordred slapped me across the back and crowed. "That sword always had a sense of humor."

Hydra smiled a toothless grin that still managed to look predatory. "I'm glad you are in good spirits because you are going to lead us through Morgana La Fey's caverns."

Mordred's mirth vanished, the sparkle of it snuffed out instantly. "No."

Hydra plopped on the ground, the cloud making a crater where she landed. "Oh, good. Certain death if we stay here."

Mordred growled and grabbed Hydra by the front of her shirt, lifting her off the ground by a few inches. "Certain death if we enter."

"True," Hydra said, twirling her fingers around the hair coming out of her ear. "But at least it's a more interesting way to go out."

I raised my hand. "I vote for least certain death." I stepped closer to Mordred. "I don't ask for stuff. It's icky…and there's a debt to repay, and feeling tied to someone else, and ugh…" I cringed. "But I'm asking you to help me. And you already said I would owe you a favor. So we have a contract, and you aren't an oath breaker."

Mordred huffed and dropped Hydra with an *ooph*. "Even if I wanted to take you to the caverns, I can't. The entrance was lost when my mother disappeared."

"Is that all?" Hydra rolled back and forth like a beetle, trying to stand. Once up, she patted her case. "Well, I have that covered, so let's go."

We walked out of the warehouse and saw the upper kingdoms ravaged by ozmosis. The bean stalk lay felled and decaying on the ground along with tree-size splinters from the remains of the giant's home.

"So…" Then I asked the obvious, "How do we get down?"

"I can't do everything." Hydra pointed to the knapsack I carried. "You figure it out."

I rolled my eyes. "I was afraid you were gonna say that. I don't suppose you still have a giant pair of underwear lying around for a parachute?"

She grinned. "For the right price, I might have something better."

"Spell's bells. I'm gonna have to give you the entire treasury of Camelot when this is over, aren't I?"

"At least," she cackled and went back inside to grab our ride down.

9

Drink Me
Dorthea

The dream ended with a pop as I woke up. I reached over to my nightstand and fumbled around inside the drawer, my eyes still closed. Feeling...feeling...nothing.

That's right. Mom took my notebook. I'm not supposed to record Rexi's story in it anymore.

Less work for me, I guess.

A smile crept across my face. Real or not, it was good to see Gwen get exactly what she deserved. Maybe instead of watching what was happening in the land of Story in my dreams, I'd write one last thing, what I thought might happen next. Make up a happy ending for Rexi. Or at least one that didn't entirely suck. Then I could close out that chapter of my life and find an ever-after of my own here.

That thought, that *control* made the morning seem brighter than any since I'd woken up in this hospital.

With a stretch, I rolled out of bed and put on my best pair of scrubs, which looked identical to every other pair in the closet. Hospital couture. My no-slip socks were all the rage on the runway, I'm sure.

Even as Bubba, the name I'd dubbed my nonverbal security guard, grunted with arms folded as I passed him, my mood could not be crushed. I whistled zippidee-doo-da as he followed me down the hall to the common room for breakfast.

Today's menu was French toast sticks. I wasn't exactly sure that counted as food. More a food-like substance. But they tasted pretty good drowned in sticky stuff and apple sauce. Bubba took my tray, swapped the metal silverware out for plastic, and then plunked it down on an empty table. After that, he resumed his post at the door.

I'd put the first dripping stick in my mouth when a little munchkin with a mass of tangled red hair ran up and plopped down beside me.

"Oh, my gosh, it's you!" She squealed in delight. "I've heard about you. Are you really a princess? If you are, where's your animal sidekick? Do you live in a castle and have a crown? Have you ever kissed a frog? Do you know any wicked witches? Is magic real? Will you sign my book?"

Overwhelmed, my mouth hung open, the apple sauce

dripping off my lip. I went to say something that would have been elegant and intelligent, but I choked. Literally. Bubba had to come behind me and whack my back.

The little girl stared at me with wide eyes. "Wow. Was that poisoned apple sauce?"

A woman ran across the room. Her hair was the same fire red as the girl's, and it also probably hadn't seen a brush in days. The little one wore hospital clothes. The older one, a rumpled blouse. "Jessica!" The woman picked up the squirming kid. "I turn my back for one second…"

She then turned to me with a look of wariness and tired apology. "I'm sorry my daughter disturbed you. It's just she has this obsession with fairy tales, and she's heard the nurses talking about you…" Her face colored. "I'm sorry. That was rude. I can't even function anymore. I haven't slept in weeks, with waiting by the phone for the hospital to call us if they found a donor. And now there's so much to do before tomorrow's surgery, and I can't get her to take any of her medications. I'm terribly sorry. This isn't your problem. We'll go."

"Awww, but I don't want to go. I want to eat with the princess." The little girl wiggled out of her mother's grasp.

Bubba and several other staff members moved from their posts toward us. I held up my hands. *See? A nonthreatening interaction. We're totally cool.*

I whispered to the half-pint, "Your name's Jessica?"

She nodded enthusiastically. "But you can call me Jessie!"

I couldn't help but smile. I looked up at her mom, at the

mismatched buttons on her shirt, at the tears threatening to spill down the dark circles under her eyes, and I knew what to do. "Okay, Jessie. Some people have called me Princess Dorthea of Emerald, but you can call me Dot. And I'm not a big fan of taking my medicine either." I stuck out my tongue and pulled a yuck face. Jessie mimicked me. "But I'll make you a deal. I would love to have breakfast with you and answer all your princess questions, but only if you promise to take your medicine when your mom tells you to. If that's okay with your mom, that is."

The mother nodded but held her breath. Jessie scrunched her nose, gnawing on her lips. "I dunno. It sounds like a trick."

"No trick. I promise. I'll even take my medicine too." I held out my hand to shake. "So do we have a deal, Lady Jessie?"

She put her warm hand in mine and shook it for all she was worth. It was so small I was afraid it might break. Her mother let her breath out in a huge whoosh, collapsing in the chair across from me.

"Let's see. Where should we start?" I thought back to Jessie's questions. "I used to live in a beautiful and grand emerald palace. And I had a whole closet of crowns. And a room just for shoes! Enough shoes to give the elves' labor union hissy fits. And thankfully, I've never kissed a frog. My best friend used to be one though. And I have kissed a chimera. I guess you could call him my animal sidekick. Just never to his face. I know far too many wicked witches, and yes, magic is absolutely real and will bite you in the butt if you're not paying attention. So be careful what you wish for."

Jessie practically vibrated with happiness in her chair.

"Let it out, kid, or you'll explode," I said before taking another bite of my breakfast.

She pulled out her book. *The Definitive Collection of All Things Fairy Tale: A Companion to the Survival Guide Series.* "Are you in here?"

I took the book and flipped through. Not surprisingly, the only mention of Emerald City was quite far from the truth. Or at least my truth. "Naw, I'm sort of undercover. But I know pretty much everything there is to know about Fairy Tale."

I expected Jessie to be disappointed at my lack of proof, but she only got more excited. She took the book and turned to the page on Cinderella. "Tell me about her."

I lowered my voice to gossip level. "Just between you and me, the reason Cindy could never go to the ball is cuz she was a lazy slob. Never ever kept her room clean. Had a horrible animal-hoarding problem too. But excellent taste in shoes, that girl."

"And her?" Jessie flipped to Beauty.

"At the moment, Beauty is the beast. Major, major anger management issues. But smartest gal you'll ever meet. She has a bit of Stockholm syndrome from being kidnapped though."

"What about her?" This time she pointed to Sleeping Beauty.

"Don't get me started on Rose. You can smell her perfume

from a mile away. And I'm still not sure how she got famous for sleeping in for a thousand years."

For another twenty minutes, Jessie peppered me with questions on everything from mini unicorns to spells to less than charming princes and exactly what a chimera was. For the first time, I shared my life without fear or judgment. Somewhere along the way, more little ones joined us until even the floor behind me had listeners.

"Tell me about Snow White," a girl who was about four years old piped up.

I fidgeted for a minute. "Maybe I should skip that one." I covered her ears and whispered to the adults. "A teen living with seven men just isn't really an appropriate story for a kid her age."

Jessie's mom laughed, long and hard. "Oh, dear, I haven't laughed in…I don't know how long."

"Hey, Dot." Jessie tugged on my shirt. "You said you used to have a crown. Why aren't you wearing it?"

I sighed. Also a story not suitable for children. I did my best to edit. "I made a wish, a very selfish wish that hurt a lot of people and changed their happy endings. But that's why I'm here—to try and set it right. That's why I'm just Dot for now."

The on-call nurse tapped her watch. "It's time for your medicine, Jessie."

"Awww…" she complained.

"You promised," I reminded. "And you can't be a princess if you don't keep your promises."

Jessie smiled and threw her arms around me. "I think you're still a princess."

I hugged her back, and then her mother picked her up and laid a hand on my arm. "You have a gift, young lady. Thank you."

A gift. That's what Dad said. My memories were filled with the curse of Emerald, and while I never thought I would say it, I was starting to prefer this life.

The nurse on duty whistled loudly. "Story time is over, you rug rats. It's time to get on with your therapies. Nope, I won't hear an ounce of whining," she said over the groans. "Thank Ms. Gayle, and please head back to your rooms."

After a flurry of thank-yous, I was soon alone again. Well, not quite. I still had Bubba in the audience. And one other person.

"You know, listening to you, I can almost see it." The guy from the roof wandered closer to me. "The purple toadstools. The ABC serpent. One would almost think you'd been there."

"Yeah, me too. I think that's the problem."

He shrugged. "What you did there was really cool and nice. And maybe you're not as crazy as I thought."

"That's a glowing endorsement, Sir…"

"John," he inserted. "No fancy title or anything. Everyone else calls me John, so I guess you can too."

"John it is. Thank you. And thank you for following the crazy girl up the dark stairs into the storm. It was very brave of you."

His blue eyes lit up as he smirked. "Perhaps I should add 'Danger' as my middle name."

I laughed but then groaned as a sudden pain hit my stomach.

"Hey," he said and chuckled. "The joke wasn't that bad."

"No, pain. It burns." I clutched my abdomen and curled up in my chair.

"I'll get someone." He started for the nurse's station, but he ran squarely into Bubba.

"She just needs her medicine," Bubba said.

"So the giant does speak," I joked before the gut-wrenching pain took my breath away again.

"Drink this." He shoved a little cup of red liquid at me.

"What is it? I've never had that before." I tried pushing it back.

He tipped it to my lips and poured. "It's new from Dr. Zelda."

I gulped it down. It was either that or suffocate from the pain.

"Jeez, dude," John said, sniffing the cup. "It's probably some opiate. It should stop the pain, but I wouldn't be surprised if it knocks you out cold."

True, because within seconds I was too tired to even stand. Bubba hoisted me up and carried me to my room.

"No one's really dead until the series finale. And even then it's debatable."

—The Completely Unauthorized Storymaker's Biography

10

Shock and Awe
Dorthea

"Nngn."

I yawned, but the inside of my mouth was so gummy and gross that I was sure someone had tried to glue it shut. I was so tired, which seemed counterintuitive since I was just waking up. I raised my arms to stretch, but I could barely raise my left. It was tethered. Restrained. My heart rate skyrocketed.

There was a quiet groan next to me.

Realizing I was not alone, my eyes shot open. The nurse practitioner sat beside my bed, hanging on to the IV pole so it didn't tip over with my squirming.

"Be still. It's almost done." She flicked the tube going into my arm to unkink it and restart the green liquid fire flowing into my veins. "I was hoping to be finished before you woke up, but I couldn't start until your new doctor calculated the new dose of treatment. And have you ever seen a doctor run on time?" The nurse shook her head and tsked. "No. I swear if Death came a calling for them, they'd stick him in a waiting room and tell him to cool his heels until he was called." She muttered something about self-important *bleep-bleeps* before remembering I was there. "You never mind I said that. It's all sorted, and you'll be feeling right as rain in no time."

"I hate the rain." The words simply popped out. I couldn't remember why that was important to me. Trying to sort out anything in my mind was like traversing through thick fog with no lighthouse. And it felt just as dangerous.

A knock interrupted my thoughts.

John stood inside my door. "You still alive?"

"Seem to be," I said, miming checking my pulse. "Are you disappointed?"

With a shrug, he said, "I went to a lot of trouble to save you, so it would be an awful shame if you keeled over now."

He made it a foot inside the room before the nurse held out her hand. "Not another step, young man. This room is under controlled protocol. Medical personnel only. Unless you've got a medical degree lying around, you should keep scooting."

With on hand behind his back, he patted himself down

with the other and then snapped his fingers. "Darn, I must have left it in my other pants."

"John," she said in warning.

He held up his hands in surrender. One of them held a small stuffed animal. "I'm going. I just wanted to leave this here. Catch." He tossed the gift from the door. It landed on my lap.

I picked up the stuffed animal, which was a small terrier toy with mangy brown fur. A mutt. I couldn't help it. I busted out laughing.

The nurse huffed. "Don't be rude. That was a very sweet gesture."

But there was no problem. John was laughing too.

"Oh, good," he said and chuckled. "I saw it and felt the same way."

The nurse looked back and forth between us two crazies. "I don't get it. Is this an inside joke?"

"Dunno," John said. "Maybe you said something about little beasts, or maybe it was something I saw on your walls. But I knew it would make you smile."

I stopped laughing and looked into his eyes seriously. "Really, thank you. It's perfect."

He held my gaze for a moment. "Don't mention it. You're making it weird."

I gasped because the nurse pulled out the IV from the port without warning. "All done," she said. "I'll turn on the TV for you on my way out." She pointed at John. "And you're coming with me."

"Yeah, yeah," he replied.

The screen on the wall flickered to life. Kansas City news at noon.

"…books completely destroyed." A news anchor seemed to be interviewing the head librarian. "It's bizarre. Perhaps it was a mold. One day the books were fine, and the next, dark spots started to appear across the pages. And those spots got worse every day."

"Can we see one of the damaged books?" the reporter asked.

"Of course." The librarian held out an older book. It looked decayed and withered. "This was in our collector's section. The first known collection of Grimm's fairy tales, handwritten by the brothers themselves. Not only is this a monetary loss, but a piece of history is now gone forever."

John and the nurse weren't paying attention, still bickering in the background, but the news story had my full attention. The book's cover was leather with a red quill engraved on the front. I'd held it often enough to know it well. *The Book of Making.*

The news reporter examined the book. "This truly is a mystery."

"It gets even stranger," the woman added as the anchor flipped through the book. "We've gone through all of our collections in the library for worry of how it would spread, but it seems that only certain sections are affected. The folklore, fantasy, and mythology section is a complete loss."

The camera panned to an entire bookcase of blackened, diseased books. I squinted to see better. Then I cried out in alarm. The spines of the tomes were not only damaged, but there was a thick swarm of glistening, black bugs scuttling out of the pages. They poured out of the book on the lectern.

"What? Are you okay?" John asked, pushing the nurse aside and rushing into the room.

I pointed to the TV. "The bugs."

John moved closer to the screen. "I don't see anything."

I pointed more urgently. "Can't you see them? They're all over the books. And oh Grimm, they're crawling all over that woman's arm!" I put my hands over my mouth to keep from gagging.

John came to my side. "There're no bugs. Just moldy books. The lady's arm is normal."

"No," I moaned, willing someone else to see what I could.

The nurse pushed John toward Bubba. "The doctor warned us this might happen. Take him out of here while I handle this." She shoved a small cup of the same sweet-smelling red liquid under my nose.

"No, I don't want—" She didn't care about consent. She tipped up the cup up the second my mouth opened. When I tried to spit out the thick liquid, she covered my mouth and held my nose.

I fought to hold out, but eventually, I ran out of air. I coughed and sputtered as the nurse moved her hand.

"See, that wasn't worth putting up all the fuss. You'll feel better soon," she said.

Lies, I thought as I dropped out of consciousness again.

"Ngn."

I yawned, but the inside of my mouth was gummy and nasty like someone had tried to glue it shut. I raised my arms to stretch, but my left arm would barely move. It was tethered. Restrained. I had a horrible sense of déjà vu.

I opened an eye groggily. "Oh, it's you again."

"Well, good morning to you too." The nurse flicked the needle, not even bothering to say it was gonna pinch.

I gritted my teeth through it. "Is it morning? Wouldn't know. Time kinda goes wibbly wobbly when you get drugged daily."

"Look, *princess*," she mocked. "You are my last case after pulling an all-nighter. I am not in the mood for your trouble. If you have a psychotic reaction to the medication again, keep it to yourself. I do not want to hear about it."

I rolled my eyes and looked away, hoping to get it over with. Notably, the TV had been removed from my room. I vaguely remembered the news program when I saw the stuffed dog on the table. I groaned.

Why'd I have to flip out in front of the nice guy? I doubted I'd see John again. My reaction probably scared him off for good. Though maybe it was better that way. I don't know what is wrong with me. I'm from another world and reacting badly to meds here, or maybe I'm just plain nuts. It didn't really matter. In the end, I still felt broken and out of place.

The doctors left orders to keep me sequestered in my room. I wasn't even allowed in the common room for breakfast, so I hadn't seen Jessie. *Jessie…* She was so young, and she was here for something. I couldn't remember what.

I couldn't remember a lot of things. I couldn't remember the last time I'd seen my parents. I kept hearing about a new doctor, but I had not had any more meetings or therapy since my last tea with Dr. Baum. I think…

"Hey, nurse lady…"

She ignored me.

I turned to get her attention and noticed the IV bag for the first time. It wasn't the usual green fluid. This time it was black. I could see it flowing into my veins under my skin.

I screamed and yanked out the needle, paying no mind to the pain. "Get it out! Get it out!" I pulled on the port and scratched on the veins, trying to expel the black ooze from my body, but only blood came out of the puncture wound.

The nurse pushed a button, and an alarm sounded. "What did I tell you? Now you've done it."

I fought and kicked and punched when Bubba and another security guard held me down. "No, not the red potion! I don't want the poppies!" I cried.

"You don't have a choice." Then nurse held up the cup. "Take your medicine."

I tried to fling out my right arm, half-expecting green flames to throw them back, but of course, that didn't happen. I was in Kansas, and all of that magic was in my head. And they were right. I was powerless.

"Ngn."

I yawned, but it was hard to swallow. Like the entire inside of my mouth was coated... Oh, I don't know anymore. I raised my arms to stretch, but my arms wouldn't move. They were tethered. Restrained. I'd been in this situation before, and it was getting old.

I looked to the side to yell for a nurse, but I was alone. The port in my arm was gone, and my hand wasn't tethered to an IV. They were strapped to the bed rails by leather restraints.

"Whaz viz?" Why couldn't I talk right? I tried again. "Lez me goo."

"You're going all right." Bubba came in and kicked the bed, jiggling the too-tight restraints.

I shook my head, looking for some way out. But there was nowhere to go. I saw my stuffed dog on the table. Or what was left of it. Its arm was ripped off, pieces of fluff yanked out and strewn on the floor.

I didn't have to ask because Bubba saw my confused look.

"That was the last straw. In the middle of the night, you freaked out and attacked it. The doctor decided you were too violent and opted to change your treatment."

"No," I moaned. He had to be lying. I couldn't remember doing that. I wouldn't have hurt the stuffed animal. It was a gift. It reminded me of…someone. My mind was mush. Clear as mud. I couldn't think straight, but I knew I needed to leave. I fought to get up, but I was trapped.

A slow smile crept across Bubba's face like a centipede. "You should be happy. You're about to get the crazy shocked out of you. Bzzt." He rattled the bed again.

This couldn't be happening. There's no way my parents would agree…

"I know you must think this can't be happening. But it is. And here's the proof." He pulled my chart of the wall. An order for electroshock treatment. Approved and signed by Dr. Zelda…and my parents.

With a whistle, two orderlies came in the room and wheeled my hospital bed down the hall and into the elevator. I pleaded for them to stop. Shouted curses. But my words came out like in a babble.

Down we went into the dredges of the basement rather than upstairs to the psych ward. The orderlies pushed me down the hall into the morgue. There was no missing the ominous irony and threat in that destination. The room looked like the Evil Queen's dungeon. Bodies lay on long metal tables. A hefty scale that was held next to one table measured a man's heart like the huntsman who'd saved Snow White.

But who would save me?

"Are you sure we were supposed to bring her here?" Orderly A asked Orderly B after they set the lock on the bed's wheels. "All of the treatment rooms are on the third floor."

The other orderly tapped the chart in his hand. "The doctor made a special request, and it ain't my job to question it. Now let's get. This place is freaking me out."

On the far side of the room, there were rows of freezer drawers and a single tray of instruments that held a pair of paddles with wires sticking out. The rest of the tray held an array of pointy tools with very sharp edges.

As the orderlies left, I screamed for them to come back, shouting until my throat was raw. Once it felt like I was swallowing glass, then I screamed some more.

Slowly, the door opened. A burst of relief flowed down my body until I saw who was wearing the lab coat.

Griz.

After that, all I felt was terror.

"It's not real. It's not real. *Notrealnotrealnotreal*," I chanted like a prayer.

"Hello, I'm Dr. Zelda. I'm sure you'll find I'm quite real, and I'll be performing your procedure today." The storm witch followed my gaze to the shock paddles. "Don't worry. I won't be using those." She held her hands out in front of her instead. Lightning sparked between her fingertips. "Now you get to see what it's like to melt into a puddle just like you did to me. Except your turn is going to take a lot longer." The lighting arced to the restraints, shooting pain up my arms. "And I'm going to enjoy every second of it."

"The biggest mistake one can make in villainy is killing your enemy too quickly. Do it slowly and make them truly suffer."

—Lord Humperdink

To the Pain
Dorthea

After the first few thousand volts ran through me, I gave up on the hope that what was happening was all in my head. Imagining it would hurt a lot less. As soon as I thought I'd pass out from the pain, Griz would stop and wait for me to recover before beginning again.

"You know, you made a big mistake by coming to this world, Girl of Emerald," Griz said, circling me.

"Like I had a choice." I spit the coppery taste from my mouth. "And what? You're going to torture me with narration?"

"*Tsk, tsk.* So unladylike. You sound just like that kitchen rat. You know, the one your true love died for. The one who stabbed you."

"Your voice makes my ears bleed. Just shock me to death. It'd be less painful than listening to you."

She rounded the bed, lowering her face to mine. "Which is exactly why I'm drawing this out. It's not to the death. It's to the pain. If I do this right and only fry your frontal lobe, you'll still feel every zap. It will be our little secret. And we can repeat this treatment every day." She smiled and nonchalantly formed three small storm balls, making them dance in her hand. "I'll watch as everyone you care about regards you with pity and disgust as you drool with a vacant expression." She emphasized her point by throwing one ball at my legs. I gasped and choked on a scream. "You won't be able to speak or move, but your mind will be as sharp as a knife, cutting you with the knowledge that you've lost everything."

Even though I knew a second blow was coming, I couldn't move or even flinch as it nailed my stomach, stealing all hope of breath.

Griz continued, "I want you to see my sister cross over and conquer this realm. To know the world of Story and your friends will be swallowed by Morte's shadow. Only then will you know how completely you've lost as you slowly disappear from every world."

While she aimed the third ball for my head, I moved the only part of my body I still had control over and shut my eyes.

Clang. "Ugh." *Thunk.*

My eyes flicked open at the sound.

Griz lay crumpled on the floor while John loomed over her, holding a metal scale in both of his hands. She didn't move.

I tried to speak, overjoyed that finally *someone* could see my nightmares, but Griz's "treatment" had sent my whole body haywire. The best I could do was groan.

"Dot!" John said, dropping the bloodstained metal scale to the floor with a clang. "Are you all right?" I couldn't answer, but he didn't give me a chance anyway. "Forget that. Stupid question. Can you move?" He fumbled with the restraints and hissed, a spark flashing the first time he touched the buckle.

My brain told my hands to grab his, but my hands ignored me. I might have seen a finger twitch, but that may have been from the residual electricity in my body.

That witch! I thought I hated her before when she gave me the cursed wishing star. But I had no idea what hate was then. Anger boiled inside me, spreading into every vein and limb. I never thought I'd wish for the Emerald curse to return to me, but I wanted nothing more than to sprout green flames from my hands and dance over Griz's ashes. Instead, without a release, my rage scorched my insides.

John snapped his fingers in front of my face. "Hey. Focus. I already committed felony assault. I don't think you should add on to it."

Those blue eyes of his were very perceptive.

"I need you to calm down and try to help me. That doctor is out cold, but someone's going to come looking for you both soon." He looked me up and down. "I could pick you up, but I don't think I could carry you out the front door without being stopped."

I collected my thoughts and my breath, steadying my heart rate and emotions. I tried sitting up. I couldn't feel the muscles flex at all. Walking out of here under my own power was not going to happen. Concentrating, I focused all my efforts on forming words. Even then, they came out like I'd been huffing pixie dust.

"Go. Out. Like. Came. In." I wheezed the last word, exhausted from those five syllables. But still, it was progress, which meant Griz hadn't paralyzed me permanently.

Hopefully.

John quirked an eyebrow, puzzling through my words. He was going to have to figure out what I meant because trying to explain it in my current condition would be like trying to scale Rapunzel's tower.

"You want me to push the gurney? Like I'm an orderly bringing you back upstairs?"

I tried to nod, but after my head dropped back against the pillow like a rag doll, I couldn't get it to move again.

John leaned in. "You don't think they are going to question a patient pushing a bed around?"

This time I looked over at Griz, my head flopping to the side. John followed my gaze.

"You want me to take her lab coat and badge."

Right on Pinocchio's nose.

"This probably won't work." He huffed, but he wrangled the witch out of her doctor's disguise anyway. "But it's better than nothing." He put a hand on my shoulder. "I don't know what is going on around here, but it's my responsibility to get you out."

I didn't have enough breath or speech function to ask him why he kept following me even though he barely knew me. Or to thank him for saving me. Again.

John wheeled me through the morgue. I finally gained enough control of myself to close my eyes and ignore the bodies.

We entered the elevator, and John pushed the button for the main floor. "Let's hope the security guards are on lunch," he grumbled.

The elevator rose, dinging and announcing each floor. Three floors, and the doors slid open.

I closed my eyes and pretended to be unconscious from the shock therapy. It wasn't like I had to act very hard.

I felt the bed move forward, turn to the left, and then abruptly stop.

"John, what in the heavens…" A guy's voice. "Son, no. What are you thinking? Go back to your room, and we can forget this."

"I can't, Nick," John said. "Look at her. Does she look like she's getting better to you?"

"No…but I'm only a nurse's assistant. There are doctors who—"

"Have no idea how to help her. She's dying." Dying? My breath stilled as John's words and each beat of my heart sounded like a tick of the clock.

The nurse's assistant, Nick, tried to say that he wasn't at liberty to discuss my case, but John wasn't having any of it. He pounded his fist on the bed rail. "Don't lie to me. I heard you talking about her at the desk. I know trying to escape doesn't make sense, but I had to do something to help her. And so do you."

I opened my eyes and looked at Nick for the first time. He was an older man with a kindly but worried expression and a yellow surgical cap covering his graying hair.

"Please," was all I could say, but I managed to extend my hand toward his.

He opened his mouth to say something and then shut it and groaned. "As you wish." He squeezed my hand and placed it back on my chest. "John, do you know the new addition they're building?"

"The wing that's for the new machine they're custom designing?"

"Yes, the Schrödinger CAT scan–MRI hybrid. I'll get her past security and meet you there. Find her street clothes so you can take her out the construction entrance without being noticed. I'm going to lose my job over this…"

"Thank you," John said and rounded the corner.

"Don't thank me yet," Nick muttered. "We've still got to get past Tweedle Dim and Tweedle Dimmer." He nodded to the big desk where two muscley guys were flirting with the receptionist. Two Bubbas! Twins. No wonder he never seemed to sleep and alternated between stints of being silent and never shutting up.

"Here we go." Nick started pushing the bed forward. I shut my eyes, playing comatose again.

I could hear the wheel squeaking. And as we got closer, I could make out the low cadence of Bubba Two's voice and the grunt of agreement of the other. "So when's your break?"

"I'm about to clock out," the receptionist's trill voice replied. "I could use a latte, but I forgot my wallet." Even with my eyes shut, I could hear that pout and her eyelashes batting. Hex, I used to be the master of that move to get my way.

"I hate to leave a damsel in distress. Why don't we help you with that?" Bubba Two's voice sounded quieter and more behind me when he replied.

I exhaled in relief.

Too soon.

"Hey!" Bubba Two called. I heard clomping as heavy foot-steps worked to catch up. "Where you going with that one? She's supposed to be in treatment."

"She, um, finished," Nick stammered. "I'm taking her to recovery."

"Recovery is on the fourth floor."

"Yeah, I know that."

I willed Nick to think of a convincing excuse for the detour.

"I'll take her," Bubba Two said, and my bed jerked to the side.

"I'm just taking the long way, sir. I'd like to put off bed-pan rounds as long as I can," Nick said.

Bubba One grunted. So Nick continued, "Plus, it sounded like you had something better to attend to."

"True that," Bubba Two said. "At least this brat will be easier to care for now, am I right?" The other Bubba grunted again. *Clomp, clomp, clomp.* After a beat, their conversation with the receptionist resumed, and my bed started rolling again.

After we rounded the corner, Nick shook my shoulder. "Can you walk?"

I pushed myself up to sit, but my arms wobbled and collapsed under my weight. That would be a no.

Nick snagged a wheelchair and transferred me into it. "This should be less noticeable." He pushed me through the lobby and the main floor cafeteria, snagging a few muffins and fruits along the way. A few minutes later, we started down a hall with fiberglass beams and large sheets of plastic. The lights flickered, and plaster dotted the floor. The unfinished addition.

It was empty except for several large wooden crates.

"He'll be here," Nick said as if reading my thoughts.

I really hoped so. But there really wasn't any reason for him to be. As far as he knew, I was simply a head case he'd met. And kept saving.

"I need to get back," Nick said, frowning at his watch. "The others will notice if I'm gone too long. Are you going to be all right?"

Nope, most definitely not. But that didn't mean I was giving up. Getting zapped by Griz may have made my body break, but it made my mind stronger. I wasn't a lost girl. While I may not see things the way others here do, that didn't change who I was, Princess Dorthea, Girl of Emerald. I had work to do.

"Go. And thank you."

"The new machine is in those crates and hasn't been assembled, but be cautious. Stay away from them. This wheelchair is metal, and the strong magnets could draw you in. With that much electricity and the rain, it would be most unpleasant, I promise." Nick handed over the bag of food he'd taken from the cafeteria and then backed up, bowing his head and taking off his yellow scrub cap. "It was my pleasure...as always." And with those odd words, he took off.

Not wanting to waste another minute in this death-trap hospital, I focused on moving my arms and rolled the wheelchair forward slowly. And I mean slowly. Slugs would have lapped me. My arms grew tired after a few yards, and my body ached each time I had to push over construction debris.

When I came across a two-by-four lying in my way, I pushed and rocked, but I couldn't get the second wheel over it. Leaning to the side, I felt the chair start to pitch, but my arms were too tired to catch me.

Someone else did.

"Whoa there, turbo," John said, hugging my shoulders and righting the wheelchair before it tipped. "Run away without me?"

I smiled, trying to shrug off how relieved I was that he'd come. "Just trying to save you." I breathed heavily and finished, "From harboring a fugitive."

"Too late. I'm already the Clyde to your Bonnie. I knocked

out that doctor and kidnapped you, so you're stuck with me."
He had changed into tan pants and a short-sleeved purple
shirt that had a weird symbol on it and the picture of a man
with a guitar. The word "Prince" was scrawled underneath.

"Yeah, about that." I watched his face, trying to read his
expression. "You saw her this time. The witch that tried to fry
me with lightning on the roof was the same witch who tried
to fry me with lightning in the basement."

"You're explaining it weird, but yeah, I saw the shock
doctor, obviously. She was a total witch and could have
killed you."

His expression was honest, but I could tell he still didn't see
anything magical or remiss about the situation. He thought
Griz was simply a homicidal doctor. Well, it was a start. I'd
take what I could get.

"So what are we going to do now?" John asked.

"We're going to find a safe place to hang out until I can
walk, and while we wait, I'm going to tell you a story. You
have to promise to listen to the whole thing. After that, you
can ditch me if you want."

"Why would I do that?" John asked. "I already said it's too
late. You're stuck with me."

We had reached the edge, where the hall ended and went
out to the street. The sun streamed down, filtering through
the clouds on this dreary day. People had their umbrellas out
as ash and sooty rain fell from the sky. The very clouds looked
like they were on fire. Most ominous were the shadowy

tendrils that wrapped themselves around a few of the buildings near the hospital.

I pointed. "That is why you should turn back now."

"What?" he asked, squinting. "I don't see anything unusual."

"Be grateful you can't," I whispered.

"Though I give advice for living, I've noticed I rarely take it myself."

—Dear Alice Manners Column, March Hair Edition

Return of the Red Queen
Rexi

Now that tyrannical Queen Gwenevere has been deposed, I promise you all safety here in Camelot as well as a new dawn and rebirth of the knights of the triangle table so that we may protect all that we hold dear. It doesn't matter what your original story was—hero or villain, myth, legend, or fairy tale. We are all the same, and we all face the same threat. We face the same enemy. I won't lie to you. The grains of sand are running low. This is the last chapter. This is the last chance to write our own fates and defend against those who would erase all of Story. I swear upon Excalibur to fight for all of Libraria. Who among you will stand with me?"

The refugees of Story roared in reply. A huge crowd had

gathered to hear their king, the dragon of Camelot who had been reborn. Or at least the guy pretending to be. Hydra let him out of the tower after we'd gotten back from the cloud. But only after he made a deal with her to keep up the ruse of being king a little longer.

Hydra pointed to my imposter and smacked me in the arm. "For all his showboating, that old faker ain't doing too shabby. You should take notes, Rexi."

I rolled my eyes. "I've heard better. I still think leaving Mic in charge is a bad idea. He's not trustworthy. It's like asking the big bad wolf to manage Grandma's retirement home."

Mordred crossed his arms, leaning back against the drawbridge. "Aye. And I maintain this entire plan is doomed to fall."

"To *fail*," I corrected.

"That too."

I had nothing to say to that because he was probably right. After Hydra summoned an UBER-Unicorn Budget Enchanted Rideshare to take us back to Camelot, the first order of business had been clearing out the mess Gwen left behind, including deciding what to do with Mic.

I suggested tossing an apple in his mouth and sending him to the orges as a gesture of goodwill. I was outvoted.

With Camelot and Avalon literally being the last line of defense against Blanc and Morte, someone needed to maintain the border and keep the people safe. The refugees had been displaced from their own fairy tales and had come to Camelot seeking a haven. And I'm not going to lie. After as many times as I'd been ordered around in Emerald, it made me feel a little good when Prince Sterling came begging for asylum. I gave him a job in the kitchens.

I figure he'd enjoy that. He can look at his reflection in the pots as he cleans them.

The only reason that Mic got the job of temporary king is that he was the only one who could fake being me, an unfortunate and necessary skill. Because I couldn't be two places at once, and if Blanc got wind that I was out of the castle, she'd attack, and that would be *The End*. We couldn't afford to let her know something was up.

"Well," Hydra said. "If there's one thing we can trust, it's that Mic will protect his sorry butushka first. And Blanc don't forget a grudge. It's in his best interest to support whoever has the best chance to protect him. And right now that would be us."

"Great," I grumbled. "And what happens when that changes?"

Hydra shrugged. "Then he'll flip faster than a burberry pancake."

I snorted. "Very reassuring. And now I'm hungry. Thanks."

She smiled. "You're welcome."

I lowered my head as a gaggle of noble women fluttered by.

"Oh, King Rex is a hunk and soooo dreamy."

"He seems sensitive, don't you think?"

"Delicate and intelligent, not at all like those other pumped-up princes."

Together, they all held hands and squealed. "And now he's *single*."

Mordred coughed to hide his mirth. Hydra didn't even bother disguising it.

"Hear that?" She elbowed me. "You're *a hunk*." She batted her eyelashes and said the last word in falsetto. "Play your cards right, and I think you could have a girlfriend. Or a fan club. Or start a boy band. I'm sure one of my heads, Mariah Fairy, would work as your manager."

"No," I said flatly. "I know we have to keep the whole stupid 'man's man' farce up because no one would listen to a scullery maid. But seriously, Hydra…you do remember I'm not actually a guy, right?"

"Bah, course I do. But no one else does, which is why this is a perfect disguise." Her hand snaked out and yanked off my traveler's cloak, exposing the costume she spoke of—a powder blue, corseted, strappy garb that Dorthea had left behind. Since I wasn't exactly the same shape up on top, I wore the dress over a white chemise. Hydra even went so far as to use her spare parts shop to give me long blond hair, which I held back with a black ribbon.

Mordred caught my gaze for a moment before coughing again and turning away.

At least he wasn't laughing outright. I felt my face grow hot and focused on tracing patterns in the dust with my comfy brown shoes. I had to draw the line somewhere. "I hate this. I look like a girl," I grumbled.

Hydra cackled. "Exactly my plan. No one will recognize you now."

I grabbed the laces to yank off the rotted dress. "That's it. Mordred's right. I feel ridiculous, and this plan is hair-brained. And it's gonna get us killed. I look—"

"Lovely," Mordred said. He squeezed my hand, stopping my fingers from ripping off this torture device.

Hydra started hyperventilating from her laughing fit.

Mordred backed off hurriedly. "Fine. Thou looks fine. I mean acceptable. A wee maiden-like really."

"Ugh. You two can both rot in spell with Tinker Bell's dirty tights." I grunted and hiked my skirt up most *un*maidenlike. "Let's just get on with the plan already."

We headed to the beach, to the water's edge where I'd traveled to see the Lady of the Lake. I poured two drops from the holy grail into the lake and said the spell, which protected the waters and kept her from entering for another few days. Shaking the inkwell to settle the liquid to the bottom, I held it up to the light. There wasn't a lot left.

Our plan had better work. We needed to connect with Dorthea, and we hoped she was doing better than us because once the grail was empty, the Water Empress would have prime access to pick off all of Story whenever she wanted.

Mordred watched me put the grail back around my neck and frowned. "Now where do we go? I have already told thee I do not know how to find Morgana's entrance to the

Caverns of Avalon. T'would be like finding a needle in a pincushion."

"I heard you. That's why we're gonna ask Morgana herself." Hydra fiddled with her suitcase.

"Problem," I said, holding up my hand. "Didn't Blanc already kill her ages ago because Gwen hired her to make the death curse that was used on Lancelot?"

"Dead depends on how you look at it." Hydra bent down and opened her suitcase. There were three heads inside. She pulled out the one with black hair plaited like a crown.

"All right, everyone. Stand back." Hydra tossed a small bag onto the ground.

Mordred stood still, bewildered. I was used to this, so I tried to explain. "Each head has its own house, and she's got to store it somewhere. Think of it like the smallest moving crate ever."

The frown on Mordred's face deepened, reaching his eyes. But he wasn't staring at the bag. He couldn't tear his gaze from the black-haired head.

Hydra offered the head up to him reverently. "Would you like to do the honors?"

"Aye. 'Tis not a kindness you offer though," he said.

"I know," Hydra answered, gripping her own red hair. "It's atonement." With a *fwuth*, she yanked her current head up.

"Aye," Mordred said softly and placed the new head solemnly on Hydra's neck. "But I fear redemption is forever out of reach."

With a gasp, the new head came to life and blinked her eyes. When they stayed open, the color caught me off guard. It was like staring into rubies. Or pools of blood.

It was the Red Queen, Morgana La Fey.

Eat Me

Rexi

On the ground the coin purse burst open, and brown sludge poured out. It boiled and bubbled, grew and groaned—until finally the sludge formed a large dome and hardened. With a snap of the woman's fingers, the brown mud cracked and flaked off to reveal a building of large crude stone. Insignias and loops covered the walls like vines.

The red-eyed woman stood still, but her head circled first right and then left, finally settling so her stare fell on Mordred. "That be you, Mordred?"

"Aye," he answered, his face unreadable. "The question better asked, be that you, Mother?"

Her lips pursed into a tight smile. "And who else would I be?"

I, for one, had been hoping it was Hydra. But just like with Gwen's head, Morgana's seemed to be the more dominant personality. I kept my mouth shut because Gwen had been a hexing, narcissistic, evil hag. Yet even she went to Morgana and her black sorcery when she needed her dirty curses cast.

"'Tis good to return, but nay," Morgana said, looking down at Hydra's grow-a-body and curling her lip. "This shan't do at all." With a scratch along her wrist, she drew blood and traced a few runes along her ribs, forming a trinity spiral. Her body shivered and shrunk, turning younger and more hourglass-shaped instead of the "rotted pumpkin" silhouette she'd had before. "Ah," she said and sighed. "Better. Do tell me, for how long hath I slept?"

"Three Story cycles…best as I have figured," Mordred answered.

Morgana's jaw hardened. "'Tis a disappointment it took thee so long to resurrect me and claim Excalibur and Camelot. Verily yet, it matters not. The bone dice hath been cast, so come greet thy mother proper."

Mordred's face twitched. "Of course." He walked over and embraced the woman. The conflict on his face was clear. I just couldn't guess about what.

As they separated, she looked at me with a tilted head. "Is this your queen?" Her nose wrinkled. "I would think thou could hast done better. Was it a forced political joining? Mother is here now and can remedy that for you."

She raised a blood-tinged finger at me.

Mordred hurriedly sidestepped in front of me. "No!" He twiddled his hands. "She's…she is…"

I'd planned to let Mordred handle this exchange, but I hadn't expected him to be such a momma's boy. "I'm Rexi, the kitchen girl. How do you do?" I bent in an awkward curtsy. Because I'd never tried one in a dress before, I got tangled in the skirts. "I hate to break up this awkward reunion, but we're kinda on a deadline. And Camelot is going to be twenty thousand leagues under the lake if Blanc has her way. We need you to show us the entrance to the Avalon Caves."

No one said anything. Mordred rumbled low in his throat.

"Please?" I added as an afterthought.

Morgana narrowed her eyes and tilted her head, looking me up and down, licking her lips. "Thou art seeking the wishing well, no doubt."

"Wishing well?" I squeaked. Nope, Hydra had not mentioned a wishing well was part of the plan. Because she knew I would in no way, shape, or form be okay with—

Mordred *accidently* crushed my foot with his boot.

"Yup," I yelped, my voice going up an octave. "That's what we need. The wishing well."

Morgana shook her head. "No, thou wouldst not survive the first trial. And I dislike leaving bodies to rot in mine cave."

Ouch. Yeah, I know I didn't look very impressive, but I was over everyone assuming I was a failure before I even got a chance to try.

"Witch of Avalon," I said in my best, uppity Dorthea voice. "As the king of Camelot, I order you to take us to the well."

Morgana stood still. For a moment I thought she'd swapped to Hydra, but it was only the calm before the gales of laughter. "'Tis the most preposterous thing I have ever heard. Mordred is the heir to the throne, not an ill-bred whelp like thou be." She nodded to Mordred. "Take out Excalibur and teach this kitchen maid to respect her betters."

"That's gonna be hard since I have Excalibur." *Boom*, I thought as I pulled the sword out of my pack.

Except I forgot that Excalibur was still in the form of a spine. The effect wasn't as impressive as I'd hoped.

"Though bones and viscera may brighten my day, 'tis a little late to offer a grim gift to appease my wrath." Morgana slid her nail down the length of her arm, gathering power.

Mordred looked like he'd been caught in between a lion and a dragon and was desperately seeking a safe place to stand. Thankfully, he chose to stand with me.

He grabbed my hand that held the sword like he had in the cloud, and as before, I focused and called upon my sword. Closing my eyes, I could feel the warmth of Mordred's hand join mine and flow into Excalibur. *Show me who you are*, I thought. When I opened my eyes, the sword of legend glowed in our hands.

A new emotion crossed Morgana's face—surprise.

"More than a kitchen maid t'would seem. That sword always did favor the most unlikely of wielders." While her red eyes twinkled and considered me anew, she seemed to glare at Mordred before lowering her head. "Very well. I serve the throne of Camelot in this age as in all others," she said, sweeping her hand grandly toward her chateaux. "The door to the caverns, my liege."

I walked over to the oak door and heaved it open. Peering in, I took stock. Bones hung from the ceiling from vines. Vials of blood and other organs that should be inside a body lined the shelves. A cauldron bubbled in the center. Hydra's witch doctor hut had similar items strewn about, but the feeling of this place was completely different. *Wicked* would be a kind description.

Most importantly, the walls were stone, not cave rock.

I turned around. "This just leads to your workshop."

Morgana pushed past me and closed the door behind us. Grabbing my shoulder, she shoved me to the ground. "'Twas that door I meant."

Once my eyes refocused, I could see a tiny door set within the big door. Like a peephole, the door was no bigger than my fist. Using my thumb and forefinger, I pinched the tiny, wrought iron doorknob, opened the door, and leaned my eye to peer in like a spyglass.

The view was completely different than before. There were bones on the ground, yes, but these were complete skeletons with small bits of mummified skin still attached. The floor was stained red, and there was a *drip, drip*, not the bubbling of a cauldron, but moisture from stalactites. These were most certainly cave walls.

I stood up and pulled the larger door open again. Like before, it opened to the workshop, not the cavern. "How is this even possible? Forget the rules of magic. This breaks the laws of Fizzics."

"Aye," Mordred said. "'Tis much bigger on the inside."

"I've seen purses and blue boxes that can do that. This door is different." I knocked on the wood. "I've seen something like this before. Except it was in the lake instead. Not a door but a whirlpool." I didn't point out the other difference. Blanc's cave den in Avalon wasn't filled with dead bodies. "I thought you were the gatekeeper. There should only be one entrance to Avalon. So how does Blanc have her own?"

"She shouldn't." Morgana crossed her arms. "I served Gwenevere once, showed her to the well. She made her wish—a death curse on the Lady of the Lake to slake her jealousy."

"I'm going to go out on a rotted limb and say that wish didn't go so well. Lancelot died. And you did too apparently." I had seen that curse, first in the Blanc Pages book and then in person when the water empress used it to suck the life force out of anything she touched.

"The queen of Camelot did not word her wish very well." Morgana lowered her voice. "And if what thou says be true, the Lady of the Lake still lives and set up shop in Avalon during my absence." She stared hard at Mordred and bit off each word. "Though *how* I know not since my death should have been avenged by my son."

"I did not know," Mordred said, not meeting Morgana's

glare. "I thought 'twas Arthur's doing and pursued him to mine own end."

There was more awkward silence, which of course, I couldn't bear. We were on the clock. "I honestly hate to break up the *Fairy Springer Show*, but we are like *this*." I gestured around our circle and continued, "And need to be like *this*." I moved my fingers an inch apart. "To get in there." I pointed to the small door and then dropped to the ground and opened it again. A cold breeze blew out.

"A conundrum," Morgana said. "Thou needs the grail to concoct mine potion to get us through the barrier, but the Lady of the Lake did no doubt steal the grail from my corpse. Because of that, she had gained her own entrance through the lake. Thou art welcome to go knocking there, for I hath shown thee the true entrance and the first trial of Avalon and can do no more."

"The first trial is to produce the grail?" I asked. I fingered the chain around my neck.

"That it is," she confirmed. "King or no, I told thee that thou wouldst not make it past—"

"'Tis time to quit the cat and rat game," Mordred said, pulling the chain with the grail from my bodice.

I swatted his hand away. "Hey, personal space much?"

Morgana's mouth dropped in surprise for a second time. "You have the grail as well? Well, now thou can enter." She held out her hand for the grail.

I put the vial back under my dress. "Yeah, no offense, but

I trust you about as much as I trust a bridge troll to goat-sit. How about you tell me what to do and I'll do it?"

Morgana laughed, not derisive, but a light trilling. "Well done and wise." She elbowed Mordred in his stomach. "Much more than a kitchen maid indeed. We should remember that."

"Trust me," Mordred said, watching me. "I could never forget."

Like a whirlwind, Morgana whisked us into her workshop and started gathering ingredients.

"Let me see. Hath been a while." Morgana hummed and sang as she went. "Twelve moldy berries, a few horned slugs." She dropped them into a bowl. "Powdered wormwood. Dragon's spit for consistency." She walked over to us, placing one hand softly on each of our heads. Then she yanked out a tuft of hair.

"Ouch," I yelped. Mordred bit his lip but did not make a sound.

Morgana placed the hair with the rest and crushed the items in the bowl, stirring it all into a paste. "Almost forgot." She grabbed some white powder from a low cabinet.

"Do I want to know what that is?" I asked, rubbing my new bald patch.

"'Tis sugar to sweeten the taste."

"We're supposed to eat that hair ball?" I gagged at the thought.

"Welcome to the first trial of will and worth." Morgana rolled the paste into three red heart-shaped truffles of eww.

"Stand tall like a knight and face this quest without

Banished

wavering," Mordred said as we walked outside, though he was a noticeable shade of green too.

Morgana gathered Hydra's suitcase and then handed me her concoction with a smirk. She'd even stenciled *eat me* in pink frosting on top.

"I hate you both," I said. Holding my nose and closing my eyes, I popped the foul candy in my mouth.

The trial was indeed of will because it took all my will not to hurk.

When I was sure the mixture was swallowed and not coming back up, I opened my eyes. We had been transported to a jungle. Mordred walked in front of me, using his ax like a bushwhacker. He made a path until we hit a wall of wood leagues high. At the bottom, there were runes etched in an arch with a small circular ball. A door.

The once very small door was not so small anymore. We had shrunk.

Morgana opened the door and entered. Mordred turned to me, waiting. "Best hurry before the magic wears off and we have to eat another."

"I'd rather face Morte head-on."

"Thou may still," Morgana said. "Now this may feel a tad uncomfortable. Growing pains and all."

Just as she finished speaking, the bone in one of my arms snapped, doubling in size and reknitting. It wasn't uncomfortable. It was excruciating. Even Mordred screamed. Only Morgana stayed silent. Mordred's and my yells echoed

117

through the cavern as, limb by limb, bone by bone, our bodies broke and stretched as if on an invisible rack.

When the pain stopped and the white flashes faded from my vision, the first thing I saw was Morgana's smirking face. "Dost thou still want to order me about?"

"No," I gasped, trying to catch my breath.

Her smirk grew like a cat's that had cornered a lizard.

Except I was a dragon.

"I want to do this." Hiking up my skirt, I swung out my leg, kicking her head off her shoulders. After scrambling to Hydra's case, I popped it open and grasped the first ponytail I could. "Thanks, but we can find our own way to the well."

Morgana's head rolled along the floor, cursing me in a language older than the trees.

With a slurp, I jammed the new head onto the homunculus body. The cavern shook and rumbled.

Please work and not kill us, I pleaded to anyone listening.

The shaking calmed, and Morgana's eyes closed while Hydra's opened. "Oh. My. Grimm, Rexi," she said. "Look at her head. It's so like, eww. You were totes kick butt. And you—" She pointed to Mordred and cracked her hand like she was cropping a horse. "Whipshhh."

Um...

I looked to Mordred for some help, but he stared as Morgana's head came to a stop at his feet.

Then he looked at me, the person who had taken his mother from him. Again.

Hydra swiveled her head back and forth between us. "Uh-oh."

"Look." I stood and walked over to him. "I had to. Hydra couldn't get through, and we needed her back. Though I might regret which head I picked—"

"It's done." Mordred avoided looking at me and grabbed Morgana's head, gingerly placing it in the case. "There are still three more trials to go." Without looking back, he walked deeper into the caves.

Hydra flipped her long black ponytail and blew her fringe bangs out of her eyes. "Is it just me, or did he get fro-sty?"

"Shut up," I snapped.

"Jeez, bite my head off, why dontcha."

Don't tempt me.

"Tale as old as time? Books covered in grime. Here are the ten cleaning tips every castlewife should know."

—Good CastleKeeping

Crushed by the Weight of the Worlds

Dorthea

Y ou realize this is hard to believe," John said, running a hand over his head.

I had just finished telling him my story. All of it. "Yup. I'm aware it sounds pretty unlikely."

As if to further prove my point, the ash-like snow continued to fall, and I had to keep shaking the dust out of my hair.

Even though John couldn't see the ash that coated his head and shoulders, he shuddered and shook it off. "No, not *unlikely*. This is wonderland level. Like 'you are having a bad trip and should bottle it up' kind of wild story."

I sniffed, a bit offended at his exaggeration. "If you think

I'm full of it, you can leave. I don't need you." I bit hard into the apple Nick had swiped for me and glared.

"Leave? Sorry, but that's not happening. Because A, you absolutely *do* need me. And B, emerald flames, chimeras, living shadows, and head-swapping witches—it's so far out there that you are either the next Harry Potter or telling the truth. And I lean toward the latter since you all but admitted to killing one of your best friends."

Verte. Accepting the truth means that I needed to face it. No matter how much it hurt.

"So if you believe I could murder someone, why are you still here?" I twisted my back, still working to gain more movement. But mostly because I didn't want to see whatever John's face might say.

"If you are honest and right about that, then there's something more to these firestorms and the darkness swallowing Kansas than just unusual weather." He stood and grabbed my elbow, helping me stand. "And if you are the only one who can see that, I'm safer if I stick with you so you can stop it."

"So what's our first move?" I asked.

"Hey," he said and shrugged. "You're the one running the show. I'm simply tagging along and trying to keep you out of trouble." He examined me, his blue eyes staring right through my core. "Or at least trying to keep the trouble to a minimum."

So very much like Kato but so different too. Being with John was like having a piece of my scattered and shattered heart returned. Kato was every bit a part of me as my limbs or organs. And if I accepted that the rest of my story was real and not in my head, I had to accept the crushing weight of the rest of the truth.

Kato died.

And he took the rest of my heart with him.

"What's wrong?" John asked, tilting my chin toward him. "I was only teasing."

"It's nothing." I shied away from his touch and looked out at the alleyway. "I think I can walk now. We should head to the library."

"Why is that?"

It would have been nice to lay out some elaborate plan to inspire confidence that I knew what I was doing. But I couldn't because I didn't. "That news story where the books were turning to mold and ash—that's the only clue I've got," I admitted.

The task before me was huge. Stop Blanc from ruining the world of Story, and if Griz was right, this world too. And do it without my friends. Or my magic. All I had was me.

Neither one of us had any idea how to get to the Kansas City branch of the public library. John was from out of town, and I was from way, way out of town. John had snagged some clothes my parents had bought me, which were a few sizes too big. Ugly and ill-fitting, but at least they weren't a hospital gown. So when we asked some people at the bus stop for directions, nobody looked at us like some escapees from the looney bin.

The library wasn't far, so we walked. The more distance we put between us and the hospital, the fewer shadows clung to the buildings and the clearer the sky got.

The mile walk shouldn't have taken more than twenty minutes, but my body was still not at one hundred percent. The trip took an hour, and when we arrived, the building was closed with a fleet of health department cars parked out front and an army of employees wearing white hazmat suits.

Even though the other buildings nearby were clean, inky black tendrils stretched out from the cracks in the historic library's mason work. They squirmed and flailed, wrapping around nearby streetlights, the large bronze cavalry rider statue out front, and pretty much whatever the inky tentacles could reach like a kraken rising from the sea.

One tentacle wriggled, moving toward John. "Move," I said, yanking him to one side.

"Invisible nasty?" he asked.

"Something like that."

"So what are we here for?" John asked. I described *The Book of Making*. "And how are we going to get in to find it?" he pressed, pointing out the boarded and caution-taped doors. Signs declared the building contaminated and off limits until further notice.

Minor details.

I looked around, waiting for inspiration. We could steal one of those marshmallow suits. Wearing a disguise had helped John get around in the hospital, but I doubted we would find two suits lying around. And we didn't need to rack up any additional police charges.

To my left, I heard a rustle and a squeak. When I looked, I saw a mouse scurrying by.

"There," I pointed, dragging John with me. "Follow that mouse. If it can get in, so can we."

We rounded the corner in time to see its tail vanish between two boards. I crouched down and peered through. Inside, the floors appeared to be decorated with black, undulating carpet. Except carpet didn't move. *Bugs.* I shuddered. Maybe we didn't have to go in there.

"Let me guess." John sighed. "Be glad I can't see it."

I nodded, took a deep breath, and looked again. Ignoring the bugs and the ooze along the walls, I took in the rest of the scene. Workers scurried to and fro, wearing masks that filtered out the ash that hung in the air. One person didn't wear the mask. Or a white suit. Instead the man wore a tweed jacket over a sweater vest. And he looked very familiar. I'd had tea with him every day for nearly a month—Dr. Baum. He looked around, watching the air, and swiping at his mustache whenever some gook landed on him.

He could see it!

I tugged on John's pants. "We've got to get in there."

"I know. We already decided that. But I'm fresh out of shrink rays."

Where was Hydra and her potions when I needed her? I looked down at my feet and missed my heels. These abominations on my feet—sneakers as John called them—were absolutely zero help prying the boards loose. Still, together, John and I wiggled one of the boards until the nails came loose and the hole was big enough to scoot through.

Well, big enough for me to slip into anyway.

"Go," John said. "I'll keep watch. I'll call if someone's coming." Before I slid through, he grabbed my shoulders and turned me to look at him. "Grab what you need and come back to me, okay?"

"Yes, bossy," I grumbled, but a reluctant smile spread across my face as I crawled into the building.

The wood scratched at my sides and creaked as I wriggled through. The sound made Dr. Baum's head jerk in my direction. He held an open book in his hands. It was the leather one with the red quill on the cover. With a wink, he snapped the book shut and walked briskly toward the rows of shelving.

Watching him made it easier to ignore the bugs crawling along my skin. I stayed low to the ground, slinking around and under tables to follow him so I wouldn't be seen by the marshmallow suits.

This is taking too long!

Of course, getting the book would take a whole lot longer if I got kicked out. When I reached the stacks, I could see the tip of a shoe peeking out. Baum was waiting for me. As I got closer, the shoe moved. While the workers were occupied cleaning sludge off books, I made a dash for it, and I was just in time to see Baum disappear around another stack. I could chase him in the maze of shelves forever and still not catch him. Or I could be smarter.

I waited, crouched behind shelves at waist height where I could see through to the next row. I waited until Baum walked past and then struck like a viper, reaching through and grabbing his book. Unfortunately, he didn't let go, and his grip was stronger.

"It's not time for this yet," he said and yanked hard.

"Time for what?" I countered and pulled on the book's front cover. I wasn't going to let go either. At this rate we would rip the book in two.

"Before you can get back what you've lost, you have to make the hero's journey."

I wasn't sure what he meant, and he didn't explain further. I didn't have the patience for his usual riddles, and he was winning the tug-of-war. I held on tight enough that as his grip intensified, I started to go through the shelving to the other side. But the opening was too small. My shoulder hit the bracket, and all my weight started to tip the shelf off its center.

A wooden groan was all the warning we got before the shelf support gave way. I jumped back, ripping a few pages of the book but pulling clear before the entire shelving row toppled over. On Dr. Baum.

"Tip #3: When in doubt, run. If that doesn't work, run faster and bring a much slower sidekick."

—*The Coward's Guide to Seeming Heroic*

True Love's Kiss. Ish.
Dorthea

The crash sent every person in the library scrambling over to my side. The closest worker helped me up, checked if I was all right, and then immediately smooshed a mask against my face and started swearing at me. I wasn't familiar with the words used, but I could tell they were equivalent to *pixing idiot* from her tone of voice.

"Stop. You've got to get—" I tried to interject.

"No, I will not stop. What were you doing? You could have killed someone," she finished.

I ripped her hand and the mask away. "That's what I'm trying to tell you!" I pointed through the stack. "There's a man under there."

"Oh, mother of…"

"Yes, mother of Grimm." I shoved the scraps of paper in my hands into my pockets and started chucking books over my shoulder. "Now shut up and help me."

The woman hollered for backup. With the additional help, we hefted the shelves. I expected to see Dr. Baum's body, crushed by the weight, but he was not there. In his place was a huddled dog. Or maybe a cat. The animal's coat was calico, but it was the size of a hound.

"I thought you said there was a man."

"There was!" I insisted.

"Does it matter?" Another worker asked, bending down to the animal. "Hey, bud? Can you hear me? You're going to be okay." He moved a few more pieces of broken wood. "Hey, what have you got in your mouth there?"

The dog or cat or whatever, previously unmoving, sprang up and leaped over the fallen shelves. In his mouth he carried *The Book of Making*.

"Grab him!" the worker next to me hollered, but the animal was too agile. It threaded in between legs and under tables. No one could grab him before he bolted. And both he and the book were long gone by the time I got to the door.

"Nope, you're not going anywhere, young lady," said a voice, filtered and altered by the air mask the person wore. "You are going to stay right here until the authorities arrive. We've already called them."

A strange growling sound came from the rear of the library.

"We'd better call animal control too," the masked person said. "Randy, go check and see what we are dealing with."

The growling grew louder and became more of a roar. Everyone dropped what they were doing, some drawing near to the sound, but most seeking a good hiding spot. While they were occupied, I slipped out the emergency exit. John was waiting for me.

"Are you okay? Are you hurt?" he said and gasped, his voice hoarse and out of breath. He patted me down to make sure all my limbs were attached.

"Yeah, I'm okay." I brushed his hands away.

He moved back and slumped against the wall. "I'm glad that worked."

"That roar was you?"

"I told you I'd call if it looked like you were in trouble." He shrugged. "So I think we can agree that didn't go as planned. Did you get what you needed?"

I didn't. But I was ashamed to say it. "I got something," I hedged.

"Don't keep it to yourself."

I was stalling when I heard another commotion out front. *I'm not gonna look a gift horse in the mouth.*

"Let's go check it out." I pulled John's shirt and peeked around the corner.

A crowd had gathered in the front landscaped area.

"Where did it go?" one person asked.

"It was here a moment ago."

"It's not like something like that can vanish."

Something like what? I wondered.

The day had grown darker, and thunder rumbled in the distance. *My favorite sound*, I snarked.

I pulled back, pressing myself against the building. "Can you tell what they're going on about?"

John was still peering at the commotion, his mouth turned and his brow crinkled. "The big statue. It's gone. Vanished in thin air."

While he was talking, I heard a huffing. And immediately regretted my earlier thoughts of gift horses. "I think I found it." I pointed behind us at the now animated statue of a man riding a horse. Black cracks covered the bronze and oozed sludge from its core.

"I don't see it," John said.

Too bad because the horse could see him. The horse's eyes flared like hot coals and focused on the pair of us. Instead of watching the horse, I should have been watching its rider. His musket was pointed right at us.

"Duck," I cried.

"It wasn't a duck. It was a hors—"

I yanked John to the ground just in time to avoid the musket ball shooting through the air right where we would have been. It pierced the brick behind us, making a fist-size crater.

John fell on his butt and crab-walked away from the bullet hole. "What in the heck was that?"

"That?" I smacked the brick. "*That* you can see?"

"Don't be ridiculous. Of course I can. That rock could have really hurt us. Where did it come from?"

Now wasn't the time to argue with him as the shadow soldier was taking aim again.

"We've got to go." I grabbed his hand and started running, pushing my muscles even though the nerves screamed.

"Where are we going?" John asked, keeping pace.

I had no idea, and it didn't matter. "Away."

Our feet pounded against the pavement, though the sound was softened by the snow-like ash that accumulated on the roads. The wind whipped it up, making it hard to see.

"A storm is coming," John said.

No, the storm was here.

The hair on the back of my neck stood on end, raised by electricity in the air.

Behind me, I could hear metal groan and stone break, the wind howling like hounds. Thunder clapped. If Griz were here, maybe the howling wasn't the wind at all.

I could hear people on the street clamor to get inside.

"It's a twister!" someone called.

John whipped his head around to see. I yanked him forward. He stumbled but kept going. "Don't look back. It'll only slow us down."

"I thought *I* was supposed to be rescuing *you*," he wheezed.

"Self-rescuing princess. We can take turns if that makes you feel better."

I'd give this world one compliment. These sneakers, though unattractive, were easier to sprint in. But I couldn't run forever. I was still recovering from Griz's lightning electroshock and poppy drug withdrawals, and I was way beyond my physical limits. We needed to hide.

"There." I nodded toward a billboard advertising the Kanas City waterpark.

"Isn't water the worst place to be in a storm?"

"Not this kind of storm!" I ran as hard and fast as I could, following the tourism signs.

The gates were closed. The park shuttered because of inclement weather. All the better. Less collateral damage.

John tossed his jacket to pad the top of the fence and gave me a boost over. He landed with a thud after his own climb, his jacket ripping on the wire.

The thunder rumbled low, and with it came a voice. "I see you."

"You won't get me, and this time I don't have to be afraid of water." I laughed triumphantly. It was convenient my hair wasn't on fire anymore.

The voice replied, "I don't have to be afraid of water either, not while I have help."

I stopped laughing.

With a *crack thud crack*, the shadow cavalry soldier rode in. "Aw, fairy-spit."

I didn't have to tell John to run as he was the one pulling me this time.

Behind us the fence clanged as the horses charged through, followed by the *clicks* of musket reloading. John pulled me down. I tripped and tumbled over. This time the ammunition hit a parking lot light with a loud boom. After a fatigued groan, the metal buckled.

Like an iron tree, the lamppost fell, landing on the one who shot it. The horse and rider fell to the pavement and shattered on impact.

"Ha! Not so tough now." I kicked the remains of the statue's head. Then hopped on one foot because it hurt.

"Uh, Dot," John said.

"I know, I know. Not the smartest idea to kick a bronze statue."

The sound of metal scraping rock beside me made me scramble away. The horse and its headless rider were rising again.

"You've got to be pixing kidding me," I yelled at the sky. Thunder and cackling were my only reply.

A new fire burned within the statue, giving it life. And fury.

"Gogogogogo," I cried.

That statue reminded me of the iron gigan mindlessly chasing me. To defeat it, I had to burrow into its core and stop its heart with the emerald curse. How would I do the same here without magic?

Then I remembered the billboard we'd passed earlier that had advertised a cliff jump into a sixteen-foot-deep wave pool.

"This way." I grabbed John's hand again and followed the

directional signs through the park. The headless horseman galloped behind.

Good. That was exactly what I wanted.

We weaved and sprinted full speed toward the fake cliff.

John didn't realize my plan until it was too late.

"Ahhh…sh—"

Splash.

It wasn't until after we hit the water that I remembered I still hadn't learned to swim. But John never let go of my hand, and he kicked us to the surface.

"What was that for?" he yelled after we both could breathe.

He'd see in a second, so I didn't argue, simply pushed him to the side before we got squished. "Don't let go of me," was all I could say before the splash of the horseman hitting the water. It didn't whinny or shriek, but it hit the bottom of the pool with a crack. Then a tidal wave hit us. We were pulled under by a riptide. With the force, I lost John's hand in the rough waters. I tumbled, but I couldn't reach him. I could see the statue, which was no longer glowing, had cooled and split. Darkness leaked out and dissipated into the water. Bubbles escaped my mouth as the last bits of air ran out.

John grabbed my hand and yanked me to him, slamming his mouth on mine. He forced air into my lungs and swam us toward the light.

We broke the surface, and he swam us to the side. Once on the land, I touched my lips, gasping, and looked at John.

"What?" he asked, ice-blue eyes staring back at me.

I don't know what I expected. Maybe part of me hoped he would have transformed into a powerful chimera in front of me. But he was still a boy. And true love's kiss hadn't broken the spell or brought my Kato back to me.

Because there was no magic in this world.

"We should keep moving," I said flatly.

"Whoa, wait a minute. We run from an invisible statue, jump off a cliff, nearly drown, and all you have to say is *we should keep moving* like this is just another Tuesday."

I couldn't really explain that the only thing I could do was keep moving. Because the rumbling thunder not only reminded me that I had lost my dreams, but also that I was living my nightmare. And if I sat here and thought about it all for even a single moment more, I would break to the point past the hope of being able to get up again.

So instead I snarked, "For me this is another Tuesday. You should see my Wednesdays. Let's go."

John groaned and said, "Fine, let's find a place so you can get your beauty rest, Your Highness."

The petty insult stung, but maybe it was better if he didn't like me all that much. Maybe that would hurt less. So I kept walking, keeping my face turned away in case John could tell the difference between pool water and tears.

"Who in the world am I? Now isn't that a great puzzle. Unfortunately, I'm quite terrible with puzzles, as inevitably a few of the pieces are always missing."

—*Ravings of a Mad Hatter*

Witz End

Rexi

After spelunking up, down, and through narrow passage-ways, we reached a three-way fork in the cavern.

"All right, Hydra. What road do we take?" I asked.

"Where do you want to go?"

"I don't know," I answered.

She shrugged. "If you don't know where you want to go, the decision doesn't really matter, does it?"

"Hydra…" I growled.

"Actually, I prefer Miss Cleo. Cleo De Nile. Okay?" She tilted her head, chewing on the end of her ponytail.

"No," I answered flatly. Gwenevere, Morgana, I could see those personalities overriding the headhunter…but not this twit. "Calling you Hydra is what keeps reminding me you might be worth the oxygen you're wasting. So I'll ask again. Which way?"

"Um…" She spit out her hair. "Hydra is fine then. And we go right."

On we went. Along the way I tried to make small talk with Mordred. "So…interesting relationship you have with your mom."

Yeah, I sucked at small talk.

He groaned. "Leave it, girl."

"Oh, so I whacked your mom's head off, and I'm 'girl' now? Not Rexi or 'your king'?"

"A pain in my rear you be. Drop it." He stomped forward until we reached another fork. "Which way?"

"Uh, left," Hydra chirped.

Mordred forged ahead.

This wasn't going to do at all. "Look, family is complicated. Trust me—I of all people get that. But we still need to work together." I jogged to catch up. "We need to talk this out." He ignored me. I tugged on his arm. He shook me off.

That was the end of my patience.

"I. Said. Stop." I came up behind him and stuck my foot in front of his. He pitched forward, rolling across the ground and taking me with him.

When we stopped, he pinned me to the floor. "Look, blasted woman. I'm not upset at you. Ye did right. I'm upset at myself for being too weak to do it meself."

"Oh."

"Aye, *oh*. So now will ye please let it be?" He tried to get up, but the buckles on his pants kept getting caught in my skirts. He rolled off with a rip. "Ack. Dresses. Hell-forged contraptions."

I agreed completely. Which was why I wore my breaches under my dress. I ripped off the skirt, leaving just the hooded, laced bodice and my pants. And while I was at it, the long hair Hydra had added needed to go. Using the blade of Excalibur, I sliced into the fake locks, and the enchantments went away. Rubbing my fingers through the shorter, cooler hair, I sighed. "Much better."

"Eek." Hydra picked up the long blond strands of hair littering the ground. "Why did you do that?"

"Nay." Mordred shook his head. "The other did not suit."

I narrowed my eyes and huffed. "What are you saying?"

"That you need not the frippery. You are as you are, and I prefer ye that way." Mordred coughed and looked around, avoiding my gaze. "Appears we are at yet another crossing. Which way?"

Hydra held out her fingers and mouthed a rhyme before pointing. "Straight."

"Hold it. Hold it." I stood up. "Did you just Happy, Sneezy, Grumpy, Doc your way to deciding which way we go?"

"No. As if." She rolled her eyes. "Everyone knows you end on Dopey. But don't you think these rocks look familiar?"

I lunged forward, but Mordred caught me around the

waist, lifting me in the air so my legs flailed uselessly. "Let go! I'm gonna kill her."

A giggle drifted on the air.

We froze. The sound didn't come from any of us.

"*Oh, don't mind us,*" the voice said. "*We were purr-fectly entertained.*" Three big white toothy grins appeared in the middle of thin air. No other shape or face, just the smiles.

Mordred lowered me gently. "Show thyselves."

"*Oh, poo. You are no fun,*" the mouth on the left said as his head came into view—a lion's face with a single unicorn horn. Slowly, more of the creature came into view. It was not three beasts but one that had three heads. A very familiar creature.

I searched my memory. It was still Swiss cheese, but some of it had returned the more I used the grail. "You're that chimera from the volcano! The one that made it erupt."

"*Not exactly. Distant relation on our mother's side,*" the head in the middle answered. He had the head of an eagle with goat horns.

"*They were the Macbethan Elders. We are the Cheshire Sphinx,*" the right head answered. His head was a bear with three horns, two on the top of his head and one out his nose like a rhino. Upon further study, I saw the resemblance to a chimera was passing. This creature had a ginormous cat body and tail, but each limb seemed patch-worked from a different creature. Lizard, horse, and a few I didn't recognize at all.

"What game do ye play?" Mordred asked the sphinx, drawing his ax.

"Can't we all get along?" asked the lion's head with one horn.

"No need for violence," the eagle two-horns said.

"For you are trying to get to the trial of wits, not courage," finished the third-horned bear.

Hydra clapped, jumping up and down. "Oh, a riddle. I'm quite good at those."

"Glad you're good at something," I muttered.

Mordred approached the sphinx. "Let's have it then, so we can be on our way."

"Can't you wait? It's been so long since we've had a friend."

"Anxious to die?"

"You must understand that only one path before you leads on. Take the other paths, and you will be Nome Ore."

"We can do this," I lied.

"Very well," the two-horns in the center said. *"We're only going to tell you once."*

"So listen close," the unicorn on the left said. *"You snooze, you lose."*

"Two of us will lie, and one of us will tell the truth. The paths in front of you are numbered one, two, three. To know the right way, you must take my brothers from me," the bear with three horns on the right said.

"You may only ask us two questions to determine the answer. Are you ready to begin?" they said in unison.

Did I really have a choice? No.

143

"Sure," I said instead.

"So are you a liar?" Hydra asked quickly.

"*No.*"

"*No.*"

"*No.*"

"Hey, wait!" I said. "That doesn't count. We didn't have a chance to discuss."

"*You said you were ready,*" said two.

"*So too bad. Go cry,*" said one.

"*You know what you need to solve this, but you get one more try,*" said the third.

Hydra opened her mouth again, but I shoved her ponytail in like a gag before she could speak. "You stay quiet."

"I know what to do," Mordred said. "'Tis like the game of Knight or Knave I played as a lad."

"All right," I said. Because I was stumped. I replayed what they'd said. What did they mean that we should already know the answer?

Mordred stepped forward. "Which path leads on to the well? One, two, or three?"

"*Me, me!*" said one-horn on the left.

"*The third path is safe,*" said the two-horns in the center.

"*All three of our paths lead to doom,*" the three-horn on the right answered.

"Well, there thou has it." Mordred pointed to the one on the center.

"Wait." I held my head, trying to follow. "How did you get that?"

"Head one and three are liars. The center is telling the truth," Mordred explained.

"That's right," Hydra piped in. "And the center was the only way we hadn't tried yet anyway."

"*Oh, well done. Good solving, you!*" the left head said.

"*If that is your answer, be on your way,*" the center said.

"*If you are sure,*" the right warned.

Mordred grabbed my arm. "I'm sure they are just trying to confuse us."

I pulled away. "Please, give me a second." We had all we needed before we even asked the good question. So the answer was in the riddle itself.

"*Two of us will lie, and one of us will tell the truth. The paths in front of you are numbered one, two, three. To know the right way, you must take my brothers from me,*" three-horns said.

But that made no sense.

Then it hit me.

"It's not that way," I called to Mordred to keep him from proceeding down the path. "The right was telling the truth. All three paths in front of us are doomed."

"That's not possible. Then there is no way out."

I paced, sounding it out. "He said to take his brothers away. So three minus two minus one equals zero. If the paths in front of us were one, two, three, then the way we came in is zero."

A light clinked on, illuminating the path behind us.

"*Well reasoned,*" said the bear.

"*You are the first to reach the trial of wits in ages,*" the eagle said.

"*Goody. Now the fun starts,*" said the lion.

"What do you mean starts? We just solved the riddle," I said.

"*You found the way out,*" said the eagle.

"*Good luck getting there.*" The lion head giggled, disappearing and reappearing.

With a rumble, the rock in front of the path fell away, creating a chasm.

"*Each of us has a riddle. Solve them all, and you pass the trial.*"

"*Then we will build you a bridge. And send you on your way.*"

With another rumble, cracks in the wall appeared and opened. At first, nothing happened after that. Then one by one, long black asps slithered out toward us.

"*Better hurry though. It's death to delay.*"

"Snakes. Why does it always have to be snakes?"

—Louisiana Jones

What You Don't Know Will Bite You in the Asp
Rexi

W atching the snakes slither out of the wall out of the corner of my eye, I estimated the size of the chasm behind me. "It's what? Two trolls' length? We could jump that." *Maybe.*

A fire whooshed up and barred the way across to the path.

"*No cheating.*"

"Rotted pox prattled discount unicorn," I cursed. "Any good ideas?" I asked Mordred.

Hydra walked toward the wall and the snakes.

"I said good ideas. Unless you plan to pick them up and toss them in the fire."

"Nay." Mordred held up a hand to stop me. "Watch her."

Hydra held out her hands, palms up, and chanted. "Iisssiiiiiissssss. Isssiiiiiiiisssss. Apep tuat Ra me Cleopatra Mekat!" Pure gold sunlight poured out of her body. The snakes hissed, bearing their fangs, but they kept their distance.

"Hex yeah." I smacked Mordred in the shoulder. "See? I told you I made a good choice swapping that head."

"Don't pat your back so hard ye burp."

I rolled my eyes. "It's 'so hard you fall over.'" He was hopeless.

"Can you guys, like, hurry?" Hydra called. "This isn't totes easy."

"*To solve each riddle, you must show us the answer,*" the heads said together.

"Aye, get on with it." Mordred watched the snakes warily, ax at hand.

"*I will go first,*" the center eagle said. "*I have a head, but not arms to flail. Though I am not alive, I still have a tail.*"

A dead snake would fit, but first, I'd need to kill one for it to count.

"I have it." Mordred dug around in his pocket and pulled out something shiny. He flicked it into the air so that it spun. "A coin."

"*That is correct,*" the center head said and lowered his eyes, fading until he disappeared.

As the coin landed, I resisted the urge to grab it, even though my years in the Sherwood gang urged me to do otherwise. I focused instead on the next riddle.

"*My turn*," the left trickster singsonged. "*I have a T at the beginning and a T at the end. And I hold T inside as well. What am I in the end?*"

I paced back and forth. "What words start and end with T."

Mordred started listing some. "Target…trivet…throat…twist…toast…treat."

"No, no, none of those have another T in the middle." I motioned for him to keep going.

"Trout, trait, tempt, trust."

Hydra swayed. "Wrong kind of T. The answer is teapot."

"T. *Tea!*" I clapped excited. "Well done, Hydra."

"I told you I was good at riddles." She swayed, and her head drooped, the light she put out dimming.

We had to hurry.

"Teapot. It's a teapot." I ran to the left head, pushing it away, willing it to disappear.

"*You must show me the answer.*"

"Spells bells!" I threw up my hands in disgust.

Mordred rummaged through the bag of stuff we'd brought from the cloud. A rubber duck. *The Real Princesses of Ever After County*, Season 4 DVD. A taxidermy spotted toad. An eyepad. And even a cauldron sink.

"Jeez, Hydra!" I yelled. "Would it have killed you to pack useful things?"

"Sorry," she said before collapsing onto the ground, the glow from her spell now barely as bright as a newborn will-o'-the-wisp.

"Nononono!" I started to run over, but that was suicide. She was still giving off enough light that the asps avoided her. But that meant they were headed to us. I ran back to the left head and threatened it with Excalibur. "I don't have a teapot, so you are going to take this as the answer."

"*Well, I would, but you aren't doing it right. Too bad, so sad.*"

That was it.

"Mordred." I reached out behind me. "Help me turn the sword into a teapot."

He was swinging his ax, cutting snakes' heads off to keep them from me. "Believe in thyself and just do it."

I held Excalibur and tried. I thought of the teapots I had endlessly washed in the Emerald kitchens. How many times I had brought Dorthea tea, chocolate wands, and burberry scones. How many times I wanted to break those teapots.

The sword began to change shape, but then it reverted.

"I can't make it obey on my own."

After swapping his ax from his right hand to his left, Mordred scooted closer and grabbed my hand. He squeezed and then gasped, his hand going limp.

His left hand was quick with the ax, but the asp was faster.

"*Aww, that's too bad,*" the left head said.

"*If you hurry, it's possible to save him,*" the third head countered.

"*Just not likely.*" The lions head spun around, giggling madly.

I took the sword and thrust it at the head. "Here's your answer." The sword shifted into a teapot as I commanded.

The head was upside down as it disappeared, making its toothy grin seem like a frown.

The snakes were coming closer. I wasn't going to make it. I had yet to solve the third riddle, and even if I did, the asps would bite me first since I had no armor to protect me.

At the very thought, the sword vanished, and chain mail appeared to cover every square inch of me. An asp struck and then recoiled, hissing angrily over its chipped fang.

"*Now it is my turn,*" the last head said. "*Higher than the brightest star, farther than any land or sea on end, what's the one thing worth betraying an oath or trust of a friend?*"

My heart was beating like a clock gone haywire, but it slowed to *tick tick tick*. I thought back to my past and what I'd done. How I'd betrayed Dorthea and Kato to try to save my own skin. How I tried to give Excalibur to Blanc to save my sanity. How Kato gave up his life to protect mine like he'd promised he would.

This was the one answer I knew without question.

I held out my empty hands. "The answer is *nothing*. Nothing is worth betraying those you care about."

The bear's head nodded. "Indeed. You have learned and grown." A bridge spanning the hole in the floor appeared. "Now you can move forward." As he disappeared, the snakes and fire went with him.

But both Mordred and Hydra still lay on the ground.

I went to Mordred first. "Hey, we did it. We can go now."

His body shook, sweat pouring off his face. When he

looked at me, his eyes were distant, not seeing me. He raised a hand to my cheek. "Beboo? Is it ye? Is it done? Did Arthur make thou a knight?" He dropped his hand and closed his eyes. "I knew thou could do it."

His breathing grew shallow.

I didn't know how to save him. But I knew who would.

Hydra's Cleo head was out cold from spell-casting overexertion, and she didn't look like she'd wake soon. I took off her head and replaced it with another's. With Morgana's.

When her bloodred eyes opened, she saw the look in mine and grew smug. "So ye need me after all."

"Save him." I pointed to Mordred.

She stood and dusted herself off. "I could, but what be in it for me?"

My jaw dropped open. "He's your son!"

"Why yes, he is. That does nay answer the question."

"Name it."

"At the well, ye must give mine son the grail. That is mine price," she said, arms crossed firm.

"But that's…" I thought about that and what it could mean.

She shrugged. "Then he dies."

Her eyes were placid red pools. I had no doubt she would absolutely watch him fade away. The riddle. What's worth letting down the ones I cared about? Nothing—not even the grail.

"Do it," I said.

One of Morgana's eyebrows curved high. "Thou agrees to the terms?"

"Yes. Yes."

"Very well." She nodded. "Place a drop of the ink from the holy grail on the center of his forehead."

I did as she asked. There wasn't much left, but I used half of what I had, which left a single generous drop.

"And now for the Ouroboros." Bending down to him, she drew a rune of a snake biting its own tail within the ink. "'Tis done."

Immediately, he seemed more peaceful. He stopped mumbling at least. "I wonder who Beboo is?" I asked mostly to myself.

Morgana answered to my surprise. "'Twas a peasant girl in Camelot. A childhood friend who foolishly wished to be knight."

"What happened to her?"

Her jaw set, and her eyes twinkled. "Arthur gutted her for befriending Mordred and then displayed Bedivere's body in the square and blamed my son for it, casting him out."

Mother of Grimm…there were no words.

"We need not your pity." Morgana walked over to the head suitcases. "I know thou wants to, so trade in my head in case he wakes. Speak not of our bargain."

"You don't want to wait and see him?"

She shrugged and picked at her nails. "He will live, or he will not. 'Tis up to him now. Naught more for me here. Yet."

She grabbed a head of white scraggly hair and swapped it herself, not leaving the choice up to me. The new head blinked. Its eyes were white and milky, blind but familiar. I'd seen it first on the beach. The first form of Hydra I'd met, the crone.

She shook a crooked finger at me. "Bah, idgit. You have made a devil's bargain."

"Maybe." I bent down and grabbed Mordred's hand. "But it was mine to make, and I'll pay for it."

"Harrumph," she grunted. "You have grown up. A little."

"Hey, jerk," I whispered to Mordred and wiped his forehead with my sleeve. "Time to get your lazy butt up. Come back to me."

His eyes fluttered, and he stirred but did not wake.

Hydra moved to the exit. "We must go. Blanc still wears our bind but continues to grow stronger. We must reach the well. Grizelda is loose in the Storymakers realm and sure to be after Dorthea by now."

I hated Griz. I still had nightmares of her pulling my soul out of my chest and stuffing it into that fire opal. "When Morte resurrected her, she seemed a bit different. Still, I think Dorth—"

"Oi." Hydra shook her head, wobbling a bit on her neck. "I know what you're thinking, but no, it's not enough. The world of the Storymakers has no magic of its own. And someone," she said and stared at me. "Someone stripped Dorthea of all her magic before sending her there."

"I had to!"

"Idgit," Hydra tsked. "I'm old, and I can complain if I want to. It had to be done. Oz ensured that. There was no way around it. That girl would have continued her temper tantrum until the world was crispy critters. The fact still remains that Griz is amok in that Kansas with powers that don't belong there, and I'm not sure how long Dorthea will be able to hold off."

I folded my arms and stared hard at Hydra, but my glare was wasted since she was blind. Undeterred, I put the strength of my glare in my tone. "I have faith in Dorthea. She may be sheltered, madder than a March hare, and a bit shoe obsessed—"

"Ha!" Hydra cackled. "A bit?"

I rolled my eyes. "Okay, a lot. The point is that she sort of lost it at the end with the curse and losing Kato, but before that, she defeated Griz without magic. With only a shoe. She'll hold out. She always comes through at the last second." Even if I wanted to strangle her most of the other seconds.

Hydra yanked her head off her neck and tossed it at me. By reflex, I caught it.

"Ugh," I said, making a face and holding it by her ears.

Her milky eyes had a trace of green and swirled while she looked at me. Though I was sure she was seeing something entirely different that no one else could. Without warning, she started cackling and then swearing. It caught me so off guard that I dropped her. Her body collected the head and put it on again, backward.

At least that way I could see her face as she walked into the next room. "We have to go now. If we are even one minute too late, all is lost. That senile cobswalled fool trotted far too close to the edge this time. Bah. He always loved cliff-hangers and suspense."

"I'm not leaving Mordred behind," I called.

"So don't," she said without pausing her walk.

"Hexing oracles. Ooof." I picked up Mordred. Sorta. More like dragged him by the wrists. "And while she's at it, she should stuff them in a cookie or something. At least then the future would be more palatable, and I'm starving."

Mordred groaned as I gently—and accidently—ran his head into a rock.

"I don't want to hear it out of you. If you've got complaints, you can walk. Besides, if it hurts, you know you're going to live. We are all going to be just pixing fine."

"Nay," he moaned. "I'm not entirely sure about that."

Truth was that I wasn't entirely so sure anymore either.

"It's impossible to be considered crazy as long as one other person shares in your madness."

—Dr. Jill from *Jack and Jill's Psychobabble Today*

A Picture Is Worth a Thousand Words
Dorthea

After escaping the headless horseman statue, John and I had taken refuge in one of the carnival game booths. It was covered and unlocked, and that was really all we needed last night. As for this morning, I woke up just after the sun, visions of Rexi and Hydra still fresh in my mind.

After bolting upright, I scrambled over to the nearest prize bin and started scavenging, chucking unwanted items over my shoulder.

A blow-up flamingo.

A giant, stuffed, white rabbit.

Packs of playing cards.

"No. No. No!" I shrieked in frustration when I reached the bottom of the bin. I was about to hurl that too when John grabbed my wrist from behind.

"Getting hit with playing cards was bad enough. I'm afraid I'm going to have to decline you giving me a concussion," he said, rubbing the goose egg popping up on his forehead. "What in the name of ice and fire are you up to?"

"I need to find a quill and page before the vision is gone."

John rubbed his head and reached out to me. Invading my space. Nose to nose, he reached…behind me. Then pulled back quickly. "Like this pen and notebook?"

Not prizes, but rather a place where the fair worker logged their hours and the big winners. "Show-off," I muttered and then started scribbling furiously. I knew John was reading over my shoulder, but I was too lost in my story to care. I had to get it all down before I forgot a single thing. I tried to include the bits and pieces I remembered from while I was drugged, but I didn't have my journal to help me.

"So all this excitement to write a story," John said.

"Yup." I kept going, taking time to draw out the three-headed sphinx.

"Meaning the world you used to live in."

"Yup." I had just started describing the part where Hydra had regained her oracle powers. From the corner of my eye, I caught John swinging the inflatable flamingo like a bat.

"So are you writing down what's happening, or is it happening because you write it down?"

"Yu—" I snapped my mouth shut. My hand slowing from runaway stallion to rocking horse as I tried to process what John said. "That's a stupid question."

"Is it?"

"Yes, it is." I huffed. "I'm mean, obviously, I'm…" I didn't even know where to begin. I had just started to believe again, to understand my place in this Kansas world. I was the misfit trying to get home and stop Blanc. This was the role that had been given to me.

Unless it wasn't.

"Look," John said. "Don't worry about what I said. It was only a thought that occurred to me."

I took the flamingo and swung it at him. "Of course I'm going to worry about it." Whack. "I mean, where do you get off judging me?" Whack. "You were in the crazy ward too." Whack. "So where did you suddenly get a psychology degree?" Whack. "Confusing me on what's real?" Whack. "And what's—" Whack. "Not." Whack.

"Jeez. Someone has anger issues." John caught the flamingo on the final swing, squeezing it so that it popped and started deflating. "I was simply pointing out that you've called yourself a Storymaker. Isn't that what you're doing?"

My mouth dropped open. I had no retort for that. So I looked for something else to swing.

John put out his arms like a shield. "Hey, stop that. I'm not calling you crazy. I'm trying to understand."

"Well, I don't *know* whether I'm creating the story or telling it." I plopped down on a pile of stuffed toys, most of my frustration and energy zapped. "Does it matter? It's like, which came first—the dragon or the egg? The dragon exists, and that's all that matters. So if that's a problem, you can go home and leave me alone."

"Okay." John stood up and cracked his back with a loud pop.

"Okay?" I froze. "You're leaving?"

"No, I don't have a problem, so I'm staying." He shrugged and picked up the notebook I'd dropped, holding it out to me.

"I don't get you." I cradled the writing to my chest and eyed John warily.

"I don't get me either." He helped me up.

"Not good enough. Dark magical forces are after us. You saw that…that statue, that thing. I know because you warned me right as it charged after me."

John scrunched up his face. "I didn't *actually* see the statue moving on its own. I saw the twister. I only saw the statue after the cyclone dumped it in the pool behind us."

I wanted to scream. After all this—even now—I was the only one who could see the truth of what was really happening.

Or I was the only one who couldn't *see the truth,* a sinister voice implied in the back of my mind.

I shut it up and pressed John again. "All the more reason for you to leave. What doesn't make sense is why you'd be willing to be chased and nearly killed for something you can't even see."

"It sounds like you've got folks who care about you and need you. And I've got nowhere to go home to, so I may as well help you get to yours."

We stood there for a moment, neither one of us speaking. I was shorter than him by a bit. Just tall enough so that his lips were at my eye level. Which made me think of our not-kiss yesterday. My cheeks grew hot. I looked away.

John put a hand under my chin and tilted my head so my gaze met his.

A loud thump broke the spell.

"And what in gobsmoggled hells? Did you make this mess? Don't think I'm cleaning it up." An old woman with wiry black hair leaned over the counter and glared at us. We didn't respond.

"Hey, I'm talking to you two hoodlums. What are you doing in there?"

My cheeks grew hotter while John stumbled over a few nonsensical syllables.

The old lady thumped the counter again, this time because she was laughing so hard. "Wahoo." She poked my side and waggled her hairy eyebrows up and down. "I'm not so old that I don't remember what it was like to be young and in love."

"Oh, we aren't," I protested.

She ignored me and ran her hand along her chin as if trying to remember days long…long…long past. "Like it was yesterday, I tell you. I was so attractive I had to beat off them young bucks with a stick." She ended her remembrance with a smile and a little twist of the hair growing out of her mole.

Could she be? Nah.

John threw his arm around me. "Yeah, you caught us. Thanks for being so cool about this. We should get home before the park opens."

The old woman pulled up her pants by her belt. "I'll let you go this once, but don't go tellin' no one. Now it's not that I don't trust ya, but I don't trust ya. So turn out them pockets."

John didn't have anything in his pockets, and while he opened his bag to show the woman, I stuffed the notebook under the back of his jacket. Then it was my turn. I pulled out the only thing in my pocket—a wad of paper. It was wet and fairly crumpled. But as I smoothed it on the counter, I remembered where it had come from.

The Book of Making.

The words were faded and blurred, made unreadable by the water. But there was a picture, details and colors smudged, but the general image was clear.

The old woman squinted and turned up her nose. "Those look like rather useless shoes. Who on earth would wear something as ridiculous-looking as those?" She pointed out the purple heels with Celtic inlay and the shiny metal plating covering the rest like high-fashion armor. "Why, them shoes look like a walking weapon. You aren't from a gang, are you?" She shoved the page back to me. "Now git before someone sees you."

As we walked out the back, she called after us. She tapped her belt and stared into the distance. "Hang onto that attraction to each other no matter what anyone says. And don't do nothing I wouldn't do." Then she winked and said, "Which ain't much."

We could hear her off-key peals of laughter long after we were out of sight.

John stopped me on the street outside the park. People were starting to mill about, starting their days. "Look, about what I said back there, about hooking up. It was just the easiest explanation. I'm not trying to… I'm only doing what needs to be done."

"Not important." I waved him away. "I know what we need to do."

"What?" he asked and hustled to catch up because I was already striding down the street.

"We're going shoe shopping."

"No matter how bright and plentiful the light, it only takes one drop of darkness to spoil it."

—Evil Queen

Inkling of Disaster
Dorthea

John was pretty unconvinced by my plan. After all, how could shoes solve anything? He couldn't understand that shoes could solve most dark days. And magical shoes—hex, I knew they could solve anything. One click, and I'd be back in Story before you could say, "There's no place like home."

Even though John thought I was being extra crazy, he suggested we look for the shoes in the mall—a wondrous place with endless stores. And the shopkeepers let you take your items home with you instead of waiting for the United Pegasus Service to deliver them.

There were stores that said you'd pay less and stores that screamed you'd pay more. In all, we stopped at five stores entirely devoted to shoes. If Griz wasn't hot on our heels, I would have thought I'd gone to heaven. A heaven of, well, heels. Pumps and stilettos. Some refined, some more edgy. Heels far too tall, ones impossible for even me to walk around that mall in. I saw so many shoes the unthinkable happened. Shoe shopping got old.

There weren't a lot of people in the stores. And the ones who were there were all talking about one thing—the tornadoes that had ripped through the downtown yesterday. Even the shopkeepers. When we could get them to stop talking about the storm and look at my picture, none had seen a shoe remotely like the pair of heels on the page. The exception was one tired girl behind the blue glittery counter of the Bibbity Bobbity Boutique. She took a second look and brightened.

"No way shoes like that would be a stock item. There's not a chance anyplace in the mall would have them. Those slick kicks have to be custom." She popped her gum and returned the page to me.

John rested his forehead on the counter and sighed. "So I endured hours of unspeakable torture for nothing?"

"Men," the rainbow-haired shopgirl said and rolled her eyes. "We have the unalienable right to shop. It's in the constitution."

"Right next to the clause that says guys have the right to complain about it," John muttered.

"Hush," I said, stepping on his foot. Which wasn't nearly as effective in sneakers. Then I asked the girl, "So where can I get custom shoes like this made?"

The girl laughed until she had to wipe tears from her eyes. "You know we are not in New York, right? Welcome to Kansas, where high fashion is a pair of stonewashed overalls."

My shoulders drooped. "It's hopeless then. I'm stuck here."

"Hey, chica," the girl said and gripped my shoulder. "I feel you. I'm just working this crappy job until I save enough to blow this haystack. Then it's off to Los Angeles or Paris maybe." She looked me up and down, wrinkling her nose at my button-down shirt. "You don't seem the type, but with a design for killer shoes like that, maybe…"

"What?"

"I shouldn't be telling you this." She leaned in close. "There's this guy. He runs an underground club and is a complete lunatic. But word is he can get anything. *Anything.* Stuff that shouldn't exist. People say he makes magic happen." She leaned back. "If anyone can get those shoes for you, Oz can."

My heart stuttered in my chest. "Oz? Oz is here?" *Of course. Dr. Baum, the doctor who wasn't a doctor.* And the mouse, the doglike beast. He was watching me, guiding me like always. He was trying to lead me to him.

The girls jaw dropped. "You know the Wizard?"

John looked back and forth between us. "I expect talk of wizards from her, but you seem, well, like an airhead. But a normal airhead."

"Feel free to hit him," I told her. "I do."

It looked like she was thinking about it, but her manager walked past. "Is everything okay, Kiara?"

"Absolutely. I'm just helping these customers with a special order." Kiara, the shopgirl, typed on her register until the manager went back in the office. "Look, spaz boy, the Wizard is his street name. Real magic doesn't exist. But the crap he pulls off is the closest thing to it."

"I really need to see him. Where can we find him?" I asked.

"His club, the Emerald City. It isn't exactly legal. So it moves from place to place. Only a few people know where it's gonna pop up next. As soon as the flash mob hits," she said and made a poofing motion with her hands, "then he goes underground again."

"Well, that's really helpful," John said. He'd been a grumpy beast since the second hour at the third store.

I didn't even bother slugging him. I simply pointed out of the store. "Go. Sit."

"Stay. Good dog," John muttered, but he headed out to the bench.

I shrugged at the clerk. "Sorry."

"Boys." She shrugged back, jotting some notes onto the back of a receipt. "Can't live with them. Can't…" She paused, trying to think of how to finish. "Yeah, I think that pretty well sums it up."

I cringed. "He's not that bad."

"Whatever you say. I'm just warning you. He's not Emerald material. If you bring him, I'm not sure Oz will talk to you." She slid the receipt across the counter. "This is the last place the club popped up."

I thanked her, took the paper, and met up with John. "She told me where we might find the club."

John stood and rocked back on his heels. "Great. So onto phase two of the goose chase? Or is it a golden goose chase?"

I sucked in my breath fast, unprepared for the bite in his words. "What is your problem? I told you everything about my world. You said you believed me. You were the one who insisted on going with me."

"I was good until this turn of events, and now I'm overwhelmed by the sheer ridiculousness of it all. How important are these stupid shoes anyway?" He frowned.

"I've told you. These shoes are the key to finding my way home. I'm sure of it."

He crossed his arms and stuck out his lip. "And what's so great about this magical home? From what you've told me, it sounds like hell. Your real home is destroyed. The rest of the land is following suit. Everyone you care about is either dead or about to be. And you're so stubborn that you can't let them go and let anyone else in."

"Huh?" *Where was this coming from?*

"You are willing to go to such lengths to try to get back, so why can't you go to the same lengths to adjust to staying? If those witches want the other world and are willing to kill you to get it, let them have it. Then they won't come after you anymore. Make it work *here*. Your parents are here. I'm here." He stepped forward, closing the distance between us. His piercing blue eyes pleaded with me. "Just let all this drama go."

I took a step back. "Wow. Either you don't believe me, or you do and you want me to leave everyone in Story to be erased. I'm not sure which is worse."

He looked down at his feet.

"I can't believe for a second I thought..." I shook my head. "You're really nothing like him."

That startled John, and then he stared at me. This time frost burned in his eyes. "That's right. I'm not Kato, your pet prince. I have no magic, no kingdom. I'm human, and that's not good enough for you. I can't compete with a ghost." He turned and walked away. "I'm out," he said, holding his hand up as he left.

"Let him go," said a voice behind me.

I whirled. It was the shopgirl, Kiara. "Why don't you mind your own pixing business?" I turned back to watch John. He didn't look back once.

"Why in Grimm's name would I do that when you *are* my business, Dorthea?"

"What?" I had never told her my name, and no one from this world used the term Grimm.

"Is everything all right?" The manager came out to join us.

"No, it's not," I insisted. "Your employee is stalking me."

"It's not stalking. We simply see you wherever you go," the manager said. "You really should listen to that boy though. Give up on Libraria. Without your magic, you are nothing."

"What's going on? Who are you?" I backed away until I ran into something. An older woman.

"The Forgotten, melted down and given new life." The elderly woman smiled. It would have been kindly if not for the black ink leaking out of the corner of her eyes. Ink just like the kind that had infected the statue. "Proof that there is no end. Just new beginnings. You can start over too."

"No. No." I turned slowly, more people approached, encircling me. "This is not a life. I will stop this."

A little girl with blond pigtails ran past the others, releasing her red balloon on the way.

I called out to warn her. "Don't come closer. Run away."

She didn't listen and drew nearer, slowing right before she reached me. A thread of black ran up her cheek, disappearing in her ear. She tilted her head and said, "You're going to die here."

I pushed her away and bolted past. The crowd tried to grab me. They yelled for me to stop, but I kept running, desperate to escape. Once I was out of the mall, I made a sharp turn and snuck down an alley.

I bent over, trying to catch my breath.

"Hey," someone said. A loader taking a cigarette break. "You okay, kid?"

Startled, I jumped away, tripping on a crate.

"Shh," the man said, dropping his voice low. "I ain't gonna hurt you. What's got you so spooked."

Aside from smelling like an ashtray and having skin that was wrinkled and cracked like old leather, the guy seemed normal. No black ooze on him anywhere.

"I'm being chased." I wheezed and coughed.

He narrowed his eyes. "You didn't steal nothing, did you? If you's a shoplifter, you should leave it here and get."

I shook my head. "No, it's not like that."

He came closer, putting out a hand to help me up. But something caught his eye. A piece of ash fell from the sky. "Snow? It's a bit warm." He held out his hand to catch it.

"No, don't!"

He ignored me and held it to his lips. He smacked his tongue. "Don't taste right."

I stood and put my back against the brick for safety. I watched him intently. It stared at the corner of his mouth, a little shadow under the skin. Then the shadow wriggled like a leech latching onto him.

The man took a puff on his cigarette. Little sparks danced around the smoke. Miniature lightning. He opened his mouth, but static came out. A moment later the static cleared, and a new raspy voice spoke. A voice of broken crystal. "There's no hiding. The Grimm Reaper and his dark grail have given me all the Forsaken I need. So it's pointless to keep fighting."

I picked up an empty bottle from the ground by my feet and threw it, cracking the dock worker in the head, knocking him down.

I bolted. Pain burned in my side. But I kept running. I didn't look back, but I could hear them coming. The shuffling of feet. Around me, those whom the ash touched stopped whatever they were doing and turned their attention to me.

Then out of the corner of my eye, I saw it. The animal from the library. The dog that wasn't a dog. It looked at me expectantly and then raced off. I followed it. The animal slowed occasionally to look back as if making sure I was following. Was it Oz? A trap? I didn't know, but it couldn't lead me to anything worse than what I was running from.

Before I knew it, I was back where I'd started the day. The animal bounded into the fairgrounds. It was vacant, not a soul in the area. Yesterday's storm had taken its toll. Some of the rides and machinery lay on their sides. The metal was bent and crumpled. Pieces of booths were splintered and scattered on the ground along with belongings people must have dropped as they fled for shelter.

The animal I was following clearly wasn't a dog. It didn't even stop to sniff at the abandoned corn dogs and candied apples. It ran toward the fun house, ducking through the curtained entrance, which was painted to look like the giant macabre grin of an insane jester.

I slowed my steps. "This is a bad idea. This is a really bad idea." Sadly, following the animal was my only idea.

I pushed my way through the curtain. In the low light, my twisted reflection stared back at me from a fun house mirror. I started into the fun house, but my foot hit air. Stumbling, I reached back for the curtain, but my weight ripped the fabric.

I fell, tumbling end over end in the dark. I lost all sense of time. It seemed like minutes. Hours. Days. I fell so long I couldn't even tell if I was falling up or down. I was weightless.

Finally, I saw a shape take form in the darkness below me. A giant book. It opened, waiting to catch me in its pages.

I didn't land with a thud. It was more like I was gently set down on my back. However, I didn't come to rest on pages but on grass. Grass so green it brought tears to my eyes. Above me, there was a tree. Its trunk was thin and braided with glittering, gemlike leaves hanging from the boughs.

I wasn't in Kansas anymore.

"Iron and ashes, Dot! Are all princesses this lazy? Sleeping all day in the sun?" The jibing was good-natured, delivered with a smile that twinkled and reached the boy's eyes. He had messy reddish brown hair, dirt-smudged skin, and blackened fingernails.

Kato. My Kato.

I sprang to my feet and flew to him, throwing my arms around his neck so tightly I might have choked him. Tears rolled down my cheeks, enough to fill a loch and drown us both.

I was home.

"Tip #4: No matter what, be yourself and hold true. Unless who you are sucks. Then lie and pretend to be someone else."

—The Coward's Guide to Seeming Heroic

Nothing to Fear but Fear Itself
Rexi

After the fourth completely accidental, head-to-rock collision, Mordred decided he was well enough to walk. Or as he put it, walking was the only chance he had at surviving the cave.

Same difference.

"Are we there yet?" I asked.

"No," Hydra replied.

We walked through the slimy caverns for what seemed like forever. Or at least five minutes.

"Are we there yet?"

"No!" both Hydra and Mordred shouted. Their echo reverberated off the walls, sending dingbats shrieking from the ceiling.

"Ahh, get 'em off! Get 'em off!" I flailed my arms above my head to keep the air space clear.

"Our cowardly lion is still afraid of the creepy crawlies? I'm afraid that you aren't going to do well in this trial," said a high-pitched voice.

While I was busy swatting, a creature had appeared in front of us. A Mock Turtle, I supposed. It had the head, wings, and talons of a mocking dove stuffed inside a turtle shell.

Hydra looked over her shoulder. "Now we are here."

The Mock Turtle flapped its wings, creating a fierce wind that shook the cave, rumbling rocks and bringing some tumbling down until three passageways stood in front of us.

"This again?" I moaned.

"Aye." Mordred looked warily at the passages, rubbing the lump on his head absentmindedly. "Which door leads to certain death?"

"All of them," the Mock Turtle said with a flap. "Or nearly certain death at the very least."

"This is the test of courage," Hydra said. "Each of us will have to gird up our granny shorts and face our biggest fears."

"Indeed," said the Mock Turtle. "There is nothing to fear but fear itself, but that can absolutely kill you. Here, all your fears become real, so think long and hard before you enter. There's no going back. You must defeat what you conjure or die." He shivered, his feathers puffing up. "It's very exciting."

I rolled my eyes. "Sounds like a hexing riot."

"You'd be a fool to dismiss him," Hydra said and paused. "Or a bigger fool than normal."

"Thanks for the confidence."

"Wherein lies the danger?" Mordred asked over top of me.

"Your greatest fears are real here. Which is fine if it's bugs and bats." Hydra walked toward the passage, cutting in front of Mordred. "If you conjure Blanc or Morte, we will be finished." Her sightless eyes stared at him...or rather into him, swirling and picking out the information she needed. She whistled. "You've got your work cut out for you, but it won't hinder us if you lose."

I winced. "Ouch. Burn."

"Be quiet, ninny. Ain't done you yet?" She moved in front of me and did her oracle bit. She whistled again. Longer and lower. "My, my, you both have more issues than *Sorcery Illustrated*. I should have worn my head shrinker." She held my cheeks between her hands. "You need to walk away from this unbroken. And I'm not sure you can." Letting me go, she stepped back. "Proceed or not. The choice is yours."

I chuckled, uneasy. "Hey, it's not like there's really a choice. I mean what do I have to lose?"

"Everything," Hydra said solemnly, no mirth or teasing in her voice.

I took a deep breath. "Then the opposite is true, and I have everything to gain."

"Well said, knight in training." Mordred clapped my back, knocking me forward a few steps. "Never let thine enemy see thee unsure. Slash and parry until they yield. Thou art my apprentice, so this should be easy as cake."

"A, I'm your king, not your apprentice. And B, it's pie. Easy as pie."

Mordred's brow furrowed. "That doesn't seem right. Hast thou ever made Blackbird Pie? Getting those five and twenty to stop squawking long enough to jump in the crust?" He shook his head. "Nay, cake is far easier."

I sighed. "Hydra, back me up on this. Hydra?" She wasn't there anymore.

"Oh, your mentor went on without you." The Mock Turtle tapped its beak. "She left a message. *If you two ever stop stalling and flirting, I'll see you on the other side.*"

I scoffed. "That's. No. It's…"

Mordred folded his arms. "Absurd."

"Hey!" I frowned. "Absurd might be a little far, pal."

"Ah," the Mock Turtle said. "I see you are not done. Well, wake me up when you have finished your banter."

"I am always ready for a challenge." Mordred hefted his ax and strode to the center passageway. "For glory!" he yelled and charged.

"And what of you?" the Mock Turtle asked. "In my experience, slow and steady wins the race. Though first, you must get started."

"Obviously." I rolled my shoulders. Stretched my legs. Made sure Excalibur was nice and sharp. Soon though, I ran out of excuses to delay. With a deep breath, I took measured steps toward whatever waited for me.

Banished

First, a narrow passage. It was dark. Okay, I could do dark. I kept moving, keeping both hands skimming the walls on either side of me. While I couldn't see anything, I could hear a skittering sound coming closer.

Breathe. Breathe. Breathe.

Something with far too many legs crawled over my hand.

"Ah! Get off. Get off." I shook my hands, but the creature skittered up into my sleeves, down my shirt, and up my neck. In my mind I imagined long fangs with dripping venom. The second I pictured that, I felt the *first* bite. Many more followed.

I changed my mind. I didn't want to face this challenge.

I started to turn around, ashamed. Mordred had run headlong into danger, and he was probably hacking a dragon to pieces right now. Hydra, well who the spell knew what that witch was afraid of? If she'd been wearing her spare-parts head, I'd say a clearance sale. But what the oracle feared, I had no clue. But it was likely worse than a few bugs.

Was this how I wanted my legend to be remembered? *Here lies the Once and Future King Rexi de Arthur Pendragon. Taken out by bugs. Rest in Shame.*

Biting my tongue, a copper taste flooded my mouth. I faced forward again. Step. *Crunch.* Step. *Crunch.* There was a light in the distance. Step *crunch.* Step *crunch.* Faster. I sped into a jog and then a run.

I burst from the corridor into the light, brushing off my arms and shaking out my clothes. There was nothing there.

"Phew." I doubled over, letting out the breath I was holding. "That wasn't so bad."

Lies. That was a nightmare.

Straightening up, I looked around for Mordred and Hydra. They weren't here. It was just me. Lots of me. I stood in the center of a hexagonal mirrored room. Each way I turned, there I was. Dozens and dozens of my reflections stretched out into eternity.

"And just what is this supposed to mean? It's not like I'm scared of my own reflection." I waved. Hundreds of me waved as well. I went over to one of the mirrors and felt the glass. Solid. "I can't go through. So what do I do?" I plopped down on the floor and stared at myself and waited. And waited.

Thoroughly bored, I walked around the room, knocking on each mirror. "Hello, is anyone there?"

One of the mirrors knocked back.

"Holy hex." I jumped back, tripping and falling on my butt. The reflection in front of me stayed standing.

"Creepy," I said. "I didn't know I was afraid of cursed mirrors."

"You're not," my reflection replied. "These looking glasses are not cursed, but they still bear the effects of Princess Dorthea's wish. You were afraid to look into them and face who you truly are."

"No, I wasn't," I bluffed.

"Good. Then you can begin," mirror-me said.

All the mirrors shimmered, my reflection changing in each

of the six walls in the hexagonal room. One was dressed as a servant of Emerald, her face distorted in bitterness. Another, the young pickpocket me, dragged long chains that bound her hands and ankles and had a broken noose around her neck. The third reflection had scars crisscrossing her skin. She stuck out her tongue and licked the edge of a storm-bolt knife. The fourth wore a gown and a solid green topaz necklace, flames flickering out of her eyes. The fifth had inky skin that was cracking and flaking away. A terrible moan came from her mouth. In that mirror I was a Forgotten. The sixth reflection was my regular self, only without a face—featureless and blank.

At once, all six reflections stepped out of their mirrors and into the room.

Oh, hex me.

My clones formed a circle, closing in around me. I couldn't step back or forward without coming in reach of one of them. Mordred had, in fact, been training me for combat. I could hold my own in a fight. But we hadn't practiced taking on a small army.

"Six against one doesn't seem very fair," I complained.

"Since when is life ever fair?" the servant-me replied, her lip twisted up in a sneer.

"At least you're *alive*," added the pickpocket.

"For now," the storm-minion finished.

"I can see you've all inherited my optimism and wit," I mumbled. "Anybody else have anything brilliant to add?"

The Forgotten merely moaned louder. The faceless-me had no mouth to speak, and my clone taken over by the Emerald curse seemed like a puppet that didn't have a mind of its own. "Oh, good, that makes group therapy so much *easier.*"

On the last word, I struck. After grabbing the end of the pickpocket's noose, I yanked and flung her out of my way. The storm minion lunged at me, but her knife got caught in the pickpocket's chains. Sweeping my foot low, I knocked the storm minion off balance. She pulled the pickpocket down with her.

I started running the second the Emerald-cursed puppet shot fire out of her hands. Staying one step ahead of the others, I ran along the mirrors, circling the room. The fire bearer had no emotion or logic. She didn't seem to notice or care who got in her way. The servant never moved. She only screamed as the flames engulfed her. The Forgotten burst apart, charred chunks flying everywhere. The faceless clone held out her arms and waited for her turn. She never uttered a sound as the life flared out of her.

The storm minion had just gotten back to her feet when the flames came for her. "I'm not going down like that!" She tossed the pickpocket in front of her like a shield, making the girl take the brunt of flames. But then the storm minion flung her knife at the fire puppet, striking her in the chest and extinguishing the flames.

"Well played," the storm minion said, tossing the burned husk of the pickpocket onto the ground. "Now it's just one-on-one."

Before she could pull out another weapon, I imagined Excalibur as a crossbow. "No, it's not. There is only me." I let my bolt fly, hitting her in the forehead, pinning her to the wall. All the other corpses, the reflections of my fear, lay on the floor. The mirrored walls were shiny and blank, showing nothing.

I had won.

"So what now? Can I go?" I turned in a circle, calling to anyone who might be listening. "I killed my fears. Am I supposed to bury them too? Fine, bring me a shovel."

Mock Turtle's voice surrounded me. "It is impossible to kill fear."

As if to prove his point, the storm minion smiled and yanked the bolt out of her own forehead. "But fear can kill you."

"Top three dark omens: A black cat is always bad news. Crossing under a beanstalk is sure to bring days of trouble. But the number-one dark omen has to be breaking a looking glass, yielding seven years of bad luck."

—Red's Reddits

21

Poisoned Apples Don't Fall Far from the Family Tree
Rexi

The storm minion hurled the bolt back at me, grazing my cheek.

I brushed my hand across the slice, my fingers coming back wet. "Who the spell designed this test?"

"Complaining it's not fair again?" The servant rose from the ground, her burns fading, her hair regrowing. If she said anything else after that, I couldn't hear because the ashes of the Forgotten had reformed, and it had resumed its out-of-key, mournful song.

In fact, the six reflections were now exactly as they had been before.

I was going to die.

But not without a fight.

Changing Excalibur back into a sword, I charged, slicing and hacking at my other selves. As I grew more tired, they regenerated faster. The servant always fought like a wild animal, biting and scratching, but she was easy to take down. The pickpocket was harder, her chains tripping me and bruising my legs. Each time the Forgotten reached me, a new vein of shadow crawled over my skin. The storm spawn waited until most of my strength was gone and then came at me from behind.

She whispered in my ear as she used her arm to crush my throat. "You are weak. You always were. And now you'll die because you forgot the basic rule. Always look out for number one."

A stream of Emerald fire came at me, scorching my side. The storm minion shrieked behind me and hit more directly. Suddenly, I could breathe. But the curse drew from my life force, bringing me to my knees. Within the flames, I could hear voices, the tainted and mad voices of those consumed by the curse.

Let go. You are powerless.

Join us and be free.

We have always been the only way to defeat Blanc.

The voices multiplied and twisted together, but a familiar one stood out. Verte's. *You cannot fight who you are. Embrace it and grow strong.*

"You are not seriously telling me that a group hug will solve this mess," I rasped, my windpipe bruised.

I staggered over to the Emerald puppet and threw my arms around her. The only thing that happened was the heat burned through my soul faster. I saw Dorthea in the mirror behind the Emerald puppet. Dorthea witnessing all the darkest parts of me. The bitter servant who hated everyone and everything. The condemned child who gave up her life to please her family. The storm minion who betrayed everyone she cared about to save her own skin. The girl driven mad by the bond that Dorthea and I shared. A blank person who was a nobody and of no importance to the story.

And not least, the blackened Forgotten, discarded and uncared for. What should have happened to me if Kato had not intervened? I let him die. Let him suffer. All so I could live. He made the wrong choice to protect me.

I looked at Dorthea and said, "I'm sorry I killed you. I'm sorry I failed and let you down. I'm sorry Kato died for nothing. I tried so hard, but this is who I am. All I can be."

Dorthea reached out, her fingers brushing the mirror and making ripples. "You didn't kill me. You saved me from becoming something else. Saved both of us. It's enough. You've always been enough."

I reached out, and as my fingers brushed hers, the mirrors shattered. The reflection clones broke apart with them. The flying shards cut and pierced my skin. The floor glittered like a piece of art, all glass and blood splatters.

I collapsed onto the ground, the sharp bits cutting though my tunic and scraping my back. As I caught my breath, a face loomed over me. Well, a beak.

"Huh?" the Mock Turtle said. "I didn't actually expect you to survive that test."

"Sorry to disappoint."

"As long as you're sorry, I suppose that apology will have to do." His frown reversed into a grim line. "Since you passed, you may leave now." With his wing, he gestured up to the ceiling. When the mirror shattered, it opened a hole.

"Unless you can carry me in that shell of yours, I'm going to wait right here for a while."

The Mock Turtle scoffed. "Then you could at least help me clean up the mess you made."

Raising my head, I looked at the disaster I'd made. "I think I'll pass."

Even now blood pooled under me. But it was slowing. The shadow veins also began to fade, forming a shadow puddle on the floor. It pulsed and stretched, growing longer. Then reflecting off a group of larger mirror shards, the shadow grew taller and took shape. A man stepped through.

I pointed, unable to find words.

"Rexi, Rexi. Lazy and undisciplined," the shadow man said, ink dripping off him. "I raised you better than that."

That voice. That honeyed voice, now cruel and mocking, was filled with twilight instead of sunshine.

Robin Hood—or the man who used to be.

Even as the shadows sloughed away, it was clear he had changed. His body was twisted, malformed. His legs, bowed and cut off at the ankle, were blackened stumps. His arms looked like diseased limbs of an ironwood tree. His fingers, spindly twigs.

But he was still strong.

As the Mock Turtle protested his presence, declaring the trial was over, Robin Hood entwined his fingers around the creature's neck and flicked his wrist with a horrific snap.

"No!" I cried out too late. "Why did you do that to him?"

"Him?" Robin Hood came closer, wobbling since his form was not ideal for stalking. "Him? You are more concerned for someone you just met than your own father?"

My gaze and resolve hardened. "You are not my father. You made that abundantly clear."

"But I still raised you. Made you who you are."

"No," I said, standing. "Verte and the House of Emerald raised me. And I made myself who I am."

"And what is that? A false king?" He spat, limping forward. "A murderer? A heartless trickster? You let me take Morte a fake Excalibur. Do you know what he did to me?"

"I can see. Maybe you shouldn't have made a deal with the devil."

"Perhaps. He knows you're here. And if I stop you, all will be forgiven." He reached behind him and pulled an arrow out of his quiver, bow in his other hand. "So be a good girl and die for daddy." He took his shot, piercing my foot, pinning it in place.

I tried not to cry out. It was useless. If I couldn't hide the pain, I couldn't hide my anger either. "You missed," I gasped between ragged breaths.

He notched another arrow. "Defiant even now. I hit my target exactly as I wanted as always." He let the second arrow fly, piercing my other foot.

I screamed, the world flickering in and out of blackness.

Robin Hood steadied himself against the wall, lifting his own disfigured stump. "I want you to experience what was done to me. Before Morte made me one of his forsaken, he removed the boots that protected me from his shadow grail. But he couldn't just take them off. No. He used that fake sword you gave me to prove his point. To show me I was nothing before him. And now I will show you that you are nothing before me."

I was going to pass out. My brain was numb from pain. I could process little else. I retreated deep within myself and found my center.

"I am a child of the trees," I mumbled.

Robin laughed. "You are a child of no one. Worthless even at birth and abandoned in a treetop bough."

"Though the wind may howl," I continued.

"You will fall." Robin raised his bow and notched another arrow. "Then you will be the one howling."

"I will not break!" I called Excalibur into my hands, a bow and arrow equal to Robin Hood's. Our arrows flew at the same time, meeting each other in the middle, splitting apart before they could reach their destination.

"Impossible." Robin blinked, his mossy eyes flickering black. "A fluke."

He shot again, my arrow meeting his bull's-eye. He raged and fired again and again. I pushed myself to meet every one of his shots. Finally, he reached back to his quiver and came up empty.

"Now what?" I asked, my voice barely above a whisper. "Excalibur will never run out of arrows."

"Then shoot me and end it." He broke his bow in half. "I was destined to die the moment I made the mistake of taking you in. You've stolen everything from me. Steal my life and earn your title as the Princess of Thieves."

I pulled the bowstring back. I aimed for his hostile and withered heart. Then I let loose. The arrow sailed toward him. But before it connected, I closed my eyes and called Excalibur back to its sheath.

I couldn't go through with it.

Robin Hood laughed, first at relief and then derision. "After all this, you still screw up at the last moment." He hobbled forward, his hands outstretched, his fingers flexing. I didn't have the strength to lift Excalibur, let alone change its shape again. "Even now. Facing your own death if I live, you can't kill me."

"No, but I can." Mordred dropped from the ceiling. "Close your eyes, Rexi."

I did, but I couldn't close my ears. I heard a thwack and the gurgle of Robin Hood's last breath.

I slumped over, Mordred catching me. "Do nay look. No one should have to kill their kin," he said.

"I couldn't. I couldn't." I sobbed onto his shoulder.

"I would think less of ye if ye could. The day ye can deal death without hesitation is the day thine soul dies as well. I do nay wish that for ye, my lass."

He moved his hand to my foot. "Are ye ready?" I knew what he was asking. I didn't think I would ever be ready, but I nodded anyway. The arrows hurt twice as much coming out as they did going in, the barbed tips ripping flesh.

"Shh. Shh," Mordred soothed, stroking my face. "'Tis done. Stay with me now." He moved his hand down to my neck. And the grail.

I grabbed his hand and stopped him from taking it. "No."

"Ye can't walk like this. Let me heal ye."

"There's a single drop left. I can't waste it here." The room was spinning. I held on to consciousness by the thinnest of threads. "Promise me you won't."

Mordred squeezed his lips together but nodded. "I'll have to carry ye. I'm not sure how to climb with ye in my arms, though I'll manage."

I looked him over. His clothes were ripped, his hands bloody and cracked. His face was pale and dripping in sweat. Mordred looked almost as bad as I felt.

"This trial was easy as cake, huh?" Then I trailed off, letting Mordred and the blackness embrace me.

"All that glitters is not gold."

—Stiltzskin

Through the Looking Glass
Dorthea

U m, Dot?" Kato said.
    "Yes?"

He held up his hand, which was firmly entwined in mine. "You realize that you are going to have to let go of me sometime."

"Nope," I said, squeezing harder. "Can't make me. I'm not going to lose you again."

He sighed. "How many times do I have to tell you that was only a nightmare? You won. Griz was defeated. Blanc is still in her prison. There's no such place as Camelot. Rexi is the furthest person from a king I can think of. The only thing more ludicrous is the idea that she would ever fall for me."

He stopped ranting and put a hand on my cheek, his thumb tracing my jaw. "And as you can see, I'm very much alive."

I smiled, enjoying his hand cradling my cheek. "Okay. But I'm still not letting go. Just in case."

"Arg. Why must you always do things the hard way?" He growled, the space around us growing colder. "You are absolutely infuriating and the most stubborn creature in the world."

I shrugged. "Someone's got to stand up to you and keep you on your toes."

He huffed, but his expression softened. "I suppose if you were any different, I wouldn't love you so."

Moving his hand to my chin, he tilted it up and then brushed his lips against mine. The kiss was sweet and soft just like I remembered them. In that moment the world stopped turning, and we were the only people who existed.

When it ended and I opened my eyes again, Kato had shifted into a chimera. He was gently flapping his mismatched wings, flying above me and grinning like an absolute loon.

I swiped at the air and stomped my foot. "No fair. You cheated. Tricking me into kissing you so you could escape."

He laughed. "Someone has to keep you on your toes. Besides, you have a dress fitting in the hall of mirrors. I know you. You won't be happy unless your dress is just so. And the shoes..." He made a face and rolled his eyes.

"Ha. Ha. Very funny." I put my hands on my hips. "Your

right. I'm not one to snub my nose at fashion, but can't you come with me? Please?"

He shook his head. "Its bad luck to see the bride in her wedding dress before the ceremony. And given our lives, I think we need all the good luck we can get to warm our hearths." He crossed his hind legs. "Also I really need to pee."

"What a romantic you are!" I scoffed as he flew off. Then I processed what he had said. "Wait. Wedding?"

"There you are." My mother stormed toward me. She looked exactly as I remembered her, crown and all.

"How did you get back from the other world?" I asked.

"Ugh. Kan-sas. Dreadful place. I thought we agreed to never speak of the wish, curse, and my temporary banishment. Oz fixed it all, and now we must get on with our happily ever afters." She grabbed my elbow and dragged me to the palace. "Speaking of, where have you been? Glinda is throwing a fit. One can only keep mice and doves focused for so long. If you don't hurry, the woodland creatures will run off, and you'll have no one to do the sewing."

"About that. I'm getting married?"

"Don't tell me you've changed your mind." Mother threw her hands in the air. "Whatever will I do with the fiddlers? They are already on the roof. And all the roses are still dripping red paint. Verte even had her face waxed for the occasion."

"Verte's here?" I asked quietly. Verte couldn't be here. I had killed her. My curse had sucked the life magic from her and scorched her to ashes.

"Of course she is. She bullied her way out of Swampy Acres Retirement Condos to be here." Queen Em hiked up her dress and started dragging me again. "And if you're canceling, you get to break the news to the Emerald Sorceress. Preferably in one of the less fragile rooms please."

Could it really be this easy? Could all the pain and anguish be wiped away? Could I really have Ever After without losing anyone? I smiled warily. "I'm not canceling. I don't need to tell her anything."

The Emerald palace had been rebuilt even better and shinier than I remembered it. The front gates stood wide open, and the stained glass shone brighter than ever. The Pied Piper cleaning services were in the entryway, playing the tune that all the dust bunnies followed, hopping through the corridors and out the door. A florist arranged bouquets, directing them with a thorny conductors stick. The flowers opened their petals and sang in four-part harmony.

The caterers placed baked goods on the long banquet table. A very familiar head of spiky blond hair poked out from under the tablecloth and snagged a tart before disappearing again.

"I saw that!" Mother stormed into the ballroom but then turned around and pointed a finger at me. "You, young lady. Hall of mirrors. Now!"

I knew that voice. That was the *obey or you're pixed* voice. And this time it brought a smile to my face. It was good to be home. It really couldn't get any better.

I was wrong.

"Voila," Glinda said. She clapped her hands, and the mice dropped their needles and scurried away.

I couldn't breathe. Not only because the dress was too tight but because it was breathtaking. Cascades of sheer green toile fell off my shoulders and pooled around my feet as my train. The dress itself was delicate with woven emerald, satin ribbons for the bodice, and the whitest, softest chiffon for the skirt, which flowed like water down my legs. Every inch sparkled like Glinda had sewn stars into the fabric.

"I know," Glinda said and sighed. "I've outdone myself. Stain it, and I will skin you alive." She kissed each of my cheeks. "Toodles. Congratulations on your big day. Don't forget to put on the Jiminy Choo shoes I picked out for you."

She left the room in a flurry of fur and feathers. Then it was just me. Standing on the raised pedestal in the hall of mirrors, I twirled around, viewing myself from every angle. Perfect. I looked like I had everything I ever wanted, the storybook life I'd always prayed for to the Storymakers.

I stopped twirling and touched my reflection. Tears welled in my eyes.

"Better not cry, you big baby. You'll ruin your makeup." Verte stood behind me, hunched over her staff, wearing her very best black and pointy hat. The green of her skin clashed horribly with my dress, but I didn't care.

I went to her, but she kept me at a distance with her staff. "I don't do hugs, and you'll get schmutz all over me."

"Grimm, I've missed you." I chuckled.

She plucked the last hair from her ear. "Bah. I never left you, ya ninny."

My smile dimmed. "I know you never left me. I can hear your voice sometimes deep inside me along with the rest of the curse." I turned back to the mirror. The dress was still lovely, but it didn't seem as bright. "It's not real, is it? None of this is real."

Verte hobbled over and perched herself on the tailor's chair. "Well, that depends entirely on you, Dot."

"What do you mean?"

She went to twirl her favorite hairy mole and then frowned to find it freshly waxed. Sighing, she settled for thumping her staff. "I'll skip the pseudo-psycho babble. Put plain, perception is reality. This is even truer since you are a Storymaker. If you perceive this realm to be real, it will be for you."

"For me…" I picked out the catch. "Meaning what for everyone else?"

"Does it matter?" She leaned forward, balancing herself on her staff. "If it's real to you, isn't that enough? If you can live here in happiness with the ones you love, what difference does it make what happens outside this bubble?"

"So this could be my reality. I can be happy. With Rexi still thieving and with you still breathing. My Kato, still alive and by my side." I wanted it. Oh, how I wanted all of it. This perfect happy ending. But could I really stay here forever? Could I choose to ignore whatever happened to the world outside?

Perhaps, but not without knowing the consequences. I had learned that lesson before. "What's outside this bubble?"

"Are you sure you want to know?" Verte asked, tracing her emerald belt. "Once you see, you won't be able to unsee."

"Show me," I said.

Verte walked to the mirror and touched it. The reflection shimmered and grew cloudy just like the emerald eye in her belt.

An image of Camelot appeared. It looked worse than when I had left it. I could see a giant barrier surrounding the castle and fields. Just outside that, an army awaited on the swampy marshland. Creatures of every kind, heroes and villains, stood twisted and slumped in formation. If I squinted, I could see the trickle of black oozing out of their eyes, ears, and nose.

The castle itself billowed smoke. Villagers, noblemen, trolls, elves, and others scurried about. It was complete chaos.

"I don't understand," I said.

"Camelot will fall because there is no one to lead them. Everyone who sought shelter there will fall as one."

"Where's Rexi?"

"I think you know," Verte said.

I remembered what I had written in my notebook. "Where's Mic pretending to be Rexi?"

Verte's face wrinkled more than usual. "Yellow-bellied, toad-boil pus bag ran as soon as the enemy was at his door."

"Will Rexi make it back in time to save them?"

Verte shook her head. "No spoilers. No flipping to the end

of the story. I can just show you the present." She touched the mirror again, changing the scene.

This time Rexi stood in the middle of a mirrored room like mine. She was cut and bleeding and broken. Surrounded by enemies.

I put my hand on the mirror. Fear slid through me. "What's happening to her?"

"She is going through the trial of fear."

"What is that?" I pointed to the girl with emerald flames. "Is that me?"

Verte shook her head. "No. That is Rexi's fear that led her to cut you down with Excalibur. That is what she was bound to become if your madness had continued. You would have controlled her life force entirely, turning her into a mindless killing machine with no sense of self."

My stomach turned at the thought. I'd forged the bond to save her. I never thought it could have harmed her.

Emerald flames shot out and hit Rexi.

I looked at Verte frantically. "If we don't help her, she'll die."

"That is one possibility. If she wants to live, she must learn."

"Learn what?"

Verte held her belt, her eyes fixing off in the distance. *You cannot fight who you are. Embrace it and grow strong.*

Rexi stared in the mirror like she had heard. "You are not seriously telling me that a group hug will solve all this."

Rexi grappled with the puppet, gasping, growing paler. Rexi's head started to droop, but she stared over the puppet's shoulder. Directly into the mirror. Directly at me and said, "I'm sorry I killed you. I'm sorry I failed and let you down. I'm sorry Kato died for nothing. I tried so hard, but this is who I am. All I can be."

I reached out, my fingers brushing the mirror. "You didn't kill me. You saved me from becoming something else. Saved both of us. It's enough. You've always been enough."

She reached out, and our fingers touched. The mirror shattered.

I jumped back to avoid getting cut by the glass. The mirrors no longer showed Rexi. They didn't show anything.

I picked up a large shard of mirror and tapped on it. "Hey. Hey. Come back. I need to know what happened."

"What do you think happened?" Verte asked.

I thought for a moment. Then I visualized it in my head. "I think Rexi finally accepted all her different sides and passed that test."

Verte winked. "I think so too."

I looked around the hall of mirrors. My reflections were all the same. They were all staring at me. The similarities between Rexi and my situations were impossible to miss.

"So is that why I'm here?" I asked Verte. "I was told I had to go on a hero's journey to earn those shoes-in-shining-armor and get home. Now it's my turn to face my fear and accept who I am?"

"Nah," Verte said. "You already accepted who you are. What you've done." I bent over to put down the mirror. Verte stopped me. "Oi. Did I say you were done yet? Your trial is not in accepting but in letting go."

I didn't ask for more details because I was afraid of the answer.

She waved her hand over the broken mirror. An image wavered, a face slowly coming into focus. A chimera that I knew so well, except not. Not my fluffy love with tawny fur and mismatched wings, but a great black shadow beast with white eyes.

"Kato," I whispered. "Or Morte now, I guess."

"Both are correct actually."

Everything stopped. Even my heart and the blood in my veins. "What?" I breathed.

She shrugged and sighed with exasperation. "Well, obviously a bit of Kato still exists in there, duh."

I held the mirror so tightly that I could feel the sharp edges slice my palms. The pain was muted by a pain much deeper.

"Are you sure?" I asked.

"Of course I'm sure. When have I ever been wrong?"

I gave her the side eye.

"Pshaw," she grumbled. "When have I ever been wrong about anything *this important*?"

If she had, I couldn't think of a time. Besides, a part of me already knew he wasn't lost forever. That I'd be able to get him back somehow. That whatever the cost, I *would* bring him home to me.

"Rule #12: For the nervous bride, impractical footwear is a must. More than being fashionable, it greatly diminishes the chances of a runaway bride."

—Definitive Fairy-Tale Wedding Survival Guide

23

True Love's Curse
Dorthea

M y mind was clearer than it had been in weeks, sharpened by resolve. "Okay, so Kato is in there. How do I save him? How do I make him like he was?"

"Those are two separate questions."

I narrowed my eyes. "What do you mean?"

"It means what it means." Verte thumped her staff against the floor. A mirror on the far wall came to life, its image splitting into two. The top half showed Kato getting fitted for a tux. Since he was in chimera form, none of the mice would go near him, so they'd called in the God Squad—the top-tier Fairy Godmothers whose services were reserved for the toughest jobs. Considering they were trying to put curlers in Kato's mane, they were going to need more backup.

Watching that vision warmed me like lying in the orchards in the sunshine. Watching the bottom half of the mirror left me so cold. It was as if I had frostbite.

The dark chimera, Morte in my Kato's defiled body, stood by a large pit, throngs of people lined up beside him. Some were crying, and some stared blindly ahead. I recognized one among them, the Evil Queen. She fought and struggled as she was escorted to the pit.

"There has been a mistake," she yelled to Morte. "I have been invaluable to the empress."

"Yes, you have," Morte said, nodding to the guards who held her, dismissing them. "And I'm sure she sincerely thanks you for your service."

The Evil Queen smiled and exhaled, dropping her shoulders. She didn't notice the fierce dragon tail on the chimera until it was too late. Morte broadsided her, knocking her into the pit. She screamed. Oh, how she screamed. And then there was silence.

A figure ascended the pit, using a staircase carved into the stone. The Evil Queen. Black ooze dripped off her, leaving trails behind her. Her limbs were twisted, and her head was bent at an unnatural angle.

"Now you may serve me." Morte's eyes flashed, and he picked up a long scroll, scratching something out. "We need to move up production. Lady Blanc will be ready to leave us very soon, and I want everything in place when that happens."

Several other chimeras flew about in response, picking up and dropping the resistance into the pit.

I looked away, covering my ears to block out the cries.

"That's…" I had no words. There weren't any strong enough to describe what Morte was doing.

"I'm disappointed you aren't enjoying the show," Morte said, his voice sharp. "I thought you might appreciate the view, one Angel of Destruction to another."

He was addressing me. Somehow. I knew it.

My breath quickened. "We are nothing alike."

Verte clarified. "He's a sly, mangy beast. He can feel you watching but cannot hear or see us."

Pity, I had a few choice words for the monster.

"I haven't thanked you for getting out of my way. This world is so much easier to rule without you in it." Morte flashed his fangs in what might have been a smile, if pure evil was capable of that. "For that, I shall give you a gift." He closed his eyes and bowed his head. When he raised it again, his eyes were open…and blue.

"Dot?" The voice was Kato's. His face transformed, his expression more gentle. Proud but tired. "If you can hear me, I regret nothing." His face crumpled, and his voice strained. "Live." The blue leaked out of his eyes, turning that cool blue to iceberg white.

"Isn't that sweet?" The voice had reverted back to Morte's

deeper, slippery tone. "I hope you liked your gift. If you continue to stay out of my way, you might receive another."

It wasn't a gift. It was a curse. Kato was close. Right there. Yet untouchable.

"Well, I must be going. Enslavement of entire stories is a full-time job, you know. Good-bye." Morte stared, and the mirror frosted over. First the bottom half and then the top. Taking both the light and dark Katos from my view.

"You wanted to save Kato and restore him to this life." Verte leaned heavily on her staff, breathing hard from the exertion of magic.

"Yes, obviously."

"You can't have both. You must choose."

"I don't understand. Aren't they the same?" I knew Verte too well. "You aren't telling me everything."

"I don't have to. You saw exactly what I did." Verte flicked my forehead. "You're just too stubborn to believe it. You're still waiting for someone to step in, wave their magic wand, and give you the perfect happily-ever-after. In that case, choose this. Stay here, believe in this reality, and forget the rest."

I laughed. "Forget?" *Impossible.* I laughed harder.

"You okay?" Verte looked at me like I was mad. She was probably right, but that didn't change the truth. I could stay here and pretend everything was fine, but I would never be happy in this illusion. There was no choice really. I wouldn't betray Rexi, Hydra, and the entire world for the fantasy, no matter how perfect it was.

I couldn't let my Kato suffer.

"So that's the trial," I said. "I have to let this delusion go."

"Correct. If you want to move forward, that's half of it." She turned and speed shuffled out of the room.

"Wait up!" As usual, I was shocked at how fast she could move when she wanted to. "What's the other half?"

"Bah." She paused and turned. "It's plain as the beautiful green schnoz on my face." She tapped the wart on her very crooked and pointy nose.

Yeah, not clear at all. But what was clear was that Verte was done talking about it. She hurried on, holding her hand in a wave. "Was good seeing you again, kid. Hope you have better luck getting rid of Blanc than I did."

Then she faded away like she was never here. But I knew better. She would always be here. A part of me. Like all the others.

I left the hall of mirrors and walked through the gem-encrusted corridors. They didn't sparkle as much, the shine dull like gum paste. Cheap imitation, all of it. Verte was right. Once I'd seen the truth, I could not unsee.

Everyone was still bustling around for the storybook wedding to top all the happily-ever-afters. A wedding that would never happen. My mother called to me as I walked past the ballroom.

"You can't leave!"

Be strong, I told myself.

Kato called to me from the staircase. "How can you go? Don't you love me?"

"Always," I answered and walked out the door.

The illusion was broken. I stepped outside into the world of Kansas. I couldn't tell how much time had passed or whether it was day or night. The sky was nearly black. The only light came from the lightning streaking across the sky.

Drawing nearer. Hunting. For me.

"The first step to healing is admitting you have a problem. Say it with me, 'Yes, these are my flying monkeys, and this is my circus.'"

—Dr. Oz's Twelve-Step Program for Recovering Reality

24

The Not So Great or Powerful Oz
Dorthea

Since I didn't know who would be a normal person and who would be a Forsaken, my first stop was to change into clothes the shadow soldiers hadn't seen. Desperate times called for unthinkable measures. In a market parking lot, there was a clothing donation box that had garbage bags of clothes inside. It looked like Snow White's hamper on laundry day.

The clothes that John had given me from the hospital were clothes that my parents had brought for me. They were oversize but at least supposedly mine. Who knew who had worn these? From the smell of some of them, onion farmers.

I rummaged through the bags, picking items that looked

the cleanest and didn't reek like the inside of an ogre's under-wear drawer. Keeping the sneakers, I threw on a pair of black sweatpants and an oversize flannel shirt. I layered a hooded jacket over that. To top it off, I twisted my hair up under a brimmed sports cap.

Walking across the parking lot, I looked at the windows. If I ignored the sign for ninety-nine-cent bananas, I could see a faint reflection of myself. I cringed. Which was a good sign. I wouldn't be caught dead in these clothes by anyone I knew. But if I got caught, that's exactly what would happen to me.

And of course, now I wanted a banana.

I had exactly no money to my name, but my stomach didn't care.

Oh, Grimm, I thought as I walked in the store. I am becoming Rexi. I tried telling myself, *It's only a banana. It's only a banana.*

I broke two off the bunch and shoved them inside my jacket pocket. Keeping my head down, I walked back toward the register, hoping to slip through an empty one unnoticed.

"Hey, that kid has a gun!"

Somebody had a gun? Startled, I looked around, worried that Griz had resorted to this world's tools inside of her tricks. Except everyone was staring at me. The shape in my pocket in particular.

They thought I was going to rob the store! *Pix.*

"No, you're mistaken. It's a banana," I said, pulling it out as proof. Instead of having the calming effect I'd hoped for, now the broad-shouldered guy behind the service desk pointed at me and said, "Thief!"

That wasn't a mistake. I ran, jumping over the turnstile and dodging shopping carts. I didn't stop running and didn't look behind me to see how badly they wanted that two bucks' worth of bananas. I kept jogging until I found a space in between Dumpsters behind the row of shops.

Ignoring the garbage beside me, I wolfed down the bananas, barely taking time to peel them first. I vowed if I ever got back to Emerald, my first royal decree would be to have the palace provide all with enough to eat and make sure no one in the kingdom needed to swipe food again. Although Rexi would probably still do it out sheer stubbornness.

Once I was sure no one had followed me out of the market, I started moving again, this time at a regular walking pace. Within a few steps, I noticed I had brought a piece of garbage with me. A page of the newspaper. I peeled it off my shoe along with whatever else I had stepped in that acted as an adhesive. Then, of course, it stuck to my hand. In the middle of shaking it off, I noticed something—my face and a headline.

"Local Disturbed Teens Escape Locked Hospital Wing. Search Underway."

The full story was on page 11A. Too bad I only had the front page. I went back to the Dumpster, but I couldn't find the rest of the paper. Dumpster diving was out of the question. I had limits to how low I'd go.

Keeping my face mostly hidden, I walked the streets, maintaining a watchful eye. After a few blocks, it became easy to tell the Forsaken from the normals. The normals twitched at the storm, anxiously looking up at the sky. They itched at their skin or fidgeted, not able to see the unnatural forces and creatures about but sensing them just the same. The Forsaken didn't break stride, never looked up, never spoke to anyone. And there numbers were growing by the minute.

The buildings had become more infected. Shadow creatures scurried up walls while the ink tendrils continued to branch out from the center of the city. It took nearly my full will not to shudder or cringe, which would be a dead giveaway that I could see what no one else could. I didn't know what Blanc and Morte were waiting for or what they needed to happen before they could cross over, though it couldn't be anything good. That I knew for certain.

Down the main drag, there was a bus stop. A woman sat on the bench, legs crossed, bouncing her knee up and down. She kept glancing nervously from the sky to the newspaper that she was reading. From her behavior, she was not a Forsaken. Maybe she would let me borrow her paper. But then I thought of the dock worker and how quickly he'd transformed.

Better to trust no one.

I waited, hanging out by a lamp pole that flickered on and off. Within a few minutes, the bus roared down the street. It was covered in dark slime. The headlights and the grill made the vehicle seem like the eyes and mouth of a great beast that had swallowed all the people inside. I wanted to warn the woman as she stood to get in, but she wouldn't believe me. I couldn't risk the exposure.

She'll be fine, I told myself as she climbed hurriedly into the belly of the beast. Or at least as fine as everyone else in this world. Which wasn't very fine at all if I couldn't figure out how to finish this scavenger hunt hero's journey and get the magic I needed to take out Blanc. I need to find Oz and his workshop at that Emerald City the girl at the shoe store had described. I was sure if I could just get home, I'd have use of the Emerald flames, hopefully without the side of madness this time.

First thing's first—the paper the woman had abandoned on the bench.

I turned to 11A.

Two local teens are on the run after escaping the security of Kansas State Hospital's neuropsychiatric ward. Dorothy Gayle, 17, had been receiving cancer treatments in the oncology center when an infection postsurgery sent her into a coma for three weeks. After waking, her doctor, Frank Baum PhD, said that Ms. Gayle was moved to the neuropsych ward as she was having difficulty returning to her normal life. She is considered a top priority for the police, as she is in a fragile state, both mentally and physically. The radiation treatments she has undergone have compromised her immune system, and it's important that she receive her medications as soon as possible. She is believed to have escaped with a young man, estimated age of 19. His identity and past is unknown. He entered the hospital after being found unconscious in the hospital courtyard with no identification. Hospital records have him listed as John Doe, and he was placed under a psychiatric hold after sudden violent outbursts that make him a safety concern to himself and others. The public has been asked to assist the KCPD in bringing the pair back to the hospital safely. If you should see them, do not approach the teens. Call the hotline listed below.

I didn't know what I was more shocked by—the fact that someone had gone to enough trouble to get me in the paper or what the article said about John. He'd never shared his last name. And I'd never even asked about his history. He said he had no home to go back to. I'd been too blinded by my concerns to follow up about what he meant by that.

It was too late to ask now, but I hoped he was okay. Wherever he was.

Folding the newspaper, I noticed some other information of interest—the weather section. It was full of stories about weather anomalies. Tornadoes downtown. Record rainfall with high rates of particulates in the air. A massive storm system was centered around Kansas City but didn't seem to be moving with the usual weather patterns. Climate change was the listed cause.

I knew better.

Kansas was landlocked, but when Blanc arrived, the tornadoes would turn into hurricanes and tsunamis.

The city grew darker in the time that I'd been reading.

Most of the streetlights were out, the magic of electricity being no match for the storm witch. I could barely make out the roaming normal people. A few people my age wore sticks of light around their necks that illuminated them.

I followed behind a group of six when they passed. Each of them wore a glow stick, and together, they made a halo of light. The shadows kept their distance and shied away from the glow.

Interesting. Was it magic or something else? The group walked into an underground parking structure, laughing and whispering excitedly as they headed down the ramp. I continued to follow them. Two levels down, the sound changed. A low *thump thump thump* vibrated the floor. And a green light shimmered just past a gate and a small glass booth.

I knocked on the booth. A guy in dreadlocks with lime sunglasses pressed his face to the glass. "Hey, man," he said. "Can't you read?"

"Yes," I said.

"Then read the sign." He turned around his swivel chair and put back on his headphones.

I knocked again, pounding until he turned around.

"You're messing with my beats, man," he said, pulling off his headphones.

"There is no sign," I protested.

He took off his sunglass and squinted. "Huh, I guess not. But if there was a sign, it would read, 'Ain't nobody getting in without an invitation.'"

I straightened my spine and used my royal command voice. "Don't you know who I am? I am a personal guest of Oz."

The guy gasped and fell off his chair. He opened a little door in the glass. "The Wizard? But nobody can see the Great Oz! Nobody's ever seen the Great Oz! Even I've never seen him!"

"Well, I have, so open the pixing gate and let me in."

"Prove it!" He sneered, looking me over. "You don't even have a light on ya."

I noticed a small blinking red light in the corner. Like an eyepod, a cam-air-a, or something in this world. I pulled off my hat and hood, showing my hair and face, and I spoke directly in the camera. "Oz! I followed your clues. I'm here for the shoes. Tell this idiot to let me in."

The guy snorted. "Like that's gonna work. Get lost, little girl."

A voice crackled and then boomed over the loudspeaker. "Let her in. Send her to the back."

The guy scrambled, tripping over his chair to get to the button. "The Wizard spoke to me! He's never spoken to me. Why didn't you say you knew him? That's a horse of a different color. Come in. Come in."

"But I *did* tell you." I shook my head and pushed through the gate. "Never mind."

The inside reminded me of a ball thrown at the Emerald Palace—if everyone was on pixie dust. Lights hung from the ceiling beams, swirling in every direction like a drunk will-o'-the-wisp. Throngs of youth swayed and bopped up and down to the bass line of a song that drowned out nearly everything else, including thought. Green fairies danced on luminescent toadstool tables, their skin glittering gold. As I passed by one, I could see her wings were cheap plastic. They'd been stitched on.

Smoke and mirrors, all of it. And not what I had expected.

I pushed through the dancing teenagers lost in their music and drinks and made my way to the back. A thick velvet curtain separated this area from the rest. A sign said it was the VIP section.

"Welcome to the Underground Emerald City," a voice boomed, and fire whooshed up in a column. "I am the Great and Powerful Oz. Speak."

"Knock it off, Oz. It's me. I need to see you."

"I'm quite busy today and not taking visitors. Come back and see the magnificent me tomorrow," the voice boomed.

What the hex? I put out my hand to push the curtain aside.

A hand grabbed my wrist. The man's fingers were covered in gold rings. Rosewater incense wafted from behind the curtain.

The gold and the smell brought back memories, but not pleasant ones.

No more Ms. Nice Princess. I yanked at the curtain, ripping it off the rod. The Wizard picked up the nearest throw pillow and hid his face.

"Pay no attention to the man behind the curtain." The voice was coming from a speaker. The fire that flared with his words was just a series of light and fog special effects, not magic.

I kicked the rig.

"I assure you I can explain," the man said in a muffled voice.

I approached him and ripped away the pillow. I saw the Wizard's face. It was him, the man from the ivory tower.

The Mimicman.

"Rule #77: Beware of wool and any sort of lambskin. Such fashion is often favored by wolves."

—Definitive Fairy-Tale Survival Guide, Volume 2: Villains

25

Dying to See You
Dorthea

"I'm gonna throttle you." I lunged, wrapping my fingers around Mic's neck.

"Ack." He clawed at my fingers, prying them off enough to free his windpipe. "I thought you were cured of the madness."

"I am. I just hate you that much." I squeezed again.

His face turned red and then blue as he tapped his hand repeatedly on the couch.

An arm wrapped around my waist and hoisted me off Mic. "You gotta let him go."

I kicked and wiggled, and as soon as my feet were back on the ground, I whirled around and slapped the owner of that familiar voice. John. My palm landed with a satisfying *whap*. John rubbed his face and the red hand-print I'd left behind.

I smirked with satisfaction. *And Rexi thought those open-handed princess slap lessons were useless.*

"I might have deserved that," John said.

"So you've been on his side all this time?" I raised my hand again.

He was ready for it and caught my wrist. "No, I deserve it because I left after promising to look out for you. I don't know this creepy gigolo."

Mic huffed hoarsely. "Gigolo?"

"You shut it." I pointed a finger at Mic. "I will get to you in a second."

John let go of my wrist and backed out of my reach. "It took me five minutes to figure out I was wrong, but when I went back to the shoe store, you were gone. I don't know what got into me. Then tonight I saw you on the street, and I followed you."

I rolled my eyes. "A likely story."

"No less believable than anything you've told me," he countered.

Touché.

"True or not, it doesn't matter. You are still a coward." I looked at Mic. "Not as bad as you though." I flashed back to the image of Camelot in flames that I had seen in the mirror. "How could you? Rexi trusted you. And you abandoned everyone."

Mic stood and rearranged his collar. "You, my beloved, are a victim of backward thinking. You are under the upside-down impression that just because you run away, you have no courage. You are quite wrong. It only means I'm smart."

I held my hand out, ready to throttle him again.

"Dot, don't." John held me by the hood, effectively keeping Mic out of reach as he scrambled over the chaise and pressed his back against the wall.

"I did what I had to do to get to you," Mic said, hands held in surrender. "Even though it meant putting myself in reach of Grizelda. Surely, that magnanimous self-sacrifice deserves to be heard."

I sat down on the nearest glowing toadstool. "Fine. Spill."

He gave John the side-eye. "Not until your new puppy quits following you around. I had you first."

"Hey, I stopped her from maiming you," John protested.

"No, you stalked me first. Then kidnapped me. Not the same." I rubbed my temples. "John, will you please go out and keep watch?"

"Watch for what?"

That was hard to explain since he couldn't see Morte's infection in the Forsaken. "Um, look for people who don't look they are here for the party."

He hesitated, glancing back and forth between Mic and me.

Mic put his hand over his heart. "I won't harm her. I swear."

"It's not *you* harming *her* I'm worried about," John mumbled and left the VIP section.

As soon as he was gone, I pulled out the drawing of the shoe and flattened it on the end table. "I need this. Tell me how to get it."

Mic picked up the page and examined it. "I've heard of shoes similar to these in Story, in the legend of King Arthur. Boots weighted in armor to keep his wife from straying from home again. The heels were forged with magic from the broken scabbard of Caliburn."

"Which means…" I prodded.

"Gwenevere's shoes were legendary, binding her to return to Camelot any time the heels clicked. There's no way I can replicate it. I could craft something similar, but it would simply be a veneer, a counterfeit." He handed the page back.

"Then what good are you?" I stood up to leave and then stopped. "Wait a minute. You got here somehow. That means you know how to get back. Then I don't need the shoes."

"I made a deal with Morte. Camelot for the use of his portal. But I'm afraid it was a one-way trip." Mic fidgeted with his golden hair. "That's what I came here to tell you. You must abandon Fairy Tale forever. It is lost. The Grimm Reaper and Empress are unbeatable together, even for you. However, you have bested Grizelda before, and with my help, we can beat her again. After that…"

"After that what?"

Mic leaned across the table, grasping my hands. "We can build a life here together. I have faith that in time you will forget that half-breed mongrel and grow to love me."

I recoiled from Mic's hands like they were leprous. "I will never forget Kato. That's why I cannot stay here. I will not abandon him. I'm going to save him."

Mic's eyes turned cold. "So you think you could fight and cast out Morte, even knowing that when he dies, Kato goes with him?"

The swirling lights, the dancing girls, the thrumming baseline—all of that was drowned out by my heart pounding in my ears.

"You didn't realize?" Mic's smile was the twisted smile of someone pulling the wings off an insect. "Kato used the last of his life magic to rescue that kitchen girl from the underworld. The only thing keeping his soul tethered to the story is Morte. Vanquish the underlord, and you destroy them both. If you care about that boy, you will let him keep what little life he has and turn your back on it all."

This. This is what Verte meant. That I couldn't save Kato and keep him around.

Kato was now part of that twisted monster. Forced to witness and take a part in all that suffering. I promised to make sure he was released. But saving him meant letting him go. Could I do that?

My stomach lurched at the thought, banana rising up to my throat.

There had to be another way. I thought through my options. Maybe I could make a deal. "What does Morte want?"

"To throw the world of Story into shadow and rule it."

"And Blanc is okay with that?" Somehow I had a hard time believing she shared power well.

"Yes." He leaned forward again. "That is what I came here to warn you about. Morte has given her unlimited use of the false grail and the shadow souls to manipulate things here for her goal."

"Which is what?"

"To start her story over, to retell it the way she thinks it should be told. You've already seen the shadow creatures and the Forsaken she had created. Next she intends to come here and force you, her Storymaker pet, to help her create a new world."

I snorted. "And how would I do that? If she's manipulating all the shadows instead of Morte, then she's stronger than I am." I shook my head. "No, even if I had that kind of power, why would I help her after all she's done?"

"Because she will rip apart this world piece by piece, town by town until you do."

I thought of my parents, John, Nick, and little Jessie at the hospital. Mic was right. If Blanc was holding them hostage—holding this whole world hostage—I wouldn't have a choice.

My shoulders slumped under the weight of it all. "So what is she waiting for? Why isn't she here already? Griz is here. You are here—"

"Morte is the king of Nome Ore, the land of the characters whose stories have ended. Using his false grail, Morte and Blanc can give those characters new life here. But first, those souls have to be on the scrolls in the *Compendium of Characters*."

"To come here, they have to die," I finished.

"And have contact with one of the grails, yes."

That made sense. Rexi pierced me with Excalibur, but it was coated with the contents of the grail to cure me. Griz died by my hand. Then I looked up at Mic. "So for you to come here—"

Mic shrugged. "I think of it more as relocating, really."

He didn't deserve it, but I felt an ounce of sympathy and gratitude for Mic. "Why doesn't Morte just kill Blanc and send her here then?"

"I really thought you would have pieced it together by now." Mic stood, gesturing grandly. "If she was so easy to kill, we would have done so ages ago instead of imprisoning her. Because of the binding and the curse of Emerald, there were only two things with enough power to send her to the underworld—the Emerald flames or Excalibur. So we had to wait for the wielders of both to be born. And for whatever reason, that meddlesome Storymaker Frank waited to plant the seed of life into the tree Camlann. He waited for you to be born as well. All to make sure the child of the trees and the child of Emerald would cross paths—the king reborn, Rexi, and the last Storymaker, you."

My mind swirled trying to make sense of it all. How intricate and detailed Oz had been, pulling the strings, manipulating all of us to be in the right place.

Rexi.

I didn't understand what it all meant, but still. "I have to warn her about Blanc."

"What? No," Mic said, his jaw dropping. "That's not why I told you about the Storymaker's plot. You're supposed to forget them all."

I looked at him pointedly. "I don't care about what the Storymaker wants. If I don't warn her and she kills Blanc first, what do you think will happen?"

Mic's eyes widened in understanding. "That would mean Rexi must slay Morte to keep him from using his tainted grail again."

Meaning Rexi would slay Kato with him.

Could I do that? Let Blanc go and trust Rexi and Hydra to figure out a way to save Kato that I couldn't see? Of course, there was no other choice.

"How do I tell them in time?"

Mic handed me a pen and a pile of napkins. "You're a Storymaker. Write it into the Story."

"Seriously?" I took the pen in my hand. "If that's the case, I have a better idea." I started writing. "Stuff happens. The bad guys lose, and everyone goes home and lives happily ever after. THE END!" I added a few extra exclamation points for good measure.

Mic smacked his head in disgust. "Did Frank teach you nothing? This is not a message in a bottle. You must tell the story, using the elements of craft at your disposal. You can't pull events out of thin air. To create a scene, you must give something in return. There must be an equal exchange."

I thought back to my practices with Oz. Pulling details from around me, memories and emotions from inside me. Closing my eyes, I visualized Rexi and the caves of Avalon. Then I started writing again.

"*Rule #99: When questing, it's perfectly advisable to take your time and relax. The biggest danger never shows up until the very end, so it's okay to let your guard down once in a while.*"

—*Definitive Fairy-Tale Survival Guide, Volume 5: Heroes*

26

Something Wicked and Squishy This Way Comes
Rexi

The first thing I noticed when I came to was that I was surrounded by warmth. Like when I was little, wrapped in a blanket of moss high up in the trees, swaying to the rhythm of the breeze. I breathed in, expecting the earthy scent of Sherwood Forest. Instead I smelled something more complex like cinnamon and leather.

I burrowed my head deeper into the smell and warmth.

"If ye keep that up, lass, I'll drop thee," a voice rumbled.

Mordred.

My eyes snapped open. He was grinning down at me. "Did ye know ye snore?"

I wacked his chest. "Put me down, oaf."

He did, and the second my wounded feet touched the floor, I remembered why I was in his arms in the first place. "Ow, ow. Pick me up. Pick me up."

He chuckled. "As my liege commands." He swept me up again, but this time I scrambled around to his back, latching onto his shoulders and waist.

"There. I'll allow you to be my steed for the time being." My dignity was preserved.

"Oh, good," Hydra piped in. "And here I was worried you might have matured through these trials." She was wearing a new head. One with smooth olive skin, the hair hidden inside a wrap of cloth. I'd never seen this head before, and I couldn't automatically place which character she was or which story she came from.

Oh joy, more surprises.

"Just tell me we are almost done. I don't think I can survive many more of those tests." I ached head to toe. Even my eyelids hurt.

"There should be one more," Hydra said. "The trial of the heart."

I gulped. "Not literal, right? No one's going to rip out my heart and examine it. More like a meta…meta—"

"A metaphor. Yes."

I sighed in relief. "Nice. All right. After that, then it's hi-ho, off to the well we go. We do what we do to get Dorthea back. Then we kick evil butt. Happily ever after. Blah, blah, blah."

Hydra cackled. Probably not a good sign. "Name one story where vanquishing the evil villain has been that easy."

"Art thou saying this has been easy?" Morte asked.

"Compared to what's coming, this has been a lovely sight-seeing tour," Hydra answered.

Hex.

"And I'm afraid that tour ends here," a voice echoed through the cave. Each drop of water from the cave's moist air shuddered. And the mark on my hand burned.

Empress of Evil. Lady of the Lake. Blanc.

Double hex.

The drips kept falling from the cave's ceiling, forming a puddle. A ripple formed. "Surely, you didn't think I'd actually let you get to the well?"

Hydra sighed. "Hoped you'd be a wee bit busy to notice."

"If Camelot had put up more resistance, you might have succeeded. But alas." Blanc shrugged, a coy smile on her face.

Mic, I was gonna kill that son of a basilisk one day.

I stared at the puddle, which was growing larger, but it was merely water. Not ink. Morte wasn't here.

Hydra whispered to me, "Be careful. We can't fight her yet. It's not time. We need her to flee…for now."

I nodded and bluffed. "So what's your plan, algae breath? We have you three to one, and I have Excalibur."

"You are half right, king without a kingdom." She pointed to my sword. "But who said I was alone?"

The puddle had grown. And instead of rippling, it roiled.

One slimy, mottled, muddy hand with daggerlike claws emerged. Then another. Each with arms oozing and scaled, more animal than human. The head, though, gave me pause. Once a very handsome face, the creature now festered and decayed, a hole in its cheek revealing something wriggling inside its mouth.

"Rex," it croaked, pulling its whole body out of the puddle.

"Dumbeau," I lamented. "What did she do to you?"

"You abandoned him, so I figured you wouldn't mind if I remade him to be more useful," Blanc said.

Hydra shifted her stance and crossed her chest in a warding. "Beware the Jabberwock."

"No matter what, every writer should remember this: Never ever interrupt a story in the middle to do something else. By the time you get back to it, Grandma will already be a midnight snack."

—Virginia "Big Bad" Wolfe on Writing

Who Let the Dogs Out?
Dorthea

B *eware the Jabberwock*, I scrawled on the very corner of the napkin. I reached for the next, but I came up empty.

"Pix! It's just getting good." I held up my hand, not looking up. "Napkin me."

Instead of a pile on mini writing squares, my hand grasped another's and tugged, which got my attention. John.

"What is it?" I wriggled my hand free. "I'm right at the part where I get to help Rexi save the day, white knight hero style, and lock up Blanc where she belongs. Somehow. Well, I was working on it. Turns out this plotting stuff isn't easy."

"Later," John said, retaking my hand and pulling me up.

"Remember how you told me to look for people who weren't here to party." He pointed to a divide in the crowd. "I think I found them."

Other partiers were starting to notice them as well—the Kansas Police, K-9 division. The partygoers rightfully gave them room, but moving to the next building still wouldn't have given them enough space. Griz's demon puppies had gotten an upgrade. The police's German shepherds had wispy gargoyle wings with curved talons at the ends. One snarled at me, drool dripping to the ground and hissing as it dissolved the concrete on contact.

I stuffed the napkins and pen in my jacket with slow movements. "We have to go."

"Cops are not good news," John agreed.

"It's not the men you must worry about," Mic said, joining us.

"You see?" I asked, oddly happy that it wasn't just me seeing things and terrified at the same time. That meant they really were real.

"More than you can know." He pointed to the neon green exit sign in the corner. "Be ready to run."

Mic took a deep breath and stepped up to the front of his stage. His booming wizard voice filled the entire underground club. "Raid."

Partygoers shrieked, fleeing in all directions. With their glow necklaces on, they looked like a swarm of will-o'-the-wisp scattering. The K-9 unit got lost in the chaos.

Using the distraction, John and I made our way to the exit. I held open the door, the cold night air hitting my face as I looked back, waiting for Mic. He stood exactly where I left him, shaking his head. A slow smile spread across his face. For the first time, it was genuine. Then he turned away.

"I am the Great and Powerful Oz, and I shall not let you pass." The flame spires at the edge of the stage flared to life, illuminating the dogs as they pounced and turned the Wizard of Is into the Wizard that Was.

Shell-shocked and unmoving, John pushed me out of the way, letting the door slam shut. "Don't waste his gift," he said and moved to the rolling Dumpster. "Help me."

I moved in a daze and helped him push the Dumpster in front of the door to block it. I'd never been a fan of Mic. Hex, I'd tried to kill him on multiple occasions. So it was unholy and unfair that he had to go out being decent. I hit the Dumpster with my fist. "You stupid, pox-ridden faker." In the end, his sacrifice would mean nothing, simply a tally mark on the body count of people who'd laid down their lives in front of mine. I screamed my frustration.

"We have to go now." John told me what I already knew as lightning cracked furiously across the sky.

The lightning was the only source of light in the whole town. Electricity seemed to have failed, and shadows ruled the night.

I needed to get somewhere safe enough to write. I'd been interrupted before I could get my message across. And even though I didn't fully grasp how this Storymaker business worked, I could feel the story taking on a life of its own. Even without my pen.

I grabbed John by the collar. "A light. Find me a light. Anything."

"Okay," he said. He didn't question me anymore. "Don't let go." Taking my hand, we maneuvered through the dark.

"How do you know where we're going?" I asked.

"I don't. I just have good night vision, I guess."

"Is this a new quality of yours?" I pushed.

"For as long as I remember." His tone was tight.

"All one month of it?"

He stopped suddenly, and I bumped into his back. "Yes. Do you want to interrogate me or find a light?"

He was right. "Go," I said.

We were off again, twisting and turning through back alleys until we reached a big shop with tools on the sign, like the Palace Depot back in Fairy Tale.

The automagic doors didn't work. John took a brick from a stack and found his own way in. A blaring siren sounded along with the tinkling of glass.

"Of course, the alarm works without power," John grumbled.

"No time." I avoided the jagged edges of glass and stepped in the shop. "They'll be coming."

Trusting John and his night vision, we wandered through the aisles while he tracked down a push-button LED, which

I assumed stood for a Luminous Enchanted Disc. It was a small light, but it was enough.

Taking the plastic light circle, I plopped on the ground and pulled out the pen. I didn't have paper or blank napkins. I had my left arm. That would do.

The crackle of glass. "Come out, come out, wherever you are," several voices intoned at once. The Forsaken.

"What the—" John said.

"Stall them. I need five minutes, and then we can bolt." I put pen to skin.

"How?"

"I don't know, but be useful and do it."

He cursed as he ran off, and from the clattering, I presumed he ran up and down the aisles, knocking crap off the shelves as he went.

I got to work. Even without writing, the story had continued to play like a movie in my head. Rexi was in trouble. I hadn't been able to sway the events the way I wanted to. I didn't have time to write out the full story. Just the part that I needed her to understand and hope it reached her.

I mumbled as I scrawled on my arm. *The water rippled, and words formed, shimmering on the surface of the puddle. Rexi, you can't kill Blanc yet. She's trying to get Morte to send her across worlds.* I paused. I'd been about to tell her that Morte needed to be defeated first, but I wasn't ready to accept that. I kept going. *Send Gwen's shoes.*

Hydra pointed to the words and chuckled. "It has to be Dorthea.

She's right. Our best chance is to trap Blanc here and then use the well to reach out to the other world and send Dorthea whatever she needs."

A hand gripped my right shoulder like a vise. My pen stilled. I slammed my other fist up, connecting with something hard enough I felt my knuckles crack.

"No more."

I looked up, knowing that voice. The face didn't match though.

"We can't have you giving spoilers," Morte's voice said from my father's mouth, black ink dripping like blood from its corner.

Morte, ever the strategist, sent my weakness after me. I wouldn't fight back now. Couldn't.

My mother came around the corner, dragging an unconscious John behind her. "Do you want me to bring this one?" she asked, voice and eyes dull.

"No, get rid of him. We only need to take the princess."

I didn't have a chance to object before a syringe pierced my neck.

"To charm untamable hair, try taking a mud bath and spraying on a dash of Rapunzel's Tangled Tamers. If that doesn't work, whack it off into a pixie cut."

—*Vanity Faire*

28

Stone Cold
Rexi

Beware the Jabberwock?" I asked. "How about beware the soggy witch?"

"Nay, this beast will fall in one blow." Mordred held his ax high.

The creature turned to Mordred. A new face I didn't recognize emerged from the mud in its stomach. It had the soft features of a young woman. "You never came back."

Mordred lowered his ax to half-mast. "Bedivere? It can nay be thee."

"Why did you let Arthur kill me?" The mournful face hardened her lips and gaze. "I died cursing your name."

"Told ya. Don't listen to its jabbering." Hydra reached into her belly button and pulled out a ball of lint. "I seen this trick before in the first Storymaker war."

"Mommy. It's me. Chrys." A third head emerged from the creature's shoulder blade. This time it was a child.

Hydra's lip quivered, and her hand wavered before stuffing the lint ball in her ear.

"Mommy, I'm cold. Where are you, Mommy?"

"I assure you it is no trick. Not this time around." Water trickled in from around the cavern, the drips echoing Blanc's voice. "My consort has given me any soul that I desire from within the underworld. I had my doubts at first, but our union has been most satisfactory. While the Grimm Reaper has been busy enjoying his time above ground, I have been playing Storymaker and perfecting my creations with his ink." The drips gurgled as if giggling madly. "Tell me—do you like my firstborn?"

I shrugged. "Ugly kid if you ask me." Using my sword on the thing wasn't an option since I could still only move forward like a broken doll. Focusing in, I transformed Excalibur back into the crossbow and took aim. In my heart, I apologized to Dumbeau and fired.

"That's cheating." Blanc's voice dripped as a stalactite fell from the ceiling, sending my bolt off course and right at Hydra.

She snatched it out of the air. "Watch it, William Tell-all." Using the tip of the bolt, she ripped at her head wrap. "I'll take care of this. Don't look."

Despite the warning, when I heard the hissing, I looked up. I only saw the mass of writhing heads on Hydra's scalp before Mordred slid in front of me, blocking my view. "Ye'd make a lovely statuary, but thou art more useful alive."

"What do you mean?" I murfed as Mordred leaned into me, my head smooshed against his chest.

"'Tis the Gorgon Medusa."

The woman that turned anyone who looked upon her to stone.

"No, Mommy. I don't want to die again," the young voice said, cracking at the end.

"I'm sorry," Hydra seemed to hiss. After a rustling and groan, Hydra added, "It is safe now."

I peeked around Mordred as soon as he let go of me. The Jabberwock stood as sandstone, the mouths petrified in eternal, sculpted agony.

I shuddered. "Dear Grimm, and I thought Dorthea's flaming hair was scary."

"Perhaps is it nay the best idea to insult such a woman. Words speak louder than actions," Mordred whispered.

Not quite, but point taken.

The dripping had stopped. Standing in the center, I hobbled in a circle. The pain was easing. "Got nothing to say now that we defeated your creation and proved your Storymaking skills suck."

A ripple ringed the center of the puddle. They disturbed the water and formed words that seemed to shimmer on the surface. *Rexi, you can't kill Blanc yet. She's trying to get Morte to send her across worlds.* The phrase dissipated, the puddle clearing before a new command appeared. *Send Gwen's shoes.*

I rolled my eyes. Seriously, after all this, that girl was still obsessed with shoes.

Now that her hair was wrapped up, Hydra pointed to the words and chuckled. "It has to be Dorthea. She's right. Our best chance is to trap Blanc here and then use the well to reach out to the other world. Then we can get her what she needs."

"Well to start with, we don't have Gwen's shoes. And I'm guessing we can't exactly swap Gwen's head and ask nicely. And second...hex, how could we kill Blanc, let alone trap her, even if she was here?"

A trickle of water flowed from the cracks in the cavern wall. "I'm sorry. Did I give you the impression I'd left? The great thing about freshly dried and petrified mud..." The trickle turned into a fountain. "All you have to do is add water."

The fountain sprayed with force, wetting down the Jabberwock. The outer crusty hardness melted only to have the Jabberwock rise up again but bigger than before. A fourth head had joined the others, though it was cracked in two. Speak of the devil, and she shall appear. The Queen of Camelot—Gwenevere.

"Even unintentionally, you were my champion after all. So I should thank you for putting her head on a platter for me. After all, she was easy to take in her weakened state."

Blanc bubbled. "Killing her myself was nice, but forcing her soul into my eternal service was the best revenge I could have hoped for."

"It's your fault," Gwen said to me. "If you had been a better student, your plans wouldn't always be such failures."

The previous heads had meant to inspire sympathy and regret. Gwen would get none from me.

Mordred held out an arm to stop me from approaching. "Nay, allow me the pleasure." He twirled his ax in his hand. "This is for all the misery ye brought upon my family and everyone thou hast met."

He pitched his arm back and hurled the ax across the distance at a speed and accuracy that split Gwen's head in half and separated it from the rest of the creature. The top half slid off and splatted on the floor.

All smiles, Mordred strode across the room to retrieve his ax. "An ax in the hand is worth two in the mud…" The last word lingered in the air as the two piles of brown muck rose again from the ground, forming a bigger one, now with five heads and twisted, conjoined bodies, jaws and claws snapping.

Little tributaries crisscrossed the floor. "Would you still like to insult my Storymaking skills?" Blanc taunted.

"Yup, still ugly, but I'll add downright nasty too," I answered. The dark grail created dark and twisted monstrosities. Just like their creators.

The time for talking was done. Instead of jabbering, the Jabberwock snarled, slicing in a wide arc. Mordred ducked, the sickle like claw just barely missing his head. Hydra was not so lucky. Her Medusa head rolled on the floor while angry hisses and rattles protested from beneath her hair wrap.

The body stumbled around, trying to find its lost noggin. The brainless body didn't seem to notice when clawed, so the Jabberwock left it largely alone. Mordred and I ignored Blanc's gurgling and Hydra's hissing. We locked eyes, and Mordred tossed me the dagger from his belt since Excalibur was still a crossbow. We both knew if I focused all my concentration on changing it, I'd lose my head in the scuffle.

"Like we practiced in the yard," Mordred instructed.

Since I'd become king, we'd spent afternoons in the courtyard, him teaching me footwork and swordplay while I taught him how not to act like a feral wolf. Both of us had limited success I'd say.

He circled the Jabberwock, sidestepping, parrying while I drew the creature's attention since I wasn't as mobile. Slash and block. Pieces of flesh and festered muck fell to the ground from Mordred's ax and my borrowed dagger. Plop. Plop. They'd fizzle before oozing and searching to shift its form again.

"Faster," I called. Hash, slash, parry, block, squish.

Our movements quickening, Mordred and I engaged in a dance of opposites, mirrored actions in perfect sync. We were faster at cutting than the Jabberwock was at reforming. *We were winning.*

"Aha," Hydra cried.

I turned. Her body had finally stumbled across the head. But the body was clumsy. And the wrap slipped from the snakes as she tried to reattach the head.

Looking away, I called out to warn Mordred, but he was busy dodging a claw and spun out of the way. So his gaze fell directly in the path of Medusa.

Mordred held out his hand to block his eyes, the tips of his fingers hardening and crusting over. Inch by inch, like a wave, the petrification covered him, the fire embers of his eyes the last to go dark.

"No!" I shouted as the Jabberwock slashed. Its claw hit the stone Mordred with a crack, breaking off a piece of his shoulder.

Without thinking, I closed my eyes and grabbed for Hydra's head, aiming it straight for the creature. I heard the crackling of the creature's mud hardening. Since the snakes were pointed away from me, I figured it was safe to look. The Jabberwock had been slain and reformed so many times, it's entire body was made of claws and heads with screaming jaws and wicked teeth.

An image of Blanc flashed in the puddle. "This is not as exciting as I thought it would be." She yawned. "I thought we already learned this doesn't work." She sent her waters to the Jabberwock. This time nothing happened. The water bubbled.

"As long as I hold Medusa's head at that *thing*, you can't reform it." I started to pat one of the snakes, and then the hissing made me think better.

"Always so contrary, you stupid girl. I suppose we are at a stalemate. For as long as you can hold it, that is." Blanc yawned again. "I have time. In fact, why don't you stay there while I see what else I can create to keep you company." She waved, and her reflection vanished. "See you soon," her voice called.

The clock was ticking to destroy the Jabberwock before Blanc got back. But I needed Mordred's help.

"Can you unstone him?" I asked Hydra.

"As long as Medusa has been alive, no one has ever broken the petrification." She grumbled, "Except that monster there."

It was worth a try. Setting the head down, very carefully and not looking at it, I went over to Mordred and splashed water on him, hoping it would work like it had with the Jabberwock.

It did not.

I pulled the grail from my bodice. "It's the last drop," I said, unstopping the bottle.

"No," someone called.

I turned around. Somehow Hydra's body kept stumbling after I'd taken Hydra's Medusa head. It found a new one. Morgana.

"You can't do that," she said. "You swore you would give it to him at the well."

I shrugged. "Well, I'm giving it to him early. What of it?"

"You cannot. It is not the oath we swore. And he will never forgive you for it."

I tucked the grail away. "He doesn't even know, but fine,

if you don't want me to use it, do some hocus pocus on him and fix it."

"There isn't time," Morgana said, grabbing my wrist. "We must leave here at once before Blanc returns."

"Not budging. If I'm going to give him the grail at the well, you'd better make sure he gets there."

"Foolish girl," she said, growling. Then she grabbed my hand and placed it on Excalibur. She guided its aim, putting pressure on the trigger. The bolt flew across the room, hitting Medusa's head directly between her eyes. The head cracked and turned gray, dulling and blowing away to dust. Mordred's stone cocoon began flaking off into dust as well, but the man underneath was safe.

"There." Morgana released my hand and Excalibur. "You should be happy now. We must go."

I couldn't decide if I was happy or not. "You are a rotted menace," I said, transforming Excalibur back into a sword. The blade flashed, but it was not the same as it was before. The blade was chipped. I didn't know what that meant, but I shoved the sword into its scabbard before I took Morgana's head with it.

She'd been willing to leave Mordred behind, only changing her tune when forced. Now Mordred was free, but Morgana had destroyed one of Hydra's heads and was in control. I didn't know how to be okay with that.

Then it dawned on me. "Wait. Excalibur broke the spell and binding from Medusa's magic."

"Obviously," Morgana said, picking up her skirts and climbing out of the cramped cavern den.

Mordred moved for the first time since petrification and pointed his ax behind us. "Aye. And my binding wasn't the only one broken."

The Jabberwock had returned to life, bigger and nastier than before. And we had no way to petrify it.

That left one choice—use Excalibur to break its bond with its creator's magic. Blanc.

Sword out, I charged at the Jabberwock, but a tidal wave hit me before I could get there. The jet of water that was focused only on me knocked me down and started to sweep me away, leaving the others untouched.

"I told you no cheating," Blanc said, creating a waterfall in front of me so that she could appear in her ephemeral liquid form.

She waved her hand at Mordred, who ran for me. A wall of water rose high, leaving Hydra, Mordred, and the Jabberwock on one side.

Blanc and I on the other.

No Use Crying Over Spilled Water

Rexi

Mordred charged at the wall, but the current of the water repelled him. Worse, the more he touched it, the thicker the wall became just like the Jabberwock, which certainly hadn't forgotten its role. The monster sliced at Mordred's back, making him howl but bringing the knight back into the fray.

"Leave them," Blanc instructed, reminding me that I had my own problems to worry about. "I should have realized the moment you entered my lake, but I was too focused on that Emerald usurper."

I tightened my grip on Excalibur and bluffed. "Realized what? That someday you'd get evaporated by me?"

"Realized that you were right under my nose the whole time, the new king of Camelot, the dragon reborn. Our fates forever intertwined."

I looked over at Mordred and Morgana, using blades and spells to keep the Jabberwock at bay. Stalling, basically, as the creature kept expanding. "I guess I drew the short piece of golden straw. But that's got nothing to do with you."

"It has everything to do with me." Blanc crooked her finger, and the mark on my wrist burned, the lotus flower glimmering, reminding me of our ties. "You've always known you didn't belong. Anywhere. Always searching for who you were."

"Said every teenager everywhere. Let's skip the heart-to-heart."

She ignored my snarky remark and continued, "It's ironic you struggled to connect to Robin Hood as a father because you never had a father to begin with. You aren't even truly human. You were created by the Storymakers from the blood of Arthur and iron of Excalibur. You are a tool, a false hero for the Storymakers to use and discard."

"That is the biggest load of pixie dust I have ever heard." I snorted. "I don't know how many times I have to say it. I'm not hero material. I'm just trying to survive. If you wanted to fight, you'd have killed me already. So spit it out. What do you want?"

"Very shrewd as always." She stepped out of the cascade of water in her true form. A single gold choker decorated her neck, the last remnant binding her powers. A bind that only

Excalibur could remove. That's what she was after. Why she'd appeared here and now.

I took my hand off the hilt. "I know you can't take this sword from me. Now it's a part of me. I'm the only one who can use it. And there's no chance in spell I'm using it to free you, so you forget trying to lure me over to your side."

She laughed. "So much alike are we. Once decided, you will stubbornly walk your path. I respect that and know it is pointless to try to convince you to be my champion. However, there is a place where we differ."

"The homicidal, power-hungry, maniac part?"

"Loyalty."

Mordred and Morgana had been holding their own against the beast. So Blanc switched tactics. She uttered a few words in a tongue I didn't understand. The Jabberwock stopped moving to listen. All the heads in its body nodded. Reforming to grow longer arms, the beast shot mud out of its body and grabbed Mordred and Morgana around the ankles, rooting them to the floor with ooze. Another stream of ooze shot out and trapped their arms by their sides.

"You see," Blanc said. "I've been letting my creation play. Letting you all see how pointless it is to struggle against me. I am the very essence of water, bringer of life and death. You are but specks of sand before me."

"And you are just a puddle. You forgot that your water powers can't hold me. I will use my sword, not on you but your creature." I walked over to the wall and started to walk through, fighting the current but breathing the liquid as it were air.

"You could do that, but your friends will still die." Blanc raised her arms and then crashed them down, the wall of water falling with it, flooding the cavern. "I've given you my mark. No water may harm you; however, they have no such protection. Choose."

The water rose, swirling around my friends like a whirlpool. I could get to them and free their bodies. I could use my limited control of water to form an air pocket around their heads, but then Blanc would find a different way to kill us all.

Mordred fought fiercely to free himself like a bear caught in one of Goldilocks's snares. Morgana was content to spit curses at Blanc. "You aqua jezebel, you stole my life once. I will not let you do that again. We will remove your binds, but I will curse you through this life and every other."

"The choice is not yours. It is hers," Blanc said.

"Nay, don't," Mordred warned. "A warrior fears not death. Only loss. A rightful king cannot afford to hold true to sentimental ideals if it means accepting defeat."

"Both of you, shut up!" I couldn't think. Couldn't magically find a way for all of us to walk out unscathed. The water rushed, splashing and slapping against the walls. It was nearly to my shoulders.

Mordred, Hydra, Morgana, Dot, and Blanc were all telling me what to do. This time I had to take my own path and pay the price for whatever came next.

"All right," I conceded. "Stop the flood, and I will cut the bind free."

Blanc narrowed her eyes. "I think not. You have proven yourself slippery. The bind."

The water was high enough that for me to keep my head above it, my feet couldn't touch the bottom of the cave. Morgana's head floated freely off her shoulders, bobbing and rocking, occasionally going under in between curses. Mordred tilted his face to the ceiling, keeping his mouth and nose clear as long as possible.

"Still the waters," I commanded. "Or I shall have no reason left to use Excalibur."

With tight lips, she seemed to consider. "Swear an oath."

I rolled my eyes. "You legend folk and your oaths. Stop the water, and I swear I will cut through the choker."

The dripping ceased, and the water calmed. Blanc slipped through the water with ease, coming closer. "You remember the spell of release?"

"Yes," I said, grinding my teeth.

Blanc's lips curled upward in satisfaction. She tilted her neck, offering the golden bind for me to release.

I thought through my course one last time. I didn't know if Dorthea was still watching through the water, but I apologized anyway. I didn't know if my plan would work or what would come of my actions, but this time I couldn't do as the Emerald Princess had asked.

After freeing Excalibur from its sheath, I brought it to rest against the bind. Steel against gold. "Libération," I said and pushed down through the choker.

Blanc's smile curved up even more. Victory was hers. Or so she thought. But I wasn't done.

"Libération for us all," I said and used all my might to keep slicing, making my way through Blanc's neck until the curve of my cut mimicked Blanc's smile, frozen on her face in death.

The water, freed from the sorceress's control, whooshed out from the chamber, and as both Blanc's head and gold circlet clattered to the floor, the Jabberwock also lost its form, the heads oozing and dribbling away. In its slurping, I swore I heard a chorus of voices saying thank you.

I stepped over Blanc's remains and made my way over to Mordred and Morgana. "It's done. I can't believe it's done."

"Foolish girl." Morgana sneered as I replaced her head on the body's shoulders. "You really think that defeating the sorceress of the lake would be so easy?"

"You think that was easy?"

Morgana tsked in disgust and walked out and onward to the well.

"I'm afraid I agree. If it seems too good to be true, you are probably mistaken," Mordred said, his eyes dark and stormy.

I scoffed, insulted. "So just because you guys never managed to defeat Blanc, you're saying I'm not capable either. I tricked her. I won. Be happy for me."

"I don't mean to diminish ye. I merely fear the Lady of the Lake was defeated because she wanted you to do so."

"That's stupid." I shoved the sword back into its scabbard. "Why would she do that?"

Mordred shrugged. "Time will tell." Coming next to me, he pulled me onto his back again. "Let us conclude our business in these forsaken caves before we find out."

I squirmed off and hobbled forward. "I'll do it on my own."

"As ye wish. I don't think the wishing well is far now."

A good thing since my sore feet would break before my pride.

Behind me, the only traces of our battle with Blanc were the two halves of the gold circlet. I stuffed them in my pocket and headed to the last trial. The trial of heart.

Crown Jewel

Dorthea

The sedative wore off, and I woke with the knowledge that I was utterly pixed.

My drugged sleep had not been dreamless. No, if it had been a nightmare, that would have been all right, but if it was a true seeing, then Rexi had done exactly what Blanc had wanted her to—break her bind and create the conditions for Morte to resurrect her. Here. In Kansas.

I also woke with the knowledge that I was not alone.

Griz stood by my bed, her breath on my neck.

I tried to scramble away, but my body wouldn't move. Not only was my body heavy from the drug's aftereffect, but I was also restrained like a mummy in a garment with a dozen metal buckles.

Wrapped up like a present for the big bad wolf.

With a sinister smile, she put up her hand on my arm. "That's fine, dear. No need to get up on my account." She snickered at her poor joke.

There was a mirror on the ceiling. I could see I'd been put on a table inside a capsule-like coffin. The top was open, and circular opening whirred near my head, ready to swallow me whole. I thrashed around, but the restraints held tight. If I couldn't move, I could still scream for help.

I cried shrill and long, the sound bouncing off the thick glass capsule I lay inside. The pitch was high enough that surely Griz's demon dogs were covering their sensitive ears.

Griz folded her arms and waited until I was out of breath, but she did nothing to stop me. "In case you didn't notice, we are in the new wing of the hospital. The MRI vault room to be precise. So you can make as much noise as you'd like, but if you keep shrieking like that, I'll step outside until your voice goes."

I'd learned from various test and treatments during my time here that vault rooms were sealed and lined with metal to contain radiation, electromagnetic fields, and a few other names I couldn't remember of things that did stuff I didn't understand. What I did understand was that the odds of anyone hearing me were nonexistent.

I sighed. "Fine. You won. Zap me and take your prize."

"Nice try, but I'm afraid you won't be taking the easy way out." After walking over to the wall, she tapped the bright copper surface, and it emitted sparks. "This world relies on alchemy rather than magic. All this metal not only keeps your screams inside but also draws my lightning as well. One bolt would bounce around and grow until it connected with something else metallic. Namely you with all those buckles. And unfortunately, my sister needs you alive. So I'll just have to torture you in other ways."

As Griz walked away, I stared at myself in the mirror. *Be brave. Don't struggle. Don't give her the satisfaction.*

I heard a blade scrape against another. I ground my teeth together to keep my fear inside.

"I read your little napkins. I know what you were planning." Griz dropped the shreds of paper like confetti. "You were hoping your pet servant would send you shoes so you could rush home and save the day." She leaned over me with shears, trailing the edge along the base of my neck. "But I'm afraid I can't let that happen."

She let the point linger and dig in below my ear. Then she lifted and snipped. A chunk of hair fell. Then another. I bit my lip and held back tears as Grizelda Scissorhands delighted in shearing me.

"There," she said. "Perfect. Not exactly the precious, pretty princess anymore, are we?"

My long locks lay around me like soldiers on a battlefield. The battle on my scalp showed some piece had been cut so close that there were small bald patches. It was a hideous haircut.

Don't cry. Don't cry.

"Aside from my own personal satisfaction, that did have a purpose." She lay the shears down by my side. They were so close, but they may as well have been a realm away. "Other than pride from your vain nature, your hair was the source of your life magic in Story. Face it. You can never go home again. Ever."

Griz was right. They were one step ahead and had beaten me thoroughly. I closed my eyes, squeezing them tight. That was the only reaction I allowed myself. I wasn't strong enough to look anymore.

"I'm sorry. There will be none of that."

"Ow!" My eyelids were forcibly pulled open. Griz kept them that way with a strip of surgical tape. Even that choice was taken from me.

"I'm not done yet." She disappeared again. "You still need one more thing." She returned with a note and a cardboard circlet. "Dear Princess Dot," she started in a sickly sweet falsetto. "Mom says today is the day I have my surgery. I'm scared, but I'll be brave like you. Then I can get better and finally go home. That's why I made you this crown. Because no princess should be without one, and maybe it will help you get home too. Maybe you'll let me come to breakfast at your palace." Griz made a gagging noise and crumpled the note in her hand.

"Jessie." My voice was low and gravelly. "Where is she? What did you do to her?"

"I never denied I was evil, and after you killed me, my hatred of you has only honed that skill."

I gulped, the pit in my stomach growing into a black hole.

"Unfortunately, I cannot take credit for anything regarding the child."

I let out my breath in a whoosh.

"She died on the operating table during the bone marrow transplant."

I couldn't breathe. I couldn't blink. I couldn't keep back the tears.

"That's more like it." Griz soothed my stubbly hair. She placed my cardboard crown with its green sticker jewel on top of my shorn scalp. "Now you are ready."

She walked over to the wall and pushed a button. The mirror went fuzzy. It wasn't a mirror at all but a plasma screen. And it showed the view outside the front of the hospital like a window. Wind blew the trees nearly sideways. Rain came down in sheets, pelting the people running out to the cars as police directed traffic.

"You have the perfect view to witness the grand arrival of the new ruler of this world. Watch her wipe this land clean of the bugs and know you are helpless to do anything to stop it. After pressing another button, she closed the capsule doors, encasing me in a claustrophobic hell. Just like Snow White in her glass coffin. Only Prince Charming won't be coming to release you with a kiss."

Her laughter trailed behind her as she left the room and was cut off abruptly when she resealed the vault.

Only when I was alone did I let myself crack. I was broken beyond repair.

Girl of Emerald, I was cursed to burn down the world. I thought Rexi had saved me from that fate, not doomed me to drown in this one.

"You're the one who's going to drown if you keep sobbing like that."

Startled, I looked around as much as I could, expecting to see Griz. But I was still alone in my vault. In my front-row seat to the end of the world. The people had all fled the storm. A single animal sat on the ledge of the hospital fountain. A rabbit. But with cat ears and whiskers. A cabbit?

"If that's you, Oz, go away. Let me mourn alone. That's the least that you owe me. I did everything you asked. I followed the bread crumbs, and look where it got me."

"Exactly where you need to be." Suddenly, the familiar, tweed jacket–wearing old man sat on the fountain edge, seemingly undisturbed by the elements. Dr. Baum. Frank. The Storymaker of Oz.

I laughed bitterly. "This? *This* is exactly where I needed to be? *This* was the whole point of your hero's journey? Well, sorry if I missed the pot of gold at the end of this rainbow."

"Not all journeys end in treasure." He pulled off his glasses and wiped away the rain. "In this instance, you, my apprentice, are the journey."

"As usual, you speak in riddles."

"This was the best Storymaking training I could give you. To tell a good story, you have to have experienced one. Only then can you create all the aspects of characters' souls to do them justice. You needed to know joy, pain, doubt, fear, love, and finally, despair."

I kicked at the tube. "Well, your lessons are unappreciated. It would be far more useful if you came in here and let me out."

Oz shrugged. "Sorry. This isn't my story. I'm afraid it's up to you to write the ending. If both worlds are to be saved, the answers must come from you."

"Arg!" I wished I could beat the crap out of that man. "I tried writing. Nobody did what I wanted them to."

"Of course not," Oz scoffed. "Good Storymakers don't have bland and blind puppets. Their characters come to life and have free will. Your job is to help them grow and tell their story. Let them play out their endings."

"I don't understand. I don't even have paper!"

"You don't need it. All you need to tell a good story is your imagination." Oz poofed back into the cabbit and jumped into the fountain, disappearing into the coin-filled bottom.

So I just lay here and tell myself a story. Totally the sane course of action. But I literally had nothing left to lose.

"Here goes." I closed my eyes and thought of Rexi.

"Rule #7: In matters of the heart, it is never advisable to look before you leap. If everyone saw how far there was to fall, no one would ever jump."

—*Definitive Fairy-Tale Survival Guide, Love's Special Edition*

Heart Attack
Rexi

Slow and steady, I stayed at the rear and followed Mordred and Morgana to the wishing well. It was like the one from every story—a dank, mossy stone circle with no bottom in sight if you peered in.

"So how does this work?" I asked. "Do I lean in and make my wish." That very word brought a bad taste in my mouth. An ill-worded wish was worse than a curse. I'd seen it.

Morgana leaned against the well. "It's very simple. You add a drop from the grail onto a gold coin, throw it in, and very carefully make what you need happen."

I wiggled and fiddled into my pocket and produced the coin from the sphynx trial. Mordred narrowed his eyes at my shrug. I hadn't been able to resist in the end. While I was pulling out the grail, Morgana objected.

"Unfortunately, we have a slight problem."

I rolled my eyes and tightened my grip on the grail. "Of course we do."

"You swore an oath. We have now reached the well, and you must fulfill your end. Give the grail to my son." Morgana crossed her arms, her smile mimicking that of the Cheshire creature.

Mordred stepped back and glared at his mother. "What is this? I know nothing of such an oath."

"The asps." I tapped my toe in frustration. "Morgana and I made a deal. She would save you from the poison if I gave you the grail once we reached the well. But if I had known that I needed it to reach Dorthea, I would have—"

"Ye would have what?" Morgana weaved her way around the well to linger behind me, stalking me like prey. "Thou would have refused the deal and let Mordred fade? I think not. I've seen the way thou looks at him."

Mordred arched his eyebrow and tried to meet my gaze. I wouldn't.

"I would have found another way." My voice was tight, trying to control my worry.

"There wasn't one, and it be done now." Morgana ran her finger along the chain around my neck. "Your oath, king of Camelot."

"I can't." I bobbed away from the Red Queen.

"Then you will be forsworn, and Excalibur will answer thee no more. It does not choose the unworthy."

I looked to Mordred for guidance. He wore a pained look on his face. "'Tis true. If ye made a binding oath, you must keep it or cede the throne."

I didn't care if I gave up the throne. Being royalty meant jack sprat to me. But I couldn't give up the only weapon powerful enough to fight Morte and win back this world. I also couldn't give up my one chance to reach Dorthea.

"I don't suppose you'll swap heads with Hydra so I can consult."

Morgana didn't answer. She just grabbed the traveler's case and dropped it in the well.

That would be a no.

I leaned over the edge, reaching after it, but there was nothing to grab. Gone. I didn't even hear the sound of it hitting bottom.

I whirled around, hand on the hilt of Excalibur. Mordred was already standing by Morgana's side, ax notched on my scabbard to keep the sword locked in.

"Nay, Rexi. I canna let you do that."

I couldn't let the disappointment show on my face, so I unleashed the anger.

"You hexing, traitorous, spineless, newt-nosed joke of a knight."

"You do na understand," he said, blocking Morgana from view.

"Oh, I understand just fine." I pulled the grail from my

neck. "This is what you always wanted, the reason you stuck close to me. Take it and rot in spell with Gwen and the rest of the cowards of Camelot." I threw the grail to the side, aiming at the well. He had to let go of his ax to catch it. Which gave me just enough time to pull Excalibur free.

I pointed it at him as he looped the grail chain around his fist. "I have honored my oath. I am not forsworn, but you both are. You swore to serve me. I find you guilty of treason. Leave the grail here and walk away. Do this, and I will let you live."

Morgana gasped, clasping her hands at her chest. "You'll let us live? How gracious of you." She laughed long and hard. "Big words for such a little girl. You may have the title and the sword, but you are not fit to rule. And once you die, the sword will choose my son as it was always meant to. Kill her as you did Arthur, Mordred. Show the sword your heart of bravery."

I was at a disadvantage, and I knew it. He was faster. Stronger. With years of knighthood. I couldn't win hand-to-hand.

I summoned Excalibur to a bow and knocked an arrow. "I'm happy to show Excalibur your heart. Up close and personal." With only a moment's hesitation, I fired.

Mordred drew his dagger and parried it before it could strike.

"You're a snake." I spat on the ground. "What are you going to wish for that's worth sacrificing the whole world?"

"My wish would save the world," he said. "If I can but

go back. Stop Arthur before his brutal reign, before Gwen, before the curse of the Lady of the Lake."

"Mordred will claim the throne and rule Camelot by my side," Morgana proclaimed.

This time I aimed at her, but Mordred knocked the shot off course again.

"Silence, Mother," Mordred snapped. "'Tis not about power. With my wish, 'twill be as if none of this will have ever happened. There will be no Storymaker wars. Morte will remain in No More, never rising. Arthur will not sacrifice all for his ideals of a peaceful kingdom ruled by an iron fist. I will not die upon that hill."

"So you want to be like Blanc. Change your story, save this world by erasing it and all our stories."

Mordred shook his head, his dagger arm lowering. "No, that's not what—"

I wouldn't let him off the hook. I had an idea. It was a gamble. I'd never trusted anyone before, but I had trusted him. And I couldn't hate him and hurt as much as I did right now unless I had felt affection very deeply first. This was different than opening myself and my feelings up to Kato. The stakes were so much higher. And I was betting that Mordred felt even a fraction of what I felt for him in return.

"Verte will never become a sorceress and battle Blanc, meaning the house of Emerald will never come to be. Mic will still be in power as the original Beast King, and the throne will never pass to Kato. In fact, he'll likely never be born. And if you never fight Arthur on the hill, Camlann and the ironwoods of Sherwood will not exist. I will not exist." I lowered my bow and gestured to the well. "If that is what you wish for, be my guest."

He didn't move, processing what I said.

Morgana grew impatient, looking back and forth between us. "What are you waiting for? Skewer her already."

"Nay." Mordred lowered his dagger and placed it on the well stones. He walked toward me, holding out his hand. Holding out the grail as an offering. "There is no point in saving the world if Rexi be not in it."

A light emanated from the well. The stones rumbled, and the handle cranked on its own, bringing up the bucket from the well's depths. Except it wasn't a bucket at all but a platform. Which looked suspiciously like a chunk of Oz's workshop floor. Especially since the man himself was standing on it.

"Well done." Oz wrung out his jacket, water dripping off it in sheets. "You have both passed the trial of the heart."

Morgana shrieked. "Love! Why must love always be the destruction of us all?" She sliced her arms and drew runes on the nearest cave wall. "Not this time."

The wall rumbled and cracked, slowly outlining a shape. A rock golem stepped free. Then Morgana instructed, "Take the grail and kill them all."

"If I had a pence for each wish thrown down a well, I'd be the richest man in the world. If I had a gold coin for each one that came true, I'd die of starvation."

—Philip, Fairywood Parks and Rec manager

32

All's Well That Ends Well
Rexi

I'd faced the Jabberwock, a nasty puppet pulled from dark magic and the earth. This blockhead was no different. Break the connection between master and servant. The end.

I nocked an arrow and let it fly at the golem. It hit the rock dead on…and ricocheted off harmlessly. Yeah, that wasn't what I had planned.

"Allow me." Mordred picked up his discarded ax and charged, jumping high and using his momentum so he could swing with all his might. He bounced off, flying backward and hitting hard against the well.

"Ummm…okay, I've got nothing." I looked over at Oz. "You can chip in here anytime."

Oz looked around and then sat up, startled. "Oh, you mean me? Why in all of Story would I do that? No, I'll just duck back down into the well and pop up after you're finished." He pointed to the handle, which started to turn, lowering him again.

The golem swung his massive arm, crushing the front of the well, exactly where Mordred had been a few seconds earlier. At the point of impact, the stone crumbled and fell into the abyss.

Hex. I was out of ideas. I needed help. A Storymaker would be nice, but Oz fled as usual without a puzzle to solve. But I did have one other Storymaker to call on. While Mordred charged the golem over and over only to be flung away time and again, I focused my energies on Dorthea and prayed for help.

Please, if you can hear me, I can't lose him.

An image filled my mind. It was unfamiliar, something from *that* world. But I didn't have time to question. I closed my eyes and formed Excalibur into the picture in my mind of a big candle with the letters "TNT" on the side.

"Move, Mordred," I yelled and threw the candle. The rock creature caught it, angry at being hit with another projectile. At first, nothing happened. Then there was a loud boom that rang in my ears and blasted the whole world away in a flash. Dust clouds made it nearly impossible to breathe.

Once some of the smoke cleared, all that was left of the golem was a pile of inanimate boulders. Hex, that's all that was left of the cave too. The blast had knocked huge holes in the walls, which seemingly lead into unending darkness.

"Iron and ashes, Dot. What have they been teaching you in that Kansas? Overkill much?" I swear I could almost sense her shrugging. I ran over to Mordred, clearing the rocks off him.

"Hey, you still alive?" I asked, hefting the biggest boulder off his gut.

He responded with an oof since I *may* have dropped the boulder a few times before sliding it all the way off. "At this rate, I may not be for much longer. But mayhap that is your purpose." He caught my gaze. "If it was, I would yield to the point of thy sword without argument."

"Pfft." I helped him stand. "What's a little betrayal among friends?"

"Friends?" His face fell slightly. "So thou thinks there is forgiveness to be had for me?"

I huffed, pretending to think very seriously on the matter. "Well, considering my past, I'd be an awful hypocrite if I didn't let you at least try to redeem yourself. But it's going to take a while."

He narrowed his eyes. "How long be this while?"

I bit my lip and glanced around surveying the damage. In reality, I didn't want to read his expression. "Um…I was thinking our whole lives might be enough."

"I'm sorry, but nay."

"Oh." I dropped his arm and tried to breathe. I seemed to have forgotten how.

Wrapping his arm around me, he drew me in close, forcing my face to his. "My fierce and feisty consort, forever after with thee would na be long enough."

The ladylike response would have been to wait for true love's kiss, but no one ever called me a lady. Gripping his tunic in my fists, I yanked his lips down to mine. There was nothing at all soft in our kiss. Just the desperation and fire of two souls that had waited ages to connect. To no longer be alone.

Now I understood Dorthea. I understood why she lost control of the curse when Kato was taken away from her. I had loved him in my way, but those feelings were a shade to how Dorthea felt about her prince and how I felt about Mordred now.

When we both ran out of breath from kissing, I rested my forehead on his chin. "Woe be the idiot who tries to pull us apart."

"Challenge accepted," Morgana croaked.

I sighed. I had forgotten about her. Morgana's head had fallen off and mixed in with a pile of rocks that were a similar size. The homunculus body was having trouble distinguishing between them. It placed a few granite pieces on its shoulder before finally getting it right.

"It is over, Mother. 'Tis time to accept this new age we live in." Mordred intertwined his hand in mine. "Thou cannot defeat us together."

"I shall have to remedy that." She made a thin slice down her arm, blood dripping off her fingertips. "Hecate por scion mortise." She flung her hands out, splattering blood to fortify her curse.

Excalibur sprang to my hand in the form of a shield before the magic had time to activate. It deflected the blood's iron missiles that were targeting us.

"Ha!" I mocked. "Missed."

Her eyebrow arched. "Did I?"

I looked at Mordred, who had a single splatter of red under his eye like a bloody tear. It sat there for a moment before his skin absorbed it, drawing the cursed drop into his veins. He smiled at me and then crumpled to the ground.

"Hey, now. Get up, you big baby. It's only one drop. Shake it off." When he didn't, I shook his shoulders.

"It seems forever may have been a wee optimistic," he murmured. "I did nay account for her oblivion curses." He held up a hand to brush my cheek, but his fingertips were no longer solid. They were fading to mist.

Morgana held out her hand. "Hand over the grail while there is still time to reverse it."

"Wretched hag." I spat on the ground. "You make the Evil Queen look like mom of the year." I bent down to Mordred, ready to hand over the grail without hesitation. Love, the biggest strength and the strongest weakness in all of Story.

"I fear it be time to ask for that boon thou owest me," Mordred whispered.

"Now is not the time." I took his other hand, which was still solid, and unwrapped the chain and grail from it.

"Nay. Now is the only time." He put his finger on the stopper to keep the ink bottle grail closed. "Do nay use the grail for anything short of connecting the world and saving Story."

"No, I refuse."

"Stubborn wench, thou promised," he insisted, his body now faded up to the waist.

"Arg!" I cursed more. "What is it with the self-sacrifice?" I stood up, putting the grail around my neck again. "All right. I agree, but only if you swear to forgive me."

"Forgive thee," he whispered. "For what?"

"This," I said, transforming Excalibur into a bow. I didn't even aim. I simply trusted that my heart would guide the arrow to its target.

Morgana.

She didn't have time to respond except for a shocked expression, which became her death mask. Her head grew older, drying out and mummifying. After the weight of her arrow tipped her head off Hydra's shoulders, it fell to the ground and turned to dust.

It was done. I'd destroyed a very evil being who also happened to be my future mother-in-law, but if Mordred was saved, if Excalibur could break the connection from her curse...

Please work, I prayed before looking at Mordred again.

At first, it seemed nothing had changed, but slowly, inch by inch, his form started to solidify. I threw myself to the ground to embrace him but fell through him.

"Ow." I rubbed my elbow. "You're not quite solid yet, I guess."

"Aye, lass." Mordred groaned and sat up. He looked over to what I'd done.

I bit my lip, worried he would be cross. Worried he would turn me away. But he was alive. Would that be enough? I gritted my teeth and clenched my fists. Who was I kidding? I'm not that gracious. He would love me if I had to follow him and nag him until the end of his days.

"And they call me the bloodthirsty one." Mordred's eyes narrowed. "I fear that I do nay desire to know thy current thoughts."

"You should never have to slay thine own kin?" I quoted back to him, squeezing his shoulder.

His eye softened. "Aye. Though it saddens me, it needed doing. Thank you for not keeping thy word and not forcing my hand."

"Speaking of which." I pointed to the well. "You can come up now. It's over," I called to Oz.

The handle turned, slowly raising the platform. Oz wore his brown jacket and held a brown leather case over his head. Presumably for protection. He lowered it and coughed into his hand. "Not exactly the way I would have done it. But I did tell you the story was yours to control. Bravo, apprentice."

Mordred lowered his head and whispered to me, "Who be he speaking to? Is he mad?"

"Dorthea, probably, and yes." Then I squinted at the case Oz was holding. I jumped up and down in excitement. "Oooh! That's Hydra's traveling case."

"This?" Oz looked at what he was holding. Then shook it. Something rolled around inside and started swearing. "Yes, I suppose it is, though from the sound of it, there's only one head left. I'm afraid it took some damage in the rock fall."

Mordred took the case. As he opened it gingerly, I muttered, "Anyone but Cleo. Anyone but Cleo."

"You saying you don't like my taste in heads, ya idgit? I'll have you know I'm putting all those heads you destroyed on your tab," came the voice from the case.

"Yes! Spare parts, Hydra. Oracle would have been better, but—"

"Bah. Just for that, I'm charging you triple."

"Send me a bill." I plopped her head back on her body, which without Morgana's magic, had promptly ballooned back to its original size.

"I don't mean to rush everyone," Oz said. "Oh, wait. Yes, I do. My apprentice is rather tied up at the moment, and the fate of the both worlds hang by a thread. But by all means, take your time with the small talk."

Oh. Big picture. I dug in my pocket for the coin and unstopped the grail. Tipping it over, I put the last drop from the grail on the coin.

Mordred stayed my hand. "Before thou throws it in, you must think of a wish. What thou desires with all thy heart."

I waited for inspiration. For the words to fill my mind. I could wish for Kato to live. I could wish for both worlds to be saved. I could wish to live happily ever after with Mordred on a far-off desert island. But in the end, I knew that all of those wishes were either too vague or would be granted at the cost of someone else's fate.

I wish the well would become a portal to Dorthea so that I can give her what she needs.

And with that wish in my heart, I threw the coin into the well.

"Rule #71: Prince Charming and other heroes are notoriously late, as they often get enchanted by their own reflection or lose track of time. That's why every damsel in distress should always bring a book or needlepoint to keep herself occupied while waiting to be rescued."

—*Definitive Fairy-Tale Survival Guide, Volume 5: Heroes*

33

There's No Place Like Home

A few beats after Rexi made her wish to the well, a glimmering coin appeared at the bottom of the fountain. The water rippled and shimmered, soon showing the surface of the wishing well as if I was inside and Rexi, Mordred, Oz, and Hydra were peering in. Well, honestly, Hydra took up most of the view.

"Hey, this thing work? Oh, there you are." Hydra squinted and pulled a face. "What in spell happened to you? That jacket, that hair! Blech. If you wait until I get back to my shop, I'll give you the family discount on some slightly used, new-to-you hair."

"Her appearance is not important. Get out of the way,"

Rexi said, elbowing Hydra out of the picture. As soon as she saw me, she winced. "Ouch, I see what you mean. Kansas must be a very strange and horrible place."

"I've missed you too." I rolled my eyes.

Rexi shrugged in what looked like a half apology. "I understand we're kinda on a time line. I've made the portal, so hurry up and get back so you can kick Morte and Blanc's butt."

"Two problems with that. First, I'm not sure I can come back. Griz cut my hair, and if it still holds my life magic…"

Everyone on that side of the well looked to Oz for confirmation. He seemed to straddle both worlds, the fountain and the well. "Don't ask me," he replied. "I'm only here to see how the story ends."

Rexi held her fist up like she wanted to smack him. Yeah, she still had some of my temper.

"It doesn't matter," I interrupted. "Even if I could go home, I can't go yet. Blanc is on her way *here*."

"How?" Rexi butt in.

"That's what I was trying to tell you earlier. She needed to die in that world by Excalibur and have Morte use his dark grail to resurrect her again. In this world."

"Hey, it's not like I had a lot of options," Rexi protested. Both Hydra and Mordred glared at her, and she seemed to shrink smaller. "What's done is done. So now what?"

"I'm going to have to beat Blanc and Griz here in Kansas while you rescue Kato and defeat Morte."

Rexi threw her hands in the air. "Well, why didn't you say so? Easy as cake."

"Pie," I corrected.

"I know," she sniped back. "But you are asking the impossible. Even if I could take out Morte and his army of twisted shadow baddies, Kato is dead. I saw him in the underworld. He used the very last of his life magic to take my place."

"He went willingly, so Morte could use his body as a host." I looked hard and deep into Rexi's eyes. Searching for that part of her that felt the same way I did about Kato. "Part of him is still in there, I know it. I'm trusting you to find a way to save him for me."

"I—" Rexi groaned. "But—" She slammed her mouth shut. "And maybe—" She growled and paced. Finally, she folded her arms and pouted. "I'm not swearing any more rotted oaths, but I owe it to you both to try. Any ideas?"

"Nope. Not one."

She rolled her eyes. "Some Storymaker you are."

Mordred poked his head into the picture. "Hath anyone else noticed that this well and connection is water?"

Blanc, the water empress. I gulped. I hadn't considered that. We needed to hurry. "I need Gwen's shoes."

Rexi threw her hands up again. "Sorry, but some of us don't travel with the latest spring collection. There's no way I can get them."

"There is one way," Mordred said slowly.

"No," Rexi answered flatly. "Better yet, spell no."

"Whatever it is, please." I had to believe Oz showed me those shoes for reason. Sure, I couldn't go home, but there had to be some reason those shoes were important. They were the key. I knew it.

Rexi roared in frustration but pulled out Excalibur. "I cannot believe I'm going to turn this holy weapon into a pair of shoes. It probably won't even work because I'm the only one who can wield it."

Oz combed his mustache. "Technically, you wished for the connection, so you can give Dorthea what she needs. Ipso facto, I do believe the sword will acquiesce and uphold the rules of your wish."

"I hate you, but not as much as I hate these blasted wishes," Rexi said in monotone. "Do like you did with the blowy-up candle, Dorthea, and I'll try."

I didn't have the illustration anymore, and if I did, I couldn't reach it since I was restrained. So I closed my eyes and pictured it in my mind. When I opened my eyes, Rexi was holding the heels exactly as I imagined.

She looked about to weep as she caressed the Celtic inlays on the side of the heel. "The hilt of my sword. What have I done to you?" She glared at me. "You'd better take care of these and send them back in mint condition. Not a scratch, not a scuff. You hear me?"

"Yes," I replied. "I never thought I'd see the day you were gaga over a pair of shoes."

She turned up her nose in disgust and dropped them into the well. "Take 'em."

I waited for the shoes. I waited for them to fall on top of my capsule. But no. They landed in the pond.

Son of a basilisk.

Now what?

I was still pondering when a new person appeared in the pool. John. He looked around cautiously like he was suspicious of everything around him. He glanced at the fountain and did a double take. Then he fished the shoes out in wonder.

"John! *John!*" I yelled.

"He cain't hear ya," Hydra said, stating the obvious. "However, for the very low price of your firstborn, I would be happy to send him a message in a bottle." She pulled a green bottle with a note out of her sleeve.

"Hydra…" Rexi snatched Hydra by her red hair and dangled her over the well.

"Or we can just consider this one on the house," she corrected.

That was more like it. "Tell him to bring the shoes to the new Schrödinger CAT scan–MRI machine."

Hydra scribbled on the note and shoved it back in the bottle. "Look out below," she said and dropped it in.

The image of my friends glitched like static.

"Hey, what's going on?" Rexi asked.

"She must have everything she needs, so your wish is fulfilled," Oz said simply. "Remember to—" The rest of his sentence was cut off along with the picture.

I groaned. "Aww, come *on*!"

I fought my restraints anew. I kicked and wiggled and nearly had one buckle out of ten loose when the door to the vault opened.

"Did anybody here order shoe delivery?" John asked, holding up the dripping wet heels. When he saw me locked away, he rushed over to the machine. "What the hell? Are you okay?"

"Decidedly not, but I'm getting there." I directed him to the release button for the capsule doors. With a whoosh, I could breathe fresh air again. "Holy Grimm, I'm so glad to see you. What happened after the Forsaken caught you?"

He jogged back over and worked on the buckles. "Your mom hit me over the head, and I woke up in the recycle bin."

"Sorry. That wasn't—"

"Really her. I figured." He finished the last buckle and helped me get the restraint suit off. "I came back to the hospital to find you, but it was chaos with ambulances because they were evacuating the patients since we're in the path of the storm."

No kidding, I thought.

"I worried they'd already taken you and had about given up hope of finding you when I heard a splash and saw those shoes we looked for everywhere. And in the fountain out front, of all places. There was this weird message attached too."

"And that was all you saw?" I asked.

He passed me both the note and the shoes. "Yeah, was there something else?"

"Don't worry about it," I said and read the note.

Hey, good-looking.

There's a shoe-desperate princess in need of rescue in some cat scanny thingamabob. Hurry if you don't want to be fried or drowned.

PS. If things don't work out with her, how do you feel about women with multiple personalities? You can text me by spellphone. 555-HEAD

I crumpled the note with a deep sigh. Rexi's wish had worked, and that's all that mattered. After setting the shoes on the ground, I slid my feet inside. A perfect fit.

"Okay, here goes everything." I clicked my heels together.

John rocked back and forth. "Is something supposed to be happening? Is this another one of those *things I can't see?*"

I glared at him. He mimed zipping his lips.

I tried again. Nothing. Then I stamped and stomped and jumped. "Work, glam you!"

I didn't know what was supposed to happen, but surely, something was. I needed my emerald flames to beat Blanc. I expected to hear the voices or feel the familiar lick of heat along the surface of my skin. A flicker at least. But there wasn't even a spark.

Maybe there really *was* no magic in this world. At least not for the good guys.

The walls rattled from the wind outside. I could feel the dread in my gut. Blanc was here. Our time was up.

"Tip #6: Before you go questing, make sure you've said fond good-byes to your friends and family. That way when you get captured, they are more likely to come rescue you."

—*The Coward's Guide to Seeming Heroic*

Family Ties
Dorthea

I pushed John out of the vault, and he tripped over the rubberized mat. "You are leaving now."

"What? No. I found an honest-to-goodness message in a bottle telling me to rescue you. I'm clearly supposed to be here." He regained his footing and stood firm, blocking the hallway.

"You freed me. That's enough. There's nothing you can do against the storm that's coming."

He looked down his nose at me. "But you and your fancy shoes can?"

"If we all want to see tomorrow, then I sure hope so. But for now I'm really sorry about this."

Before he could question me, I stomped on his foot, and

when he bent over to cradle it, I kneed him in the face, knocking him out.

I grabbed John from under his arms, and dragged him across the floor into the nearest room, which took effort because the boy wasn't light. In the room there was a monitor that showed the vault and a desk with a keyboard, a bunch of buttons, and a microphone. This was a control room to manage and monitor the CAT scan machine.

I deposited John under the desk so he would be shielded and quickly checked him over for permanent damage. His nose looked a bit more crooked than it had a few minutes ago. He also had a bump on his head, but that wasn't from me. It oozed black. Back at the hardware store, he'd been hit by a Forsaken. Infected. There was nothing I could do about that at the moment. Hopefully, defeating Blanc would cure all the Forsaken. It had to.

I left him there, locking the door from the inside before shutting it behind me. John should be safe. Well, as safe as anyone could be right now.

Retracing my steps from my earlier escape, I looked for the construction exit. It would be easier to fight or hide from Blanc out in the open, harder to drown outside than cornered in a building. Unfortunately, Blanc and Griz must have expected that. The exit was blocked by shadows. The flowers from the pots that flanked the outside entrance were tainted and overgrown. They snarled and snapped at my head, looking for their next meal.

Okay, not that way.

I took off down the hallway. The lights flickered. I didn't pass a single soul. Everyone must have left the building during the evacuation. That was good. It would limit the collateral damage.

I ran to the lobby, hoping that one of the three entrances would be clear, but the glass was covered in dark, inky vines. They appeared dormant, so I tiptoed closer. As soon as I got within a foot, they woke up, squirming from the bottom of the door to the top. They hissed and backed away from my shoes, angling for my head like a kraken looking to wrap around a ship.

Standing in the center of the lobby, I looked north, east, south, and west. In each direction the hallways looked dingy like mold grew on the walls. But I knew the growth wasn't as mundane as fungi.

If I can't escape the hospital, maybe I should hide somewhere and figure out how these shoes work.

Within the lobby there was a gift store, so people could buy flowers and stuffed animals before visiting a patient. The Caterpillar's Garden. The lights were turned off, but the door was unlocked. I stepped inside and turned the deadbolt.

The store was fairly small. Flowers and baked goods on one side, toys and fantasy items on the other. There was a selection of candy and pipes behind the sales counter. But there weren't many places to hide. I ducked under the tea and tart table, hiding behind the cloth.

Even through the fabric I could see the flash as the emergency lights started strobing. With a metallic pop, the fire sprinklers on the ceiling began to spray water everywhere. The gift shop stayed dry only because it was too small to have its own sprinkler. Outside the room though, water fell in sheets against the display window.

Blanc's voice filled the air with each drop of water. "It will be easier for you if you come out. There is no escape. This whole dismal town will be underwater in a matter of hours. You have no magic. Your Storymaker skills can only influence other worlds. Build me a new world to rule, and I will return this one to you."

Even if I hadn't heard Griz snickering in the background, I'd have known that Blanc was lying. Blanc fueled her powers with life magic. She'd leave this world all right, but only after she'd sucked the magic from every living creature, leaving them as empty shells.

Pulling my knees to my chin, I looked at the shoes Rexi had sent me. I tugged and prodded every inch of them, trying to find their secret. "Come on. There's got to be something special about you. You're made from Excalibur for Grimm's sake." Maybe I was just supposed to stab them with the heel or blind them with their shiny metal sides?

I rolled my eyes at myself. If that was my best plan, I was pixed.

Okay, what did I know? According to the well and Oz, I had everything here that I needed to defeat Blanc and Griz.

So what did I have? A pair of sword-forged shoes that shadows seemed to shy away from, which would help my feet escape but didn't do much for my head. Aside from what I had on me, I also had a hospital with all its tools and equipment.

I thought of the sisters weaknesses, which ironically was each other. Griz would melt at water. And water was charged by lightning.

Before I could complete my thought, Blanc's voice returned.

"I tire of this, so I shall speed up the process. Speak," she commanded.

Yeah, no. Not that dumb.

But Blanc wasn't talking to me. I heard a smack and a yelp from a man. Then I heard, "All right, stop."

It was my mother's voice.

"Dorothy, wherever you are, run!" she shouted. There was another smack, and Mom went silent.

"That should be convincing enough," Blanc said. "I've removed the shadow infection from their bodies, so they will feel every ounce of pain my sister inflicts on them. They will drown knowing you failed them. You have a minute to respond."

When Blanc was done talking, the sprinkles shut off again. If the shoes warded off shadows, maybe they would ward off water. I didn't have a choice but to find out.

I opened to door to the gift shop. Water puddled on the linoleum, but it parted in front of me, repelled by the shoes.

"Yes," I breathed. Of course, shoes from Excalibur would expel magic. I ran for the security desk and hit the PA system.

With a loud ping, it activated. "You win. Bring my parents to the vault room. I'll give myself up if you let them go." I released the button and ducked below the counter for safety.

Within minutes I head footsteps splashing down the hall. "Keep moving," Griz ordered my parents.

I peeked out from around the reception desk to see her riding behind them on a very large shadow demon dog, which kept her feet from getting wet. My parents trudged forward, my mother with her head held regally like going to the gallows was exactly where she wanted to be.

"I don't like this," Griz said, looking beside her. "The Emerald brat has something up her sleeve. I know it."

There stood Blanc, practically glowing in a shimmering gown that looked like falling water. Her long white hair swayed as if she was swimming in the air. "You overestimate her, sister. The girl's flames were the only threat to me, and those have been stripped from her. She's no longer a danger. She is nothing except a tool to grant my most fervent desire."

"She didn't need those flames to kill me. You don't know her like I do. She's got help. Otherwise, you would be able to sense her in the water." Griz frowned, obviously unconvinced.

"She's simply adept at hiding. The only reason she was able to defeat you was lack of attention, which was a grave mistake on your part, but I am not you," she admonished, but then she quickly added, "But I mean no offense. You did the best you could."

Banished

Griz smiled. "None taken, dear sister." As Blanc passed her, the false smile fell off Griz's face.

"Not quite fair that she gets all the reward for your hard work," my mother said.

"Shut up." Griz gave my mom's shoulder a spark.

They all walked down the hallway of the new wing.

I waited until I couldn't hear the splashing anymore. The minutes passed like days. Finally, when I couldn't wait any longer, I stood up.

It was my turn. The hunted was now the hunter.

"With family it's really all about the Golden Rule. Do unto others before they do unto you."

—Agatha, *Stepsisters: Not So Ugly on the Inside*

35

Twisted Sisters

Dorthea

The door to the vault was slightly ajar. I would get there in a minute. First, I knocked on the door to the control room. I heard the muffled sounds of someone shifting around followed by a crash and swearing.

Yep, he was still there.

"I need you to stay put and watch the monitor for my signal. I'm counting on you." I didn't wait for John's answer before entering the vault.

"Dot, no!" my mother yelled as soon as she saw me.

Griz yanked the shadow leash that held my parents. "Quiet."

Blanc stood apart from them, gliding over the floor. "So you *did* have the courage to come. That's very noble of you."

"Yes, I'm here, so let them—"

Griz interrupted and pointed to my feet. "See, I told you she was up to something. Somehow she made magical shoes." Probably remembering what happened the last time I'd faced her with a high-fashion weapon, she sidestepped out of my direct line of sight using my mother as a shield.

A corner of Blanc's lip turned down. "Yes, that footwear seems unlikely to be the regular attire here."

"Get rid of them," Griz said, still hiding.

"No, these shoes aren't special. I just have good taste," I insisted. "Now release my parents."

"I'd be happy to," Blanc said. "But first, I'm afraid you must part with your shoes."

"I can't. That wasn't part of the deal. My parents for me. Simple."

"See?" Griz said. "She's trying to trick us. She'll kill us both with those shoes."

"Let me handle this." Blanc glared back at her sister and then turned to me. "I'm making a new deal. Hand over the shoes now, or you watch your parents die."

Water shot from Blanc's body, encasing my parents' heads in water bubbles. Griz scrambled away to steer clear of the liquid.

I raised my hands in surrender and lowered my head. "Okay, okay. You win. Please. Stop."

As I bent down, Blanc released the water, which splashed to the ground. "I knew you'd see it my way."

I took off both heels slowly and held them in my hands.

"Just so we're clear, I'll toss these to you, and at the same time, you let my parents go."

"I don't know…" Griz said.

Blanc ignored her. "As a show of good faith, since we will be working together on my new story, I will accept this offer."

"All right. One. Two…" As I cried, "Three," I tossed both shoes, one to the left and one to the right. Blanc and Griz released their holds on my parents to catch them.

"Hurry." I ushered my mom and dad out the vault door.

"Let's go, Punkin," my dad said urgently, holding my hand.

"Not yet." I pulled free and hit the button to slam the door, sealing myself in with Blanc and Griz.

Standing on the rubber mat, I held my hands palm out. "I did what I promised. You have the shoes, and I'm still here."

"Yes, that's very wise of you." Blanc smiled and examined the Excalibur shoe.

I turned to Griz, who was also looking over the shoe in her hands. "So I guess the next step is for you guys to decide who gets to wear the heels."

"There's no decision to be made. I will, of course." Blanc held out her hand expectantly.

Griz scoffed. "Why is it always automatically you?"

"Because I'm the elder and the strongest," Blanc answered matter-of-factly.

Griz threw her head back in disgust. "It's always the same since we were kids. You get everything while I get nothing."

While the two got in each other's faces, bickering back

and forth, I looked directly into the camera and held up my hand. *Wait.*

I yawned. "Not that it's any of my business, but I agree with Blanc. You're kind of a screwup, Griz."

Her face twisted into a hideous snarl. "Nobody asked you." She flung her arm back and hurled a crackling lightning bolt at me.

Blanc cried out as I ducked. The bolt hit the copper-lined walls, conducting the electricity throughout the room. Even through the rubber mat I stood on, I felt the current scorching my insides. It brought me to my knees. The lightning traveled along the walls, the ceiling, the floor, seeking out a better target. It found one. The iron and steel shoes forged from Excalibur acted like a lightning rod, giving both sisters a full blast.

Griz laughed it off. "I'm made of lightning, you idiot."

I pointed to Blanc. "But she's not."

Sparks of light zipped through Blanc's body, turning her skin translucent. The electricity was making her lose her solid form, reverting to liquid.

"Help," she said, reaching for her sister to ground her.

As soon as the water touched Griz, she shrieked. But it was too late. She began melting, getting shorter and shorter as her skin oozed into a puddle. Blanc's watery body mixed together with Griz's. I could no longer tell where one sister ended and the other began. And my Excalibur shoes were trapped in the middle of their mess. Together they thrust out a hand, calling for the shadows in the room to assist them. The shadows came, mixing with the sisters to bring them a single, more solid form. The hideous form gurgled and lurched forward.

"Not over," it gasped.

"Yeah, it is." I glanced back at the camera and yelled, "Now!"

In the control room, John pushed a button and the Schrödinger CAT scan–MRI machine lit up, whirring to life.

I remembered exactly what Nick had told me in that hall. Keep steel away from the machine because it used powerful magnets that would draw you in.

There was nothing the sisters could do. The metallic shoes were embedded inside them, and they drew closer to the machine with each revolution of the magnets. Blanc and Griz were sucked into the tube of the machine, one withered, shadowy hand clutching at the side of the capsule, refusing to go down easy.

"We'll get you!" the sisters screeched.

"Sorry. I'm the Storymaker, and I say *the end.*"

I slammed my hand down and snapped the lid shut, breaking off their sludgy fingers. As soon as I did, the capsule slid backward, automatically feeding into the machine for imaging. The whole system went haywire, sparking and hissing. Black smoke billowed out. The machine began to overheat, its parts melting and sealing the unit closed as it shut down.

Behind me, the vault door opened.

"Are they alive or dead?" John asked.

I steadied myself against the wall. "I'm not going to open it and find out."

"Good plan."

Giving up on the whole upright thing, I slid down the wall to the floor. "I can't believe it's finally over."

"I don't really know what *it* is. I don't really understand what I saw. Those women were here, and then there were flashes of light, and they vanished. But if you're crazy, so am I. It's like the more time I spent around you—" John's light-blue eyes grew dark. He rubbed his short hair. "I...I..." When he pulled his hand from his head, it was dripping ink like blood.

"John!" I shouted as he collapsed, falling onto my lap. I maneuvered him gently to the floor, my arms still around him, and I called, "Mom! Dad! I need help." When no one came, I peered around the doorway. I could just see my mother's legs splayed on the floor.

"Oh my." Oz coughed, fanning away smoke from the top of the broken machine. "Interesting solution. Not what I would have thought of."

"Where did you... Never mind. What's happening to them? Help me heal John and my parents. I beat Blanc and Griz. This world should be safe!"

He shook his head, actually looking sad for once. "You did. And very well. Unfortunately, Blanc and Griz were not the source of the shadows."

Morte.

"What do I do? I have no way back to Libraria to stop him." I gingerly moved John out of my arms and scrambled over to Oz, grabbing his hands. Pleading. "Please. You have to send me back. Or go back yourself and help Rexi defeat Morte. Or give me something magic to fix all this mess."

He shook his hands free and reached into his tweed jacket. "There is nothing I can do. There is no magic I can give you. You've had the power inside you all along. You simply had to learn it." He pulled out *The Book of Making* and laid it in my open palms. "You have to finish the story."

I took the book and clutched it close, praying he was right. With a deep breath, I opened to the first blank page, which was marked by a fresh quill.

Then I set out to banish the Darkness once and for all.

"Tip #7: When questing, it takes a village. Find a well-populated one so that the peasants with pitchforks can do your dirty work."

—*The Coward's Guide to Seeming Heroic*

36

Cooperation Is a Hard Cell
Rexi

"Thou knows what needs to be done."

"Yeah," I mumbled. "Take out Morte and his super shadow army all while keeping Kato intact." I just had no idea how to do that. I sighed. "We're gonna need an army. The walk back to Camelot through the caverns is pretty long, so that should give us an opportunity to come up with a plan for where to find one."

"Nonsense," Hydra said. "Ain't got time for that." She pushed a stone into the wall of the cave. The well shifted, rotating to the side to reveal a secret passage. Yet Hydra was able to defy the laws of physics. Mordred and I gaped. Hydra shrugged. "What? Shortcut back to the castle dungeon."

"And you didn't think that would have been useful to tell us, I don't know, maybe before we started this journey?" I would have wrung Hydra's neck if it wasn't so gooshy.

"Bah," she said, descending the stairs. "Then it wouldn't have been a quest. This way you got to find your will, brain, courage, and heart. Which yous gonna need to finish this."

I had a feeling I was going to need a whole lot more than that to defeat Morte.

As if she heard my thoughts, Hydra added, "And something to purify all that ink."

My shoulders drooped. I had an empty grail and no Excalibur. This would not go well.

Mordred squeezed my arm. "We will be victorious."

"How do you know?"

He kissed the top of my head. "Because we have no other choice. Let us go now, lass."

The pathway connected to the catacombs, which ran under Camelot. We continued past the arena and popped up outside the dungeons just like Hydra said.

But the cells weren't empty. Quite the opposite.

Beast snarled at Grumpy, who snarled back. Hook swiped at Pan, who hovered just out of the captain's reach, taunting him. Malevolent took up way too much space in dragon form in her cell, and Rose took a nap on the hay in the corner.

"What are they doing here?" I asked. "Morte doesn't keep prisoners."

"Nay, he doesn't," Mordred agreed. "'Tis a holding pen to keep the characters contained until he can get around to dropping them into the pit."

"I'm sure he's a busy tyrant." Hydra nodded knowingly. "Taking over the world isn't a simple task. The devil is in the details."

It was then that Hook noticed us. Me in particular.

"You. Blondie. Get us out of here." He squinted. "Did I kill you once?"

"Yes. Yes, you did." I smirked. "Which is why I'm going to have to pass on letting you out."

"Rexi," Mordred said. "Thou needs an army. Whine and thou shalt receive."

I rubbed the bridge of my nose. "If this is the best help we can get, we're pixed."

Hydra perked up, sensing a deal. "If you don't want 'em, I'll claim 'em as spares. Sell 'em cheap to whoever's buying."

"I may not want them to be my arm, but I'm gonna enlist them." I walked to the cells. "Okay, listen up."

The storybook characters continued their squabbling.

"Allow me, sire." Mordred put a hand to chest and pushed me back. With a reverberating clang, he hit the bars in front of Hook's cell with his ax. "Thy king speaks. Pay heed to your liege, or pay head to my blade."

That worked. The dungeon fell silent.

And I suddenly had several dozen story misfits and refugees staring at me with disdain. All except Rose, who was still snoring like a huntsman. I coughed nervously, thinking back to Mic's grand speech.

"The time has come where we all, villains and heroes alike, must share the same story. We must work together to win back our world…"

Captain Hook rolled his eyes and started picking the green off his teeth with his hook.

I groaned. "Hex this. In case you haven't noticed, we're all pretty pixed. Grimm's not listening to your bibitty boohoos. I've seen what's in store for you. Twisted shadow puppets, that's what. If that's the ever-after you want, you're welcome to rot here and wait for Morte. If you want to get off your butts and do something to rewrite your fate, then I'll open these cells, and we can go out there and save ourselves."

Rasputin pushed Anastasia to the side and pressed up against the bars. "That's vell and good for the heroes, but what about the villains? I will not change who I am for you."

"I'm not asking you to. Heroes fight for the greater good. Villains fight down and dirty to save themselves." I shrugged. "Everyone still fights against Morte and his shadows, so I don't see the problem."

Before me, everyone was on their feet and growing rowdy in agreement.

Emotion swelled within me. If I didn't know better, I'd say it was pride. "All right, everyone. Here's the plan. We need you to disable Morte's shadow army. Hack 'em, hex 'em, do what you do, be who you are and own it. Leave Morte to us."

Mordred smiled and winked at me. "Being you seems to be exactly what the situation needed."

Hydra grunted. "You did okay, I guess."

"Thanks." That was as much of a compliment as I was going to get, so I ran with it. "Now how do we magic these cells open?"

Hydra reached into her pockets and pulled out a ring of keys.

"Wait," I said. "You just happened to have the exact set of keys we needed?"

"No, ya idgit." She pointed to the wall where there was an empty hook with a sign over it that said, "Keys." "I swiped 'em while you was busy with yer pep talk."

With a shake of my head, I took the keys from her hand and unlocked each door, cell by cell. Once free, Mordred led the fairy-tale riffraff, charging out of the dungeon with a shout, spirits high.

"Our turn next." I looked over at Hydra. I still had no clue what I'd do once I found Morte. With a deep breath, I prepared myself to find out.

"Hold up," Hydra said. "I gots something for you."

I crossed my arms and waited. "And how much is it going to cost me?"

"Triple," she said and cackled. Then she straightened her face and pulled out an arrow. "But three times zero is zero. So it won't cost you anything. Though I wouldn't mind a shadow skin rug when you're done with Morte."

I laughed and took the gift. It was better than nothing. "Here goes the most important few minutes of my life."

"It's not where you go but who you meet along the way. If you're lucky, you'll find someone hard to say good-bye to at the end of the journey."

—Toto, *The Long Yellow Road Home*

The Last Good-bye
Rexi

I climbed the stairs and stepped out into the courtyard. The sunlight blinded me at first, but I could hear the sounds of battle. Metal scraping, glass breaking, screams of pain. When I blinked open my eyes, I was greeted by a familiar furry face.

"Bob!" I threw my arms into his mane as he drew a paw around me in an embrace.

"I am glad your hearth burns bright and your flame has grown. You are no longer the same child who—"

"Mocked you during your tour of Chimera Mountain and stole your food. Yup, and you're only half as stuffy as you used to be." I elbowed him in the chest.

"Well, yes. But more importantly, I am at your service."

"You know what I have to do, right?" I stared at him, watching his reaction.

His muzzle dropped, his eyes downcast. "Yes, that monster cannot be allowed to defile our Beast King Kato's flame any longer."

I pulled Bob's face to look at mine. "I want to save him. Please tell me you have some secret guardian potion of exorcism or something."

"If there was such a thing, I would give my own life to make it. However, the last service I can give to my lord is to be your second as we free him from his prison."

My heart sank. So there really wasn't a way to end Morte and save Kato. *I'm sorry, Dot.*

I nodded. "Then let's finish it."

Bob grabbed my hood in his teeth and flipped me up, tossing me on his back.

Hex. Of course, I was going to have do this a million feet in the air. Bob launched into the sky, and I tried not to hurl while keeping a lookout for Morte.

"There," I said, one hand covering my mouth, the other pointing to the black blur in the sky.

"Hang on, little ember." Bob leaned forward and roared, picking up speed. He rammed Morte broad side, his horns ripping through his black fur.

Morte howled and snarled. "You are no match for me, little hero. Die like the insect you are." He cracked his dragon tail like a whip, hitting Bob in the face, sending him plummeting.

I held on to Bob's mane with all my strength in fear of the ground several hundred feet below.

Bob growled and righted himself, so I wasn't dangling anymore. "Fear not. I have not gotten this old by avoiding battle."

He charged again. Morte readied for Bob's horns, but Bob changed and sliced his claws across Morte's belly instead.

"Hurry! Get out of range," I instructed. "Morte's been a chimera all of a month, while you've got a few hundred years of flying experience on him. Make him chase you."

Bob roared in agreement and sped off, forcing Morte to chase him. When Bob doubled back and got close enough, he'd strike Morte and then retreat again. I simply tried not to fall off through all the barrel rolls and loop de loops.

I had one arrow but no bow. And with Blanc and Dorthea gone from this story, I had no power of water or fire to forge one. I could only watch and guide Bob as he wore Morte down hit by hit, his black blood dripping across the field.

Below us, my mishmash army fought against Morte's chimeras. His battalion picked off the untainted, carrying them in their claws to the pit of the false grail, dropping them in. Voilà, endless soldiers.

As Bob made another run at Morte, a different chimera caught him by the tail. I recognized those broken horns, scarred face, and hissing serpent—Griff. While Bob reared instinctually, kicking with his back paws, Morte seized his chance. Baring his fangs, he grabbed Bob by the throat, shaking his head back and forth.

Morte was close enough now that I didn't need a bow. I leaned over Bob's side and thrust the arrow into the shadow chimera's chest with all my might. He yelped and released Bob, who tumbled through the air.

"My embers are fading," Bob said, "but I will do what I must so you can end this nightmare." He rolled on his back, nudging me into the hollow of his arm, wings crossed in front of me like a shield while we fell like to the earth.

Even with his protection, the landing jarred me to the bone and stole my breath.

Bob gasped.

He was dying, and there was nothing I could do but see him off. I buried my face in his paw and bid him farewell with the words I'd heard Kato use once. "Though your flame be gone, may your hearth's light shine on forever."

He smiled and spoke haltingly. "It was an honor to fan your flames." Then the rise and fall of his chest ceased, the warmth of his body slipping away.

Through blurry vision, I saw Morte land nearby. He was unsteady on his paws. He had not come through the aerial battle unharmed. He had slices and tears over his body, and my arrow still protruded from his chest.

As I stood to face him, the grail chain weighed heavy on my neck. It was the only thing that could cleanse this world of the shadows. I held it and peered in, wishing it was full. There was not a drop, but the interior of the container was slick though. The opening was too narrow to fit my finger inside to swipe at the remainder of the grail on its walls, let alone use the last of the grail as a weapon.

I would have to be the weapon.

I walked over to Morte as he swayed and kicked him in the snout. "Hey, you big pussy cat. Is that seriously all the fight you've got?"

I saw his tail coming at me and ducked, but I didn't see his paw in time to avoid getting tossed twenty leagues. I'm pretty sure I broke a rib or two. But they didn't keep me from walking.

Morte turned slowly, scratching at his chest. "Little hero, still trying to make it into the compendium."

"No, just trying to wipe your ugly mug off the face of the universe." I charged him again, feinting right. We dodged each other for a minute in a game of chimera and mouse. I was the mouse.

Morte pounced and pinned me to the ground under his claws. "Now that I've finally caught you, what should I do with you?"

"Eat me," I growled. It was less of an insult and more like my last hope. If he ate me along with the grail, I'd purify him from the inside out. I'd be dead, but at least I'd go out on top.

"Gladly," he replied, licking his lips.

I waited to meet my fate, but he was still scratching at my

arrow with his hind leg. The area around it was irritated. And the fur was brown, not black.

Kato's fur! But I hadn't dipped the arrow in the grail. How could that be? Then I got a good look at the arrow. It was steel. Like the ones I'd shot using Excalibur. I remembered Hydra pocketing one during the Jabberwock fight. My sword had been chipped after that.

If a small piece of Excalibur could bring back a little Kato, then maybe…

Twisting my body, I pulled my leg up and stomped down on the arrow with all my might. It slid straight into the chimera's heart.

Morte shrieked and wobbled off me, stumbling away before finally falling on his side. He glared at me with hate in his wide, white eyes. "No. I refuse to go back. I will not return to No More, forgotten by all."

He huffed and pushed back onto his legs. My gamble had lost. Behind him I could see Griff swooping down from the sky. Soon I'd be dropped in the pit.

But I would not give up. It was my turn to glare defiantly. But the eyes I saw in the shadow chimera were no longer white. They had turned ice blue. He smiled. "Rexi."

I ran—or rather hobbled—over to him. "Kato. Kato! You're back!"

His smile dimmed. "No. Your holy arrow has given me but a moment of control to hold Morte at bay." He opened his mouth to me.

I pulled the grail from around my neck and put my arm forward and then pulled back and shook my head. "I don't want to. That was when it was Morte, but now it's you. I can't."

He nuzzled me with his nose. "It must be done. Good-byes come to each one of us, and it is our turn. It's okay. I'm proud of you, Hearth Sister."

Mordred came running from the side, alarmed I was so close. As he grasped the situation, he held out his hand for the grail. "I will bear this burden for you."

"No. I promised Dorthea *I* would save him." I placed the grail on Kato's tongue. "Be free."

He nodded once and chomped down, glass crunching between his powerful jaws. He breathed in deeply and huffed, a smile on his face. "May your embers burn bright, for my light will shine on elsewhere."

Then he closed his eyes. Kato was gone, though Morte wasn't done with his body yet. He gasped and rolled his white eyes. Mordred dragged me out of the chimera's grasp.

"What have you done?" Morte wheezed, choking and holding his throat.

I didn't have a snappy retort. I simply leaned on Mordred while I watched the shadow dissipate from his body like the new morning dawn had broken. Finally, the tawny-furred and mismatched winged chimera lay before me. The King of Shadows had been banished.

Griff and his minions fled when they saw the black ink clearing and the darkness receding from the shadow army.

We had won, but at a heavy cost.

I looked at Kato and Bob and all the storybook characters that would have to find some way to rebuild their homes and happy endings.

"I told thee we would win," Mordred said.

I turned to tell him off, but something was missing. Kato's body. All that remained were a few glittering blue embers wafting on the wind.

I smiled broadly.

"And what be that knowing smirk for?" Mordred searched my face, crossing his arms.

I looked through the battlefield anew. Villains helped heroes wipe the ink off themselves. Heroes treated the wounded. Characters from the same stories, once enemies, helped one another. At least for one day. Tomorrow they'd be back to cursing one another. But in that moment we all shared the same story.

I shrugged at Mordred, grinning even wider. "Nothing. Just a little reminder that everyone deserves a happy ending. Speaking of which, if I'm king, does that make you queen?"

Mordred's jaw dropped, opening and closing like a merman out of water.

With a chuckle, I let him trail after me to the castle, while he argued his case for how we could be co-kings. I didn't care about titles. I never had. Just as long as he held to his promise. To stay with me. Forever after.

"And I woke from my adventure, sad that it was over and mourning the loss of a dream that I could never return to. Then I realized there were many nights ahead of me, each one a chance to discover a new dream."

—Excerpt from *Over the Rainbow and Back: A Memoir*

38

Lost and Found
Dorthea

I blew on the ink, allowing the last words to dry. *Forever after.* I'd done the best I could. It would have to be enough.

"Did it work?" I asked Oz. But he was gone.

I closed the book, set it down, and scooted over to John, taking his hand. He groaned, stirring.

There was still enough smoke in the room that my eyes watered. Or I was crying. Impossible to tell. The tears fell like glittering blue jewels, landing on his knuckles. "You're okay. I'm glad."

He sat up, still unsteady, and rubbed the wet on the back of his hand. "I feel like I've been hit by a drunk dragon, but I'm more than okay." Then he opened his eyes, their blue managing to show both frost and warmth. "Hey, you."

I gasped and brought my hands to my mouth. "It can't… Is it really? But you're John."

He shrugged with a lopsided grin. "If you get to have a new name in this world, why can't I?"

My hands were all over him, inspecting every inch of his body. Looking for fur or horns or any remaining shadows.

"Iron and ashes," he said, grabbing my hands. "Give a guy a break. I've been mostly dead all month."

"But how?" I replayed the last battle in my mind. "Was it Excalibur? Or the grail? Or—"

"I don't care," he cut me off, leaning his forehead on mine. "All I know is that in any world, in any life, I will always find you."

Clasping my hands, he brushed his lips against mine. Again. And again. A barrage of kisses to make for every day that we had been apart. And then one lingering kiss that we savored. Our promise that we would never be apart again.

After we separated, I looked at him in awe, seeing what was mine to keep.

He smirked and waggled his eyebrows. "I know. No switching into a chimera. Score one for Kansas."

I smacked him on the arm for being a dork, and he retaliated by kissing me.

Or he almost did before my mother cleared her throat not so gently.

My dad stood beside her, shuffling his feet. "Not to interrupt, but we've been standing here for a few minutes."

I jumped up and hugged them both.

"I think you have some explaining to do, young lady," Mom said.

I laughed. I was deliriously joyful. But our success, Rexi's and mine, didn't feel real. Maybe it wasn't. I didn't care. This was the happy ending I was meant for. True, I could never go home again. But I had everything I needed right here to make a new home. Together, we all walked out of the crumbling hospital and into our strange, new world.

"Well, Mom, it's a long story. But how about I start with *Once upon a time...*"

"*Rule #1000: There comes a time in every story when the last page has to be turned. Instead of mourning the end, simply look at it as the opportunity for a new story to begin.*"

—*Definitive Fairy-Tale Survival Guide, Volume 1*

The Un-epilogue

The man in the tweed coat closed the cover of his book, caressing it gently. He sighed with satisfaction and stretched. He'd been working on this story for many years and was pleased that his plotting had come together so well in the end.

Whistling, he picked up the book and placed it in an empty space on the shelf. The book did not slide in gently, as if it was resisting being put away. "Come now. Don't be greedy," he whispered, patting his mustache. "Your time is done for now. There are others who need their happy endings." Almost with a sigh, the book whooshed into its place, looking at home among the countless other tales in the Storymaker's library, on shelves so tall they reached toward the heavens.

The man grabbed his hat and headed for the door. Pausing, he wished all his stories good night. "I'll return. But for now I must go out in search of inspiration. There are new worlds to build. New stories to write." He smiled and gazed upon the most recent book in his collection. "Or perhaps a new

adventure with a few old friends instead." With a chuckle
and a wink, he turned out the lights.

Acknowledgments

I wouldn't be where I am today without Odyssey of the Mind, which took my creativity and set it free. A big thank-you to all my fans and readers that encouraged me through this series. You kept me going when I thought I had nothing left. To everyone at Sourcebooks that believed in my vision and let me break all the rules to tell a great story. I look forward to telling many more. And most of all, thank you forever after to my family for putting up with my crazy.

About the Author

Betsy Schow is the *Today Show*–featured author of *Finished Being Fat*, *Quitter's Guide to Finishing*, as well as the Storymaker's Saga—*Spelled*, *Wanted*, and *Banished*. Her career in both fiction and nonfiction makes sense because she's been mixing up real life and fantasy for as long as she can remember. If someone were to ask about her rundown truck, she's one hundred percent positive that mechanical gremlins muck up her engine. And the only reason her house is dirty is because the dust bunnies have gone on strike. She recently moved to Maryland with her own knight in geeky armor and their two princesses (who can totally shape-shift into little beasts). When not writing, she is actively involved in Odyssey of the Mind, a program that helps teach kids to think like there is no box. Catch up and connect with Betsy at betsyschow.com.